CW00548211

SUSAN
BABBACOMBE'S

SUSAN Scarlett is a pseudonym of the author Noel Streatfeild (1895-1986). She was born in Sussex, England, the second of five surviving children of William Champion Streatfeild, later the Bishop of Lewes, and Janet Venn. As a child she showed an interest in acting, and upon reaching adulthood sought a career in theatre, which she pursued for ten years, in addition to modelling. Her familiarity with the stage was the basis for many of her popular books.

Her first children's book was *Ballet Shoes* (1936), which launched a successful career writing for children. In addition to children's books and memoirs, she also wrote fiction for adults, including romantic novels under the name 'Susan Scarlett'. The twelve Susan Scarlett novels are now republished by Dean Street Press.

Noel Streatfeild was appointed an Officer of the Order of the British Empire (OBE) in 1983.

ADULT FICTION BY NOEL STREATFEILD

As Noel Streatfeild

The Whicharts (1931)

Parson's Nine (1932)

Tops and Bottoms (1933)

A Shepherdess of Sheep (1934)

It Pays to be Good (1936)

Caroline England (1937)

Luke (1939)

The Winter is Past (1940)

I Ordered a Table for Six (1942)

Myra Carroll (1944)

Saplings (1945)

Grass in Piccadilly (1947)

Mothering Sunday (1950)

Aunt Clara (1952)

Judith (1956)

The Silent Speaker (1961)

As Susan Scarlett
(All available from Dean Street Press)

Clothes-Pegs (1939)

Sally-Ann (1939)

Peter and Paul (1940)

Ten Way Street (1940)

The Man in the Dark (1940)

Babbacombe's (1941)

Under the Rainbow (1942)

Summer Pudding (1943)

Murder While You Work (1944)

Poppies for England (1948)

Pirouette (1948)

Love in a Mist (1951)

SUSAN SCARLETT

BABBACOMBE'S

With an introduction
by Elizabeth Crawford

DEAN STREET PRESS

A Furrowed Middlebrow Book
FM90

Published by Dean Street Press 2022

Copyright © 1941 The Estate of Noel Streatfeild

Introduction copyright © 2022 Elizabeth Crawford

All Rights Reserved

The right of Noel Streatfeild to be identified as the Author of the Work
has been asserted by her estate in accordance with the Copyright,
Designs and Patents Act 1988.

First published in 1941 by Hodder & Stoughton

Cover by DSP

ISBN 978 1 915393 18 0

www.deanstreetpress.co.uk

INTRODUCTION

WHEN reviewing *Clothes-Pegs*, Susan Scarlett's first novel, the *Nottingham Journal* (4 April 1939) praised the 'clean, clear atmosphere carefully produced by a writer who shows a rich experience in her writing and a charm which should make this first effort in the realm of the novel the forerunner of other attractive works'. Other reviewers, however, appeared alert to the fact that *Clothes-Pegs* was not the work of a tyro novelist but one whom *The Hastings & St Leonards Observer* (4 February 1939) described as 'already well-known', while explaining that this 'bright, clear, generous work', was 'her first novel of this type'. It is possible that the reviewer for this paper had some knowledge of the true identity of the author for, under her real name, Noel Streatfeild had, as the daughter of the one-time vicar of St Peter's Church in St Leonards, featured in its pages on a number of occasions.

By the time she was reincarnated as 'Susan Scarlett', Noel Streatfeild (1897-1986) had published six novels for adults and three for children, one of which had recently won the prestigious Carnegie Medal. Under her own name she continued publishing for another 40 years, while Susan Scarlett had a briefer existence, never acknowledged by her only begetter. Having found the story easy to write, Noel Streatfeild had thought little of *Ballet Shoes*, her acclaimed first novel for children, and, similarly, may have felt Susan Scarlett too facile a writer with whom to be identified. For Susan Scarlett's stories were, as the *Daily Telegraph* (24 February 1939) wrote of *Clothes-Pegs*, 'definitely unreal, delightfully impossible'. They were fairy tales, with realistic backgrounds, categorised as perfect 'reading for Black-out nights' for the 'lady of the house' (*Aberdeen Press and Journal*, 16 October 1939). As Susan Scarlett, Noel Streatfeild was able to offer daydreams to her readers, exploiting her varied experiences and interests to create, as her publisher advertised, 'light, bright, brilliant present-day romances'.

Noel Streatfeild was the second of the four surviving children of parents who had inherited upper-middle class values and expectations without, on a clergy salary, the financial means of realising them. Rebellious and extrovert, in her childhood and youth she had found many aspects of vicarage life unappealing, resenting both the restrictions thought necessary to ensure that a vicar's daughter behaved in a manner appropriate to the family's status, and the genteel impecuniousness and unworldliness that deprived her of, in particular, the finer clothes she craved. Her lack of scholarly application had unfitted her for any suitable occupation, but, after the end of the First World War, during which she spent time as a volunteer nurse and as a munition worker, she did persuade her parents to let her realise her dream of becoming an actress. Her stage career, which lasted ten years, was not totally unsuccessful but, as she was to describe on *Desert Island Discs*, it was while passing the Great Barrier Reef on her return from an Australian theatrical tour that she decided she had little future as an actress and would, instead, become a writer. A necessary sense of discipline having been instilled in her by life both in the vicarage and on the stage, she set to work and in 1931 produced *The Whicharts*, a creditable first novel.

By 1937 Noel was turning her thoughts towards Hollywood, with the hope of gaining work as a scriptwriter, and sometime that year, before setting sail for what proved to be a short, unfruitful trip, she entered, as 'Susan Scarlett', into a contract with the publishing firm of Hodder and Stoughton. The advance of £50 she received, against a novel entitled *Peter and Paul*, may even have helped finance her visit. However, the Hodder costing ledger makes clear that this novel was not delivered when expected, so that in January 1939 it was with *Clothes-Pegs* that Susan Scarlett made her debut. For both this and *Peter and Paul* (January 1940) Noel drew on her experience of occasional employment as a model in a fashion house, work for which, as she later explained, tall, thin actresses were much in demand in the 1920s.

Both *Clothes-Pegs* and *Peter and Paul* have as their settings
Mayfair modiste establishments (Hanover Square and Bruton
Street respectively), while the second Susan Scarlett novel, *Sally-Ann* (October 1939) is set in a beauty salon in nearby Dover Street.
Noel was clearly familiar with establishments such as this, having,
under her stage name 'Noelle Sonning', been photographed to
advertise in *The Sphere* (22 November 1924) the skills of M.
Emile of Conduit Street who had 'strongly waved and fluffed her
hair to give a "bobbed" effect'. *Sally-Ann* and *Clothes-Pegs* both
feature a lovely, young, lower-class 'Cinderella', who, despite
living with her family in, respectively, Chelsea (the rougher part)
and suburban 'Coulsden' (by which may, or may not, be meant
Coulsdon in the Croydon area, south of London), meets, through
her Mayfair employment, an upper-class 'Prince Charming'. The
theme is varied in *Peter and Paul* for, in this case, twins Pauline
and Petronella are, in the words of the reviewer in the *Birmingham Gazette* (5 February 1940), 'launched into the world with
jobs in a London fashion shop after a childhood hedged, as it
were, by the vicarage privet'. As we have seen, the trajectory
from staid vicarage to glamorous Mayfair, with, for one twin, a
further move onwards to Hollywood, was to have been the subject
of Susan Scarlett's debut, but perhaps it was felt that her initial
readership might more readily identify with a heroine who began
the journey to a fairy-tale destiny from an address such as '110
Mercia Lane, Coulsden'.

As the privations of war began to take effect, Susan Scarlett
ensured that her readers were supplied with ample and loving
descriptions of the worldly goods that were becoming all but
unobtainable. The novels revel in all forms of dress, from under-wear, 'sheer triple ninon step-ins, cut on the cross, so that they
fitted like a glove' (*Clothes-Pegs*), through daywear, 'The frock
was blue. The colour of harebells. Made of some silk and wool
material. It had perfect cut.' (*Peter and Paul*), to costumes, such
as 'a brocaded evening coat; it was almost military in cut, with
squared shoulders and a little tailored collar, very tailored at

the waist, where it went in to flare out to the floor' (*Sally-Ann*), suitable to wear while dining at the Berkeley or the Ivy, establishments to which her heroines – and her readers – were introduced. Such details and the satisfying plots, in which innocent loveliness triumphs against the machinations of Society beauties, did indeed prove popular. Initial print runs of 2000 or 2500 soon sold out and reprints and cheaper editions were ordered. For instance, by the time it went out of print at the end of 1943, *Clothes-Pegs* had sold a total of 13,500 copies, providing welcome royalties for Noel and a definite profit for Hodder.

Susan Scarlett novels appeared in quick succession, particularly in the early years of the war, promoted to readers as a brand; 'You enjoyed *Clothes-Pegs*. You will love Susan Scarlett's *Sally-Ann*', ran an advertisement in the *Observer* (5 November 1939). Both *Sally-Ann* and a fourth novel, *Ten Way Street* (1940), published barely five months after *Peter and Paul*, reached a hitherto untapped audience, each being serialised daily in the *Dundee Courier*. It is thought that others of the twelve Susan Scarlett novels appeared as serials in women's magazines, but it has proved possible to identify only one, her eleventh, *Pirouette*, which appeared, lusciously illustrated, in *Woman* in January and February 1948, some months before its book publication. In this novel, trailed as 'An enthralling story – set against the glittering fairyland background of the ballet', Susan Scarlett benefited from Noel Streatfeild's knowledge of the world of dance, while giving her post-war readers a young heroine who chose a husband over a promising career. For, common to most of the Susan Scarlett novels is the fact that the central figure is, before falling into the arms of her 'Prince Charming', a worker, whether, as we have seen, a Mayfair mannequin or beauty specialist, or a children's nanny, 'trained' in *Ten Way Street*, or, as in *Under the Rainbow* (1942), the untrained minder of vicarage orphans; in *The Man in the Dark* (1941) a paid companion to a blinded motor car racer; in *Babbacombe's* (1941) a department store assistant; in *Murder While You Work* (1944) a munition worker; in *Poppies for England* (1948) a member of a concert party; or, in *Pirouette*, a ballet dancer. There are only two exceptions, the first being the heroine of *Summer Pudding* (1943) who, bombed out of the London office in which she worked, has been forced to retreat to an archetypal southern English village. The other is *Love in a Mist* (1951), the final Susan Scarlett novel, in which, with the zeitgeist returning women to hearth and home, the central character is a housewife and mother, albeit one, an American, who, prompted by a too-earnest interest in child psychology, popular in the post-war years, attempts to cure what she perceives as her four-year-old son's neuroses with the rather radical treatment of film stardom.

Between 1938 and 1951, while writing as Susan Scarlett, Noel Streatfeild also published a dozen or so novels under her own name, some for children, some for adults. This was despite having no permanent home after 1941 when her flat was bombed, and while undertaking arduous volunteer work, both as an air raid warden close to home in Mayfair, and as a provider of tea and sympathy in an impoverished area of south-east London. Susan Scarlett certainly helped with Noel's expenses over this period, garnering, for instance, an advance of £300 for *Love in a Mist*. Although there were to be no new Susan Scarlett novels, in the 1950s Hodder reissued cheap editions of *Babbacombe's*, *Pirouette*, and *Under the Rainbow*, the 60,000 copies of the latter only finally exhausted in 1959.

During the 'Susan Scarlett' years, some of the darkest of the 20th century, the adjectives applied most commonly to her novels were 'light' and 'bright'. While immersed in a Susan Scarlett novel her readers, whether book buyers or library borrowers, were able momentarily to forget their everyday cares and suspend disbelief, for as the reviewer in the *Daily Telegraph* (8 February 1941) declared, 'Miss Scarlett has a way with her; she makes us accept the most unlikely things'.

Elizabeth Crawford

CHAPTER ONE

"WE ARE this term losing a head girl who has been in every way splendid. For me, and for the staff, and the school, next term will be the poorer because Elizabeth Carson is not with us."

The Carson family were sitting in the front row of visitors. George Carson had not been married twenty years, and owned a family of five, without having learnt that a parent must disguise all feelings when inside his children's schools. Not that George was a man given to showing his feelings. He had worked in Babbacombe's stores since he was fourteen, and that was thirty-six years, and as Babbacombe's insisted the customer was always right, a Babbacombe face learnt how to get under control. Still, just this once it was an effort to look as if you could not hear what was being said, when your heart was pounding with pride. His Beth to be spoken of like that—"next term will be the poorer because Elizabeth Carson is not with us." He wanted to lean over and squeeze Janet's hand and say "Hear that, Mum? That's our daughter she's talking about."

Janet Carson was a little self-conscious in the children's schools. It was such a struggle making their income do, and the children wanted so many clothes there was not much left for mother. Coming into the school hall, and being shown to the conspicuous front seats, she had been conscious that this was the third annual prize-giving she had been to in the same brown coat. She had been so sensitive to being looked at in it again this year that she had nearly had it dyed black, only she was sure the stuff would not stand it, and she had no shillings to throw away on dyers. But now, with what the headmistress was saying, she might have been dressed in sacking for all she knew or cared. She just sat with her shiny-fingered gloved hands tightly clasped, and swallowed. Terrible if she disgraced the girls by crying right there in the middle of the school hall. And what was there to cry for, anyway? Wasn't this the day she had known was coming from the moment Beth was born? The headmistress wasn't saying one word more than Beth deserved—not enough, really. But she wouldn't know all the things there were to say; it was her mother who knew that.

Edward felt his ears growing red. It was sickening the way his ears grew red; a fellow's ears ought to be part of himself, like his nose. After all, his nose didn't sniff unless he meant it to, so why should his ears grow red all by themselves? Pretty good all that about old Beth. It would be a bit of all right if Mr. Cart, his headmaster, said things like that about him when he left school. Not much chance of that, though; all he had to say so far was, "Don't dream, Carson; keep your mind on your work." It was different for Beth—she was the sort you'd expect those kind of things to be said about. Bit of all right, old Beth.

Girda was not sitting with her family: she was sitting in the gallery with her form. She was grinning from ear to ear, her hands just twitching to clap. It was splendid about Beth, and a very good thing, too, because perhaps now all the teachers had heard what was said they might mind her mistakes less; they might say, "Perhaps Girda Carson will turn out all right; look at her sister."

Paul and Eve sat on each side of their mother. It was a grand evening because they were out of bed at nine o'clock instead of in it for Eve at six thirty, and Paul at seven. Besides, they wore their best clothes, and putting on best clothes in the evening made you feel like a party. Actually, except for being pleased about the hour and the clothes, they were bored. A lot of old gentlemen had talked, and a lot of girls had been given books. Paul had been troubled with his legs, which would swing, and it had needed a lot of looks and pats from his mother to remind them not to. Eve had found it difficult to leave her frock alone; she had not meant to fidget, but she had found a loose thread and pulled it out, and then a mark which she attempted to rub away with her thumb, and that had led to her trying to pleat the hem. She had needed a lot of pats, too, before she could make her hands stay quiet. But now it was different; the headmistress was talking about Beth; Beth, who was like Mum and Dad—somebody so important that you couldn't think of a world without them; Beth, who, unlike Girda and Edward, was always the same—a person who made you feel safe. Paul and Eve leant forward and beamed at each other across their mother.

Beth was sitting in the front row with the other prizewinners. On her knees were the six books she had won. She was staring down at their dark-blue covers and the embossed school shield; but she was not seeing them. "The school next term will be the poorer because Elizabeth Carson is not with us." And how much poorer things were going to be for Elizabeth Carson! This year as head girl had been such fun. It would be different if she were going on to do something she wanted. Something first class in the secretarial line she would have liked; but of course it could not be: there was no money in their family for things like that, especially as Dad had managed to have a job for her at Babbacombe's just waiting.

The headmistress had finished, the girls were clapping and stamping, they were looking at her, her friends on each side were nudging her. She had never heard such loud clapping—it was the loudest since she had been in the school. It was grand to finish like that. Just for a moment tears stung the back of her eyes, then she blinked and threw up her chin. School was not everything; she might miss it—she would miss it. But it was no good thinking like that: she belonged now to the grown-up world outside.

The family lived at number ten Penruddock Road, Battersea, a little squat mid-Victorian house with a narrow strip of garden which finished at the railway embankment. They went home by omnibus; it did not take them all the way, but as far as the Battersea Bridge Road, and from there they walked. Relieved from being on their best behaviour, the younger members of the family were full of conversation.

"I bet you can't get a hat on, Beth," said Edward. "Your head must be swollen three times its size after all they said about you."

Beth flushed, for the omnibus was full of people.

"Shut up."

"My word, I'd be proud if somebody said all that about me." Girda's voice was shrill. The other passengers looked at them all and smiled. "Even being your sister I was quite proud. All the girls kept nudging me."

"Me and Eve clapped like anything," Paul broke in.

Beth was by now crimson, conscious of amused eyes on herself and her pile of books, but unconscious that most of the glances were affectionate and envious. She did not grasp that they saw a pretty girl with brown curling hair and big brown eyes, who had evidently done well at school, and was just the kind of daughter that everybody would like to have. Janet, seeing Beth's embarrassment, tried to quieten her family.

"Pull your skirt down, Girda. Don't keep jumping about like that, Paul. All right, Eve; I heard the speech, too."

Edward grinned. He was very good at imitations. He rearranged imaginary pince-nez and spoke as it were over the bridge of his nose.

"We are this term losing a head girl who has been in every way splendid. For me, for my staff—"

They all had to laugh, the inflection was so perfect. "Though, mind you," said George, wiping his eyes, "you haven't any right to go taking off Miss Rigg like that. She's still Girda's headmistress, even if Beth's finished with her."

That took the laughter out of Beth. It was as if a goose walked over her grave. Somehow with her father's words it felt as if a door were closing behind her—the door of the safe and secure days of childhood. Janet, who was sitting next to her, partly sensed how she was feeling. She tucked her arm into hers.

"I can do with a bit of supper when I get in. Feeling as proud as I felt tonight makes you peckish." She looked down at her knees, her eye caught by the lighter edge of her coat where the stuff was wearing thin. "I wish I could have got myself up a bit. Down our row that girl Ruth's mother was sitting; she had a black crêpe-de-Chine frock and ever such a nice fur coat."

Beth gave her mother's arm a squeeze.

"Nobody's got a nicer face than you, whatever you've got on; and Ruth's mother works in a dressmaking business. I expect she gets her clothes cheap." She gave a little laugh. "Anyway, you'll have that fur coat soon, perhaps by next winter prize-giving. The savings box is doing well, and now I'm earning I shall be able to put in a bit more."

Janet laughed.

"My fur coat!"

A fur coat for Janet was George's most cherished ambition. The wives of the rest of the staff at Babbacombe's seemed to have fur coats—he had seen them at the firm's parties. Years ago, before Girda was born, he had come in one day with a moneybox. It had been a cold winter's night, and Janet had been having a bad time carrying Girda, often sick and wretched, finding it difficult to crawl about doing the housework and looking after two babies. All day while at work George had been trying to think of something that would cheer her up. It was no good bringing her anything to eat—like as not she wouldn't be able to keep it down. Perhaps some flowers—no one loved flowers more than Janet. It was on his way to the flower department that he saw the moneybox. It was in the banking and accounting department—a proper bank moneybox, with places for notes and the different-sized coins. He had the book made out in Janet's name, and started her box with five shillings, which at that time he could ill spare, and carried it home to her in triumph and put it down on the mantelpiece.

"There's the beginning," he said; "and when that's full you'll have a fur coat, my girl."

There had been very few Fridays since then that George had not managed to put a bit in Janet's box, and as the children got older they had helped too. The halfpenny that Eve found on the sand when they went for their fortnight to Bexhill; a shilling out of the half-crown Girda earned by sitting on a wall for a lady artist to paint her; five whole shillings out of the pound that Edward had earned as a prize for an essay on the children's page of a newspaper; a bit of almost all that came Beth's way. But somehow no matter how fast the money had gone in, and however full the box had become, something had always happened, and out it came again.

With the years it had become a superstition with Janet that if her box weighed more than a certain amount, ill luck was on its way. There had been that winter when they had all been ill with influenza and Paul had nearly died of pneumonia. The doctor's bill from that had crippled them quite enough, and it was her box that supplied the extra invalid nourishment and the money to get Paul sent away. Then they had that trouble about Edward's eyes. He had not been allowed to use them for six months, and when he was allowed to use them again, he had been ordered very expensive glasses. Edward did his best, and meant to be careful, but he was a terrible boy with glasses. It seemed to Janet that it was almost every week that she was off to the optician to have them mended, and every time that happened it was a bit out of the housekeeping, and, adding those times together, sooner or later it was ten shillings out of her box. Besides, it was not only illness which was a drain; there were secret ways in which the money went. Sometimes it was to help out on the family's clothes, sometimes it was plants for the garden, lately there had been a pound taken out for Beth's room.

Beth's room was almost as much a pleasure to Janet as to Beth. Number ten Penruddock Road was a squeeze for a family their size. There was the big front bedroom which had belonged always to herself and George and the newest baby. There was the room over the kitchen for Beth and Girda, and the one over the dining-room for the boys. The idea had come to her one day when she was talking to George.

"Eve's getting too big to be sleeping with us; I'll have to put her in with the girls, and that means that room isn't big enough. I think when we get back from the holiday I'll have to move us in there and give the three of them this room."

George was fond of the bedroom. He and Janet had shared it since their wedding, and it was in there the five children had been born. But he made no complaint; what the children needed, as far as possible he and Janet gave them—that was understood; no need to do a lot of talking about a thing like that.

Janet had broken the news of the planned change to Beth when she came in from school. Beth was busy at that time working for the school certificate. She liked to think over her work while she dressed and undressed. Girda was a sufficient hindrance, but the thought of Eve full of chat from about seven in the morning made her heart sink, and involuntarily she let an "Oh Mum!" escape her. She covered her lapse in a second, saying with a grin, "What a nuisance! But what must be must."

Janet had said no more at the time, but over her housework and in her kitchen she did a bit of thinking. The result was Beth's room in the attic.

It was not much of a room, being reached by a ladder from the passage, but it was her own. Janet had got Edward to help, and had dragged the accumulated rubbish and the family trunks down to the coal shed, where there was an unused place with a concrete floor. She had done wonders with the pound from her moneybox. She had bought paint and distemper and turned the drab place cream-coloured. She had bought a gay cretonne and made curtains for the window and one for a railed-off corner for Beth's clothes. There had been an old dressing table, and with the remains of her cream paint she had turned it and a kitchen chair into decorative bits of furniture. She had not let Beth see the room till it was done. She had leant down through the trap and called down the steps.

"Come on up, Beth, and see your own place."

Beth had come up, and had stared round so pleased she could not speak for a moment. Her face was enough for Janet; it was almost an anti-climax when she flung herself in her arms with a breathless:

"Oh, darling Mum."

Number ten Penruddock Road was lit by a street lamp. To pass-ers-by it might not seem much of a little house, but the Carsons loved it. It was home, and they knew of charms it possessed which were hidden to strangers: how in the spring there was a laburnum in the front garden that was the envy of the street; how at the back, where the garden ended in the embankment, you could shove your arm through the fence and pick ox-eye daisies. Beth knew of her attic room, and Edward of how the shed was big enough for his carpentry. They all knew of something which made that house and garden the best of their kind in London.

"Give old Puss a call, one of you," said George, feeling in his pocket for the key. "Don't want him caterwauling to come in just as I'm getting into bed."

"Not all of you," Janet broke in hurriedly; "remember we're late, and think of the neighbours."

"There he is," Eve shrilled. "I see his eyes shining like little fires."

Paul scrambled under the privet hedge.

"Puss, puss."

Janet was after him.

"Oh, Paul, think of your best suit."

Paul had hold of puss.

"I had to fetch him; he's had an awfully dull evening. Haven't you, Penny?"

Penny was a ginger tom with one of those gamin faces which endears a cat only to its owners. The children had called him Penruddock after the street, and reduced it to Penny as more friendly. To George and Janet he was just puss.

On the mat, when George opened the front door, lay a letter. Letters were not very common in the Carson household. Janet had too much to do to keep up a correspondence with her family, and George had no near relations. They all studied the envelope with interest.

"It's for you, Dad," said Edward.

George examined the stamp.

"It's come from Somerset."

Janet laughed.

"Open it; it won't bite you. You go up with Eve and Paul, Girda, and see they get quickly into bed. Now, no arguing," she held up a warning finger to Eve. "I'll be up with your supper in ten minutes, and there'll be an extra biscuit; but if you aren't both tucked up, then the biscuits'll come down again."

"Can I help with the supper, Mum?" asked Beth.

Janet gave her arm a pat.

"No, you run up and see how your books look in your room; I know you're dying to. Edward'll give me a hand, won't you, Edward?"

There was soup for supper. Janet, having settled Paul and Eve for the night, put the tureen on the table and called the rest of the family. As she stood waiting for them she felt a consciousness of the moment. Of the two little ones in bed upstairs. Of George with his pipe in his armchair. Of Girda and Edward arguing whether pea soup was nicer than tomato. Of Beth leaning over her father's chair telling him of how well the new books looked in her room, and of the pleasure in George's eyes as he answered her.

"I am lucky," thought Janet, feeling a throb of happiness so sharp that it hurt. "A nice family like mine and a husband like George. My word, I'm sorry for women who haven't a husband and children."

George put his pipe in its tray on the mantelpiece and came over to his seat at the table.

"That letter was from Miss Pole," he said.

Janet wrinkled her forehead.

"Pole?"

"Yes." George ladled out the soup. "She was the sister of Brenda that married poor Gerald."

Edward passed a plate to his mother.

"Our half-uncle Gerald?"

George nodded.

"That's right—my half-brother. He married a girl called Brenda Pole, and she died when their child Dulcie was born. Her sister

Rosa came then to see after the house, and when Gerald died too she took little Dulcie to live with her in the country."

Janet cut bread for her family.

"Is it that Miss Rosa Pole who's written to you?"

The soup was all ladled out. George took up his spoon to eat his own.

"That's right. She says Dulcie is seventeen. I hadn't reckoned she'd be that old."

Janet spread her bread with butter.

"Must be: she was born very nearly the same time as Beth. I remember you wanted to go up and see Gerald when Brenda died, only Leeds was so far and we hadn't the money. What's Miss Pole write about?"

George said nothing for a moment, then he laid down his spoon.

"She says Gerald's business fetched quite a bit when he died. He had a sweet and tobacconist's business, you know. There was enough, it seems, to send Dulcie to a boarding school, and she's got about a pound a week for life. She's through with school now, and wants a job."

Janet looked across at him.

"What sort of job?"

George felt in his pocket and brought out the letter. "Dulcie is now finished with school and says she finds the country dull; she wants to live in London and get some 'congenial work.'"

Beth grinned.

"I like that—'congenial work.' I suppose you can pick and choose if you've got a pound a week."

Janet was staring at George.

"Why has she written to you?"

George found another place in the letter.

"As she is your half-brother's child, will you take her as a paying guest, and help her to find work? She . . ." He broke off, obviously considering the rest private.

"Gosh!" said Edward. "We needn't have her, need we?"

"Goodness, no!" agreed Girda. "It would be foul."

"I might get her into Babbacombe's." George's voice was troubled.

"Do we have to have her, George?" Janet's tone was anxious. "I know the money would be a help, but I do like us being just ourselves. Then there's the question of a bed. I don't know where we'd put her."

George gave his head a worried shake.

"I didn't get on well with Gerald, but he was my half-brother." He glanced at Beth for help.

Beth swallowed. Perhaps only Janet knew the extent of the sacrifice she offered. "Of course we must have her, Mum. She can share my room."

It was not until George and Janet were undressing that Janet asked for the unread part of the letter.

"What did Miss Pole say about Dulcie?"

George sighed as he found the letter and read:

"'She is a difficult girl—very fond of gaiety, and too much for me to manage.'"

Janet felt her heart sink, but she disguised it and came over to him.

"Don't look such an old long-face. She's only a kid. I expect I can manage her. Besides, there's Beth. I reckon sharing a room with Beth will cure anybody of being difficult."

George leant his face against hers.

"I hope so, but you didn't know my half-brother Gerald. One shouldn't speak ill of the dead, but if she takes after him we're in for a peck of trouble."

CHAPTER TWO

BETH was not starting work for another week, so it was she who went to the station to meet Dulcie. She was not feeling cheerful. She had spent a dismal morning moving her possessions out of her attic to the boys' room, and the boys' things up to her attic. Janet had once again robbed her moneybox, and had worked a trans-formation in the boys' room by making dainty flowered cretonne curtains and bedspreads to match. But in spite of these charms Beth (in strict privacy) had shed a few tears at saying goodbye to her attic. She knew her mother was right: Dulcie could not be asked to climb a ladder to her bedroom. She realised, too, that, thanks to her mother sitting at the sewing-machine early and late, the bedroom for herself and Dulcie was looking charming—fit for any girl, however many boarding-schools she had been to.

Waiting at Paddington for the train to come in, Beth tried to put her thoughts where she imagined they ought to be. She must not even feel inside that she did not want Dulcie, or Dulcie might sense it, and that would be simply awful, for Dulcie was an orphan. Beth, with her love for her father and mother the *leit motif* of her life, could not imagine any state so lonely as that of being an orphan.

"I do wish I had more control of my thoughts," she told herself, as she strode up the platform. "I keep saying 'I will make her feel wanted'; and then another bit of me says, 'Oh, goodness, I *do* wish she needn't come! I wish I still had my own room. I wish—"

What Beth might have wished next was swept out of her mind because she fell full length on the platform. She was pulled up, feeling shaken and very dusty, by a young man, who had a dachs-hund under his arm.

"I say," he said. "I'm awfully sorry. It was Scissors here. He wasn't looking where he was going."

Beth, brushing her skirt, examined her stockings, and was pleased to find that they had not been cut. She smiled at the dachshund.

"It wasn't his fault. I wasn't looking either. Why d'you call him Scissors?"

"Because you can never find him when you want him."

Beth laughed.

"It's funny you know that. It's true about scissors—when one wants to sew they're always missing."

"I was thinking of nails when I christened him. You know, toes and fingers."

There was a pause then. Beth filled it in as best she could brushing her clothes, but she was very conscious of the young man, of his well-cut blue suit, of his grey eyes that screwed up when he smiled. His hair was brown—she could not see much of it under his hat. She liked his long narrowness—long and narrow in body, long and narrow in face. He looked as if he were always doing something energetic.

He could not get much of a view of Beth: each time she looked up for a second she found another bit of dust and began to brush it off. Her hat had come off when she fell; he had picked it up when he had picked her up. Hatless he had a good view of her hair. He liked its colour—like a chestnut, with the same lights on it. He wondered if it curled like that naturally, or had a permanent wave. He came to the pleased conclusion that it was probably natural: she looked too much of a kid to have taken to permanent waving. He liked her eyes. There had been a song his mother had been fond of, called "Brown-eyed Sue". He wondered if her name was Sue. It might be; it would suit her.

"Awfully dirty, stations are," said Beth.

He looked at the platform.

"I doubt if it would be fit to eat the old meat off if the seven maids with their seven mops swept for half a year."

She finished her dusting and took her hat from him and put it on.

"I'd like to see them. It would brighten the station. Oh, there's the train."

"So it is." He took off his hat. "Goodbye."

"Goodbye." She gave the dog a pat. "Goodbye, Scissors."

In the crowd she lost sight of the young man and the dog. She never consciously noticed young men much. She was surprised at herself for peering through the people for another glimpse of this one. She would have been still more surprised if she could have heard the young man whispering to Scissors:

"Clever dog, Scissors. We'll buy you a bone on the way home. Your taste is impeccable; you knocked down the nicest person we've ever seen."

As the two girls did not know each other by sight, it had been arranged that Dulcie should stand by the engine until Beth found her. Beth, pushing through the crowd, saw Dulcie before Dulcie saw her, and her heart sank. "Oh goodness," she thought, "I'm afraid that's her."

Dulcie was fair. She had a mass of very arranged curls. To Beth, who had not yet taken to it, she seemed frighteningly made-up. The hand she held out to shake hers had startling blood-red nails. Beth had on a simple dark frock; it had looked quite nice when she had started out—or at least she had thought so—but now she not only became painfully conscious that it was still dusty, but she felt it looked as if it had been made at home, as it had. Dulcie had on a black crêpe-de-Chine frock with white collars and cuffs; it had a little white lace at the hem to look like a petticoat. On the back of her head was a black straw hat tied under her chin with black ribbons. Her skirt barely covered her knees, her stockings were so sheer her legs looked bare. She had on exaggeratedly high-heeled shoes with no toes. Through her stockings her toenails showed painted with the same enamel as her fingers.

"Are you Dulcie Carson?" Beth asked.

Dulcie nodded, her eyes raking Beth in a not kind way. "Yes. You must be Beth, I suppose."

"Yes. I'll get a porter. I suppose your box is in the van."

"I have a porter; he's seeing to them. I've three boxes in the van and a couple of suitcases."

"Oh." Beth was so overcome at the vision of so many boxes crowding in their bedroom that she could not think of anything else to say. Dulcie, however, took command. "Shall we go? I told him to put it all in a taxi."

Beth's eyes opened.

"Oh, but it's miles. It will be much cheaper to let the company deliver them; we could manage two suitcases on the underground."

Dulcie gave her a scornful look.

"What, live with a couple of suitcases for days? Of course I couldn't. I want to change and have a bath as soon as I get to the house. I always feel a mess after a journey, don't you?"

Beth, feeling a raw schoolgirl, gulped.

"Well, I've only been to Bexhill. We go there for a fortnight every summer. Of course we change into beach things as soon as we get there, but the sea has to be our bath. The landlady would die if we wanted hot baths in the middle of the day."

"I hope your mother doesn't mind them."

Beth struggled to speak nicely.

"Well, nobody ever does have baths at teatime in our house, but of course she won't mind."

Driving along in the taxi, Beth's spirits sank lower and lower. Everything Dulcie said made her feel more sure she was not the sort of person she was going to like without a great struggle. She had an unhappy feeling, too, that neither were her father and mother going to like her. "It's like bringing home a bomb," she thought miserably as the taxi turned into Penruddock Road.

"Is this the house?" Dulcie asked as the taxi stopped. "You don't mean to say you all squeeze in there."

"Oh yes, there's plenty of room really. I'll go in and see if Edward's about to help with your boxes."

Janet was in the kitchen making a pot of tea. She looked round with a cheery smile.

"Hullo, darling; where's Dulcie?"

"Seeing her luggage off the taxi."

"Taxi!" Janet's eyes opened. "She must be feeling rich."

"I think she is," Beth agreed miserably. "She looks it, anyway. Where's Edward? There's a lot of boxes."

"Out in the shed at his carpentry." Janet leant out of the window. "Hi! Edward!"

Edward stuck his head out of the shed door and peered short-sightedly.

"What is it?"

"Go and give the taxi driver a hand with Dulcie's boxes."

"Gosh!" said Edward. "A taxi! All the way from Paddington?"

Girda's voice came from her bedroom window.

"Has she come?"

Edward hurried up the garden.

"Yes, in a taxi."

Girda's voice rose in an excited scream.

"A taxi! All the way from Paddington?"

Paul and Eve were playing at the end of the garden. Girda's voice reached them. They came running into the house.

"Mum," Eve squeaked. "Cousin Dulcie has come in a taxi!"

"I'm going out to see," said Edward.

Janet went into the hall. Dulcie was coming in. In one glance Janet took in all the cheap pseudo-smartness of her niece's appearance, but it did not dismay her as it had Beth. She only felt an infinite pity.

"Poor little thing!" she thought. "That Miss Pole must be a fool to let the child make such a little guy of herself." She gave Dulcie a hug.

"How are you, dearie? Tired after the journey?" The taxi driver and Edward struggled by with one of the boxes. "What a lot of boxes! I hope you'll find room for your things. You and Beth are sharing a bedroom."

Dulcie raised her eyebrows.

"Are we? Didn't Aunt Rosa tell you I was going to pay to live with you?"

Janet laughed.

"If you paid a thousand a year we couldn't give you a room to yourself—we haven't got one. Take her up, Beth, and help her arrange where the boxes are to go."

With a little pride Beth showed Dulcie into the bedroom. It faced west, and the afternoon sun was streaming in; it made the new cretonne look gay. But Dulcie was not impressed; her face was sulky as she looked round.

"Only one cupboard? I hope you haven't many clothes."

"Not many. If there isn't room for you I expect Mum will put up a curtain for the rest."

Dulcie was peering at the chest of drawers.

"I shouldn't care for that; it would look like a maid's bedroom."

Beth thought of her beloved attic. Her eyes flashed. "Would it? I've never seen a maid's bedroom."

"Haven't you? We had a lot of maids at school."

Somehow two of the boxes and the suitcases were squashed into the bedroom. The third box was put in the passage. Dulcie went down to pay the tax-driver. A moment later the driver's voice was heard raised in fury.

"Threepence! Drove you all the way from Paddington, humped three great boxes up the stairs, not to mention the suitcases, and you give me threepence!"

Dulcie's voice was ultra-refined.

"Don't be impertinent."

"Impertinent! I—"

Janet, purse in hand, hurried to the gate. She held out a shilling.

"I'm sorry," she said gently. "My niece is a country girl; she does not know much about London yet."

Dulcie's face was scarlet.

Janet put her arm round her.

"Come along into the house." She turned to the taxi-man. "Thank you, driver. Good afternoon."

The driver looked at Janet's and Dulcie's backs, then he spat on the shilling.

"Country girl! Strewth!"

Edward and Girda, their eyes goggling, came to Janet in the kitchen. Edward shut the door.

"Gosh, Mum, have you seen her? She's got painted fingernails."

"And toes," said Girda. "And such a lovely frock! Is she very rich, Mum?"

Janet recalled Dulcie's flushed face, and the taut fury of her body as she led her into the house. She picked up the teapot smiling.

"No, just a little schoolgirl with no mother to teach her how to behave. You must all try to make her feel at home."

George when he came back from work could not view his half-brother's child with the same tolerance that Janet did. He remembered her father Gerald, with that same vapid face and rather showy good looks, the same fondness for cheap clothes in bad style, and certain ways which he called "being smart" and George called downright dishonest.

"I daresay Gerald was like that," Janet agreed. "But that's no reason to go painting the daughter with the same brush. Her mother was all right as far as we know. She's probably a nice little thing really. What we've got to do is to train her. She's been brought up stupidly, that's all."

"I hope you're right," said George gloomily. "But I don't take to her."

That night after supper George talked to Dulcie about work. He waited until Janet and Beth had washed up and Janet was in her armchair opposite him with her basket of darning, Beth on the windowsill busy on a frock for Eve, and Edward and Girda had been sent to bed. Then he took a consoling suck at his pipe and looked disapprovingly at his niece lolling in a chair with a picture-paper.

"Your Aunt Rosa told you, I suppose, that I'd spoken to the staff manager at Babbacombe's for you."

"Yes. I'm glad. I've decided to be a mannequin, or perhaps arrange flowers. I'll see which seems most fun."

George gasped. Mr. Smith, the staff manager, was a nice man, but a stern one; he could not see him having any use for a girl who talked about "which is the most fun."

"I don't think you're the cut of a mannequin—you're a little thing, they have to be tall; and there's no vacancy that I know of in Flowers. I told Mr. Smith you'd go in any department."

Dulcie pouted.

"I don't want to do something boring."

"Work's scarce, you know, and you've no special training."

"I just couldn't do the same drab job every day. I'd go mad."

George set his chin.

"You know, my girl, you've got the wrong idea of business. It isn't going to be what you want, it's going to be what you can get."

Dulcie nodded.

"Oh, I do see that; only you see I'm rather different from the ordinary girl."

George's eyebrows shot up.

"Why?"

"Oh, well, I've been to a boarding-school, and I've got private money—"

Janet felt George was going to lose his temper.

"The thing is, Dulcie dear, what job can you get for which you can be certain to give full value for the money you earn?"

Dulcie shrugged her shoulders.

"I don't see that. My idea is what job can I get with least to do and most money and most fun. That's why I thought of a mannequin."

Janet caught Beth's eye. "Take her up to bed," she signalled, "before your father has apoplexy."

When the door had shut on the two girls George gave the table beside him a thump.

"That's what I mean. Gerald's child all over. Get rich quick. I wish we'd never agreed to have her in the house."

Janet laid down her work. She came and sat on the edge of his chair and rubbed her cheek against his hair.

"And do you know what I think? We're a couple of selfish ones. Here we've let the years go by and we've never bothered about the child. Well, now's our chance to make it up to her."

CHAPTER THREE

BETH started work on the Monday morning. She was to begin as a junior in the Gowns department. The thought of Babbacombe's gave her a sinking feeling inside; it would be worse than being a new girl at school, only school did not matter so much, because you paid to be there; now Babbacombe's were paying you; even though it was only a beginner's wage of fifteen shillings, how awful if she were stupid and they felt they were wasting their money!

Always when thinking of her first day at Babbacombe's Beth had been comforted with the knowledge that her father would be with her. She and he had always been such friends it would make the first morning less alarming that they were together. Now the pleasure of that was spoilt because Dulcie would be there too, for George had been told to bring her along for an interview with the staff manager.

When she had something ahead of her, Beth liked to dress slowly and silently, gathering her forces as it were for the day. Dulcie was at no time a silent dresser, and that Monday morning she was maddening.

"What's Mr. Smith, the staff manager, like?" Beth was at the dressing table combing her hair.

"Old."

Dulcie opened the wardrobe.

"I rather like old men, and I think they like me. They often look after me in the street. Do you think I'd better wear black? It's supposed to please men."

Beth gave a wriggle of disgust.

"Mr. Smith is going to see you about a job. I should think your brains will matter more than your clothes." Dulcie looked smug.

"That's all you know. In everything in life a woman's charm is what counts. I read that in a magazine."

Beth joined her at the wardrobe and took out her working frock. All the girls in Babbacombe's wore green—a dark green in any material. Back in the summer sales Janet and Beth had gone out to buy her frock. A study of the papers had shown Janet that when it came to sales, bargains, even within the reach of themselves, could be had at quite good places. So it was not to one of the second-rate shops they went, but to a good firm in Knightsbridge, and there right away they found the very thing. It was a model going cheap because it had been worn a lot by the mannequins and had become soiled. Janet, feeling the heavy, moss-coloured cloth between her fingers, decided it was well worth the extra that would have to go on the cleaner's bill.

As Beth fastened her frock, Dulcie looked at her in surprise, and with a faint ruffling of her complacency. From the moment she had glanced at Beth she had marked her down as negligible. She thought her hair quite pretty, and of course she was lucky it curled naturally, but she was certain it looked drab beside her own golden permed head. She thought there must be something the matter with a girl of seventeen who did not make-up. If she knew what she looked like, she often thought, she'd do something to her face. Why, she looks as if she were still at school. She had many a smile over Beth's clothes. Of course everybody could not be like her, with a nice sum saved up for her while she was at school to spend on a wardrobe, but all the same it was a joke to look like Beth. Why, half the time she was wearing out her old school things; that was a bit too much for somebody just starting work.

Beth, utterly unaware of Dulcie's appraising stare, was straightening her frock in front of the glass. It was an amusing yet simple garment. It had about it a faint remembrance of the days of the bustle. It had buttons all down the back, and what seemed to be a sash but was really a length of moire silk let in to the front breadth; the silk finished behind in a stiff bow. The moss green suited Beth's colouring, it brought out the lights in her hair, and enhanced the peach-off-the-wall colouring of her cheeks.

"Course it's quiet," thought Dulcie, "but it's got something. I wonder what?" With less pleasure in herself than usual, she pulled on a black satin frock trimmed with imitation gold leather.

Beth's arrival down to breakfast in the new frock was the cue for family criticism.

"Ooh, Beth," said Paul. "You look like a cucumber."

Eve walked round her slowly, her eyes wide with amazement.

"Don't you like it, pet?" asked Janet.

Eve nodded.

"Yes; only Beth looks like a grown-up lady."

Girda sighed enviously.

"It's lovely. I do wish I could have a really good frock. All the other girls in my class have."

Edward grinned at Beth.

"Oh, Modom! Let me dust a chair for you, Modom. What time are you expecting your Rolls Royce, Modom?"

They all laughed: Edward's voice was like the commissionaire's at the cinema up the road. Besides, a new frock was a proper subject for a family joke. The laugh stopped suddenly as Dulcie came into the room. Janet, feeling the girl might notice the change of atmosphere, smiled at her kindly.

"Good morning, dear. Are you feeling all ready for your interview?"

George gave a disgusted glance at his niece's clothes and painted face, then he swallowed down his feelings, and gave a nod towards Dulcie's chair.

"Sit down, my girl, and make a good breakfast."

Mr. Smith's office was on the top floor at Babbacombe's. It was reached by the staff lift. George, feeling flustered, pressed the button and took the two girls up.

"You'll go in first, Beth, and then I'll bring Dulcie in afterwards. Don't be shy."

Beth edged towards her father and, without Dulcie seeing, gave his hand a squeeze. He looked down at her and smiled. They said nothing, but they understood each other. She was saying:

"Don't fuss. I'll be all right—you know that."

And he was saying:

"Of course you will; only having Dulcie with me upsets me. You understand."

Mr. Smith was at his desk. He looked up as Beth was shown in, and gave her a quick, approving glance.

"Good morning. All ready to start work?"

"Yes."

"Well, your father is a good servant of the firm's, and he will have talked to you about the way we like our staff to behave."

"Yes."

"In many ways I think it's easier for our girls when they come to us as apprentices. But you are a scholarship girl and have had unusual educational advantages. Now, that acts two ways. It means that you ought to be smart and do well, but it also means that being a junior will come hard on you. You'll be at everybody's beck and call. You know that?"

"Yes. I shan't mind."

He smiled.

"That's good. Now you go to Gowns and report to Mrs. Nunn, the buyer. She's expecting you." He got up and shook her hand. "Mr. Babbacombe is a good employer, as you'll learn. He expects service, but he gives a lot for it. Not perhaps in money—though the pay's as good as any—but there's no staff in London looked after like ours. But there's one thing Mr. Babbacombe never forgets himself and never lets anyone else forget. Babbacombe's exists to serve the public, and the public, no matter how difficult they may be, are always right. You remember that."

Beth nodded.

"I will. Good morning."

Hurrying down the passage to the lift, Beth wondered if all your life people talked to you like that. She had supposed work would be very different from school; but here was Mr. Smith making just the sort of speech Miss Rigg made to new girls.

George, hat in hand, ushered Dulcie into Mr. Smith's room. Mr. Smith looked up and gave a nod.

"Morning, Carson."

"Morning, sir."

"This the niece?"

"Yes, sir."

In a flash Mr. Smith took in Dulcie and had given George a glance to say "All right, it's not your fault. We'll do what we can." His voice took on a brisk note.

"Well, Miss Carson, what can you do?"

Dulcie looked at him from under her eyelashes.

"I'd like to be a mannequin."

Mr. Smith's voice hardened.

"I didn't ask what you'd like to be, I asked what you could do."

Dulcie changed her tactics, her face grew pathetic.

"Well, so far I've only been in a boarding-school. I'm not very old."

Mr. Smith's lips curled.

"Our apprentices start at fourteen and usually know what they want." He looked up at George. "I can do one of two things with her. There's a vacancy on the lifts. She's got the appearance for that. She'll start at twenty-five shillings, and the top wage is thirty shillings. As you know, there's no future in the work. Alternatively, we need a junior in Handbags. What do you think?"

Dulcie did not wait for George to answer. She broke in with shining eyes.

"Oh, I'd love to be a lift girl. Do I wear special clothes?"

Mr. Smith nodded.

"Green suits in huntsman's style. But you heard what I told your uncle; there's no future, and it's only a job while you're young."

Dulcie blinked at him.

"Well, I hope I shan't want a job always. I might get married."

Mr. Smith thought that likely; his experience was that the Dulcies of this world always did, and a fine mess they often made of it.

"Very well, I'll give you a month's trial." He scribbled on a slip and handed it to Dulcie and pressed a bell. "That's for Miss Jenkins; she'll show you where to go."

The first days when you are a stranger in a world where everybody else knows each other are a strain. Beth was naturally quick and adaptable, but her start at Babbacombe's tried her high. Mrs. Nunn, the buyer, was a difficult woman. She had an unpleasant, lazy husband to cope with, and the good salary she earned was eaten up in keeping her home going and educating the children. The resultant struggle to make two ends meet while presenting an appearance to match her job made her a victim to nervous indigestion. She put up a struggle to be considerate and not to snap, but she frequently failed, and her girls were scared of her. The assistant buyer, Connie Jones, had got her job by a piece of luck owing to somebody else's illness. She was not really efficient, and she knew it, but she was saving to have enough to help buy a house so that she and the man she was engaged to could get married. The vision of that house spurring her on made her cringing and subservient to Mrs. Nunn's least whim. She did not want to be unfair to anybody, but if something went wrong she must never be to blame, for fear of jeopardizing her job. Below Mrs. Nunn and Miss Jones were the salesgirls, all different, and all with idiosyncrasies to study. Beth was at the beck and call of everybody.

"Go and hang up those afternoon dresses I had down for that customer."

"There's a lot of things in fitting-room K; go and put them away."

"Telephone down to the workroom and tell Mrs. Fosdick I've got a lady for alterations in fitting-room Y."

"Run up to Accounts and see if Lady Fraser's bill is sanctioned; she wants to take the things away with her. I have rung through, but they seem to have gone to sleep up there."

"Get these packed, and tell them to put the blue on top, and not to put any string round the box, as the customer's going to Gloves for matching."

"Madam says she was sitting on the settee in the corner and she has dropped a charm off her bracelet. Have a good look and feel down the settee."

For all and everything Beth had to smile and look pleasant and forget how tired she was. It was her feet which suffered most. She had to wear shoes with fairly high heels. The high heels alone were tiring to a girl who had been used to spending hours a day in school uniform, flat-heeled shoes. But it was the carpet that really got her down. Miles of it, thick and clinging, dragging at her feet with every step she took. Just for a moment or two on her second day in the shop she sat down. A fellow-junior, called Jenny, gave her a horrified dig in the ribs.

"I say, get up before Mrs. Nunn or Miss Jones see you."

Beth sprang up.

"I thought we were allowed to sit. I mean I thought it was the Shop Act or something that we had to have something to sit on."

Jenny laughed.

"So they say, but it doesn't work out that way. You won't get sacked for sitting, but if you sit you'll get the sack."

During her first days at Babbacombe's Beth reached home so exhausted that she could only eat her supper and crawl into bed. Janet was quite worried.

"I wish Beth didn't get so tired, George. D'you think she's outgrown her strength?"

George shook his head.

"No. Give her time. Of course it is tiring at first, with all the standing, but she'll settle down. You see, what with the strangeness, and wanting to do her best, she's probably putting more energy into what she does than is wanted; after a time she'll get sorted out, find the best way of doing everything."

In those first days Dulcie added to Beth's burden. While waiting for her lift uniform she was given the list of the goods on the different floors to learn by heart. Beth, lying dead tired in bed trying to get to sleep, was driven distracted by a continued mutter:

"Ground floor: confectionery, cooked meats, hardware, food market, ribbons, flowers, haberdashery, lampshades, linens, lace, handbags. First floor: boyswear, menswear, inexpensive millinery, perfumery, gloves, post office, library, rest room. Second floor: model millinery, furs, artificial flowers, knitwear, blouses, coats, inexpensive gowns, clothes for misses. Third floor: costumes, gowns, inexpensive coats, skirts, outsize department, juvenile, baby linen, lingerie, beach wear, corsets. Fourth floor: sports, toys, sportswear, furniture, furnishings. Fifth floor: restaurants only."

Then the muttering would pause.

"Oh, dear, I've left something out. I believe it was shoes. Did I say 'shoes', Beth?"

On Saturday morning there was an entirely different atmosphere in Babbacombe's. The sun was shining: it looked as if for once there would be a fine weekend. Girls meeting each other whispered of bathing parties, of motoring down to Brighton, of dancing at a roadhouse. Beth, too, felt cheerful. Her first week was over. It had seemed frightful, but today she felt for the first time that she was sorting things out. She was beginning to know to which cupboard or stand the different things belonged. She was getting the girls sorted out, getting names to them and being called by her name instead of "Hi, you" or "Hi, what's-your-name."

In the middle of the morning a Mrs. and Miss James arrived about a set of bridesmaids' dresses. Miss Jones served them. They chose a certain maize-coloured frock, but the girl wanted a sash added to the model. Miss Jones beckoned to Beth.

"Run down to Ribbons, dear, and bring back a selection of browns about this colour." She produced a scrap of silk brought by Mrs. James. "Be quick, because they're in a hurry. Bring the widest, so they can see the effect."

Beth, her hands full of the matching ribbons, decided her quickest way back was by the staff lift—Ribbons was not far from a staff door. She was lucky the lift was down and empty; she was just pressing the third-floor button when a man's voice called, "Wait for me," and the doors were flung open. Beth gasped: it was the man she had met on Paddington Station.

"Hullo," she said, pressing the button. "I didn't know you worked here. How's Scissors?"

"Grand! How extraordinary that you work here!"

"I didn't when I saw you. I've only been here a week." She sorted her bundles of ribbons, preparing to get out, and at that moment the lift stuck.

They were halfway between the second and third floors. Beth pressed button after button. Then she shook the gates.

The young man smiled.

"No good, I'm afraid."

She frantically tried all the buttons again.

"It can't be. We must be able to do something."

He felt the doors, and then tried the buttons.

"No."

"But it's awful."

"No good getting in a tailspin," he said cheerfully. "It's quite safe."

"Safe!" Her voice was full of scorn. "D'you think I'm frightened?"

"What else?"

She looked at him in disgust.

"I'm working in Gowns, and there's a customer waiting to see these ribbons."

"Well, let her wait. Who cares?"

"I care. And you ought to care. Babbacombe's employs us, and we ought to mind what upsets their customers."

He gave her an interested look.

"Fancy that, now." He hammered on the lift doors. "Somebody will hear us and get the engineers."

He was right: in a few moments they were heard by a passing member of the staff. The young man nodded at Beth.

"What did I tell you? Trust Uncle David; he's always right. Shall we sit? If I know anything of mending lifts we shall be some time."

Beth looked at the floor.

"It's rather dirty."

He took off his coat and laid it on the floor.

"There you are, modom; Babbacombe's for service. Can you squeeze up a bit, and we can share the coat?" He opened his cigarette case. "Will you?" She pointed to a notice over his head which said: "No Smoking Allowed." He sighed, "I'm afraid you're one of those people who lets herself be browbeaten and dictated to for a miserable weekly pittance."

Beth had not met many men, and certainly none like this one. She was not sure if he was teasing her or whether he meant what he said.

"As a matter of fact I don't smoke, but if I did, I wouldn't have one where it says I can't."

He lit his cigarette.

"Why not? The word 'can't' makes me truculent. I go round the country forcibly holding myself back from pulling the emergency thing in trains, and I've never been able to stop myself spitting in tubes, and as for throwing bottles out of express trains, it's become a vice. I should think I must have killed half a dozen or so men working on the line."

Beth laughed.

"Aren't you silly? All the same, I wouldn't smoke here. After all, it's Mr. Babbacombe's lift, and he can do what he likes with it."

He shook his head.

"You've a sadly misplaced respect for Mr. Babbacombe."

Beth flushed. She did not want to sound priggish, but she hated to hear their employer run down; after all, he provided their weekly wages.

"My father's worked here for thirty-six years, and he says Mr. Babbacombe's a very fine man."

"What's your father do?"

"He's a salesman in Hardware."

"And doesn't earn a penny more than four pounds a week, I'll swear."

"Four pounds a week is pretty good. Besides, it comes out better than that sometimes, with bonuses and commission."

He looked at his cigarette end.

"Babbacombe's is a company, you know. Even in the slump their preference shares never dropped under seven and a half. Do you understand that? Heaps of men and women who've never done a stroke of work in their lives are getting seven and a half per cent on their money, while your father has worked for thirty-six years and gets four pounds a week."

She wriggled uneasily, her schoolgirl sense of honour and "standing up for the school" conflicting with her mind, which liked to thrash things out.

"I don't see that what the shareholders get from Babbacombe's has anything to do with shop rules." She looked at him curiously. "Why d'you work here if you feel like that about the store?"

He blew out a ring of smoke.

"I don't work here."

"You don't? Then what are you doing in the staff lift?"

His eyes twinkled.

"Did you know Mr. Babbacombe had a wastrel and ne'er-do-well son?"

Beth's eyes opened.

"You mean—"

He nodded.

"Yes. I'm David Babbacombe."

Beth's sense of humour came to her rescue; she laughed.

"I'm awfully sorry I've said the things I have, but I couldn't know who you were."

"Why be sorry? You've said all the right things. My father would be charmed if he'd heard you."

His voice sounded bitter. She gave him a puzzled glance.

"Are you going up to see him now?"

"Yes. I'm a remittance man. I'm going for a cheque."

Beth examined his lean, athletic figure in shocked surprise.

"Don't you work at anything?"

"No. A little beachcombing now and again, and I've a nice hoard of silver cups won for this and that."

Beth forgot he was Mr. Babbacombe's son and only felt that she liked him too much to want to despise him.

"I should have thought doing nothing but playing games was pretty dull."

He tapped some ash clear of his coat.

"Oh, it's all right."

Beth hated that.

"But it isn't. It's miserable. You might as well be a cabbage."

He looked down at her, smiling.

"You are a nice person. Shall I tell you the sad story of my life?" He pointed over their heads, where hammerings showed the engineers to be at work. "Those fellows will be some time."

"Yes, do."

He hugged his knees.

"You know, it's not all beer and skittles being born with a thing like Babbacombe's stores in the family."

Beth thought of the security of his background and marvelled. "Isn't it?"

"No. It's like the child-marriages they used to have. I was married to the stores when I was born. Taken all over it when I was four. Dragged round it every holidays, when I was at school, and expected to go into it when I left Oxford."

"Didn't you want to?"

"No. My tastes happen to run quite a different way. I like designing aeroplanes."

"Can you?"

"I don't know." His face was suddenly eager. "I'll tell you a secret. I've been working a couple of years on a seaplane. I sent the idea in to the Admiralty last week."

"Oh, I hope they take it!" She hesitated. "But if that's what you want to do, your father doesn't mind, does he?"

"That's all you know. You see, I'm the only son. He's set his heart on my coming in as a director later on."

"And you won't?"

"I did try. I put in three years, but I couldn't get enough time on my own stuff."

Her face was understanding.

"I suppose you were always stopping away."

"Yes. I know I made a howling mess of everything I touched."

"And then you gave it up?"

"No. My father kicked me out. You see, he didn't know I was working on my 'plane, and he thought I was just wasting my time."

"Why didn't you tell him what you were doing?"

His eyes grew hard.

"Not me. I asked to go through some aeroplane works starting at the bottom, but he wouldn't hear of it. I could have an aeroplane if I wanted one, but I had to come into Babbacombe's. Some day I'll show him what I can do without him."

"But didn't you say you were going up for a cheque?"

"Yes. I told you I was a remittance man."

"Then you haven't done without him."

"Oh, well—"

Beth's voice rang with scorn.

"I'd hate to do that—I mean I'd rather do anything than take money that I didn't earn."

He flushed.

"But working on my model cost quite a bit."

"If you'd stayed in Babbacombe's you could have earned quite a bit, couldn't you?"

"But then I'd have had no time."

She raised her eyebrows.

"Can't you work on a model at night?"

He got up, his hands thrust in his pockets, his shoulders hunched. He looked, Beth thought, like Paul when he was cross.

"Well, I suppose I can do what I like with my own life," he said.

Beth turned scarlet. Whatever was she doing criticising him like this? What must he think of her, a stranger, except for one meeting on Paddington station, dictating to him as to what he ought to do?

"I—I'm awfully sorry. It was cheek. It was only I was interested."

He did not answer that. The lift gave a jerk. She got up and picked up his coat; it was very dusty. He held out his hand.

"Thank you."

"If you'll hold these ribbons," she suggested, "I'll give you a brush."

He smiled.

"When we meet, one of us is all over dust."

There was a shout from an engineer.

"Hi, you in that lift. Press a button, will you?"

"Which floor?" David asked Beth.

"The third."

David pressed, and as if it had never stuck the lift glided to the floor above. He opened the gates.

"Goodbye," she said. "Thank you for lending your coat."

He held her arm.

"As a matter of fact I'm not sure it's going to be goodbye. Look out for me. I might come back to Babbacombe's. You never know."

CHAPTER FOUR

JOHN Babbacombe—"the old man" or the "O.M." to his workers—was a character. He was a little man whose once ginger-coloured hair was now grey, but still retained sufficient of its original colour to give a pink tone. He had the poorest opinion of his own appearance.

"Try and build me up a bit," he always said to his tailor. "A scrap like me in the chair at the shareholders' meetin's gives 'em the jumps. 'No good trustin' Babbacombe's,' they say; 'why, the chairman's no bigger'n a rat.'"

The tailor tried to do as he was told, with the result that old John had a shrunk look. But neither his shareholders nor his work-people found his size took away from his power—a dictator, was old John. He had an undeniable air. If he was seen walking through the stores, his people nudged each other and made a great effort to appear busy and efficient. Those, such as George, who had known him over the years, mixed respect for him with deep affection. They knew the size of the heart in the little man: how he might strut a bit, and put on a few airs, but how under it all was plain, Ginger Babbacombe, who had been kicked round the shop when he was a kid, and knew all about working conditions at first hand, and was apt, in a showdown, to see the workman's side of a case.

Old John was at his desk when David came in. He looked up and nodded.

"Hullo."

"Hullo, Dad."

The old man fidgeted with a pile of papers: he did not want to raise his head so that David should know how pleased he was to see him. The young devil was a lazy hound, but he could afford to have a lazy son, and there could not be much wrong with a boy who could do so well at sport. Besides, he would not waste his time forever. He'd reach sense in the end.

"Cheque wanted?" he asked gruffly.

David sat on the edge of his father's desk.

"There was. When I parked the old car outside this magnificent store about half an hour ago, I was on my way to ask for a couple of hundred."

"Well, what's stoppin' you?"

David opened his cigarette case and leisurely lit a cigarette.

"A girl."

Up shot old John's eyebrows.

"What girl?"

"One of your staff."

Old John's face grew pink.

"How often have you heard me say I won't have you lookin' at my work-girls?"

David nodded.

"And how often have you heard me say 'But I don't want to, Papa'?"

"Who is she?"

"She works in your Gowns department, and she got stuck with me in a lift."

"I'd take a bet you had something to do with it sticking."

David shook his head reprovingly.

"You've got a dirty mind. It wasn't that sort of goings-on at all. Matter of fact she spent the whole time telling me off."

Old John chuckled.

"A bit of that won't do you any harm."

"She despised me because I took money from you that I didn't earn."

Old John gave a snort.

"I'd like to see any job that you could do that would earn a tenth of what I give you."

David rubbed his nose.

"You know, she was a girl of sense. I'm not sure she wasn't right. How would it be if I came back into Babbacombe's?"

John's heart gave such a pleased thump it caught his breath. It was all he could do to keep his voice level.

"If you think I want any more of that, you're wrong. I can afford to keep you hanging around a damn sight better than I can afford to have you demoralising my staff. When you worked here there wasn't one day but what you sneaked off early, and there wasn't one man over you but reported that your heart wasn't in your work. That's a fine example for my workers. I reckon the only use you were was to add to the sports trophies down at our club."

David nodded.

"True, too true. But suppose the leaf has turned over, showing a clean bottom never before exposed. Or suppose the prodigal son, sick of sitting around with swine and eating husks, has come home?"

Old John made a curious sound, half snort, half laugh.

"It would take a bit of swallowing."

David dropped his light tone.

"Happens to be true. The loafer's through with loafing. Got a place for me?"

Old John tapped his desk thoughtfully. This was not the way he had seen things working out. He had visualised a gradual boredom before David put his shoulder to the wheel. This change of heart in a lift with one of his staff did not sound the real thing. Sadly he shook his head.

"Too sudden, my boy. You take the two hundred you came for and go away and think things over."

David's tone was firm.

"No. I want to start now. I hadn't cottoned on to myself before. It's a bit stiff when a kid can turn round and call you names and you can't answer because you deserve them."

John gave his son a look, an idea coming to him.

"If you were to start again I'd want you to begin where I began, at the bottom."

David nodded.

"All right. What is the bottom job? I'll take it."

John had to hold himself down in his chair, he was so excited, but he was not showing David any of that.

"The bottom carries bottom pay. Course I can go on allowing you—"

David shook his head.

"No. I'll take whatever the pay is and make do. I've plenty of clothes and no debts, and I'm living at home."

John chuckled.

"What about all your theatres and dining-out?"

David tapped his cigarette ash into a tray.

"I can manage without them for a bit. I might get a rise later on."

John, so eager that his hands shook, leant forward.

"Look here, my boy. If you're serious, I'll put you into whatever department has a vacancy and I'll pay you a couple of pounds a week. If you stick it for six months—and when I say stick it, I mean do the job well, clock in on time, and get a good chit from the buyer—I'll take you into the firm. How's that?"

David got up.

"Grand! When do I start?"

John lifted a telephone receiver beside him.

"Give me Mr. Smith, please, miss. That you, Smith? We got a vacancy for a young man?" There was a pause, then John chuckled. "Oh, is there? Good. Well, hold it. I've got the man for it. I'll send him over to see you right away." He replaced the receiver and looked up at David with a grin. "Your job's waiting. You're in Cooked Meats."

Mr. Wills, John's secretary, came hurrying into the room in answer to a ring. David had gone, and John, alone, had let himself relax. Unexpected happiness is as much a shock as unexpected sorrow. Mr. Wills thought his employer looked smaller even than usual, and a little pale.

"Yes, Mr. Babbacombe. Can I get you something? Brandy, perhaps?"

"No." John's eyebrows shot up. "What for?"

"I thought—"

John twinkled.

"Look a bit winded, do I? You ever back an outsider?"

"No, Mr. Babbacombe. I don't bet."

"Pity. You back an outsider that nobody believes in except yourself and see it win. Nothin' like it."

"Yes, I'm sure, Mr. Babbacombe."

John remembered why he had rung.

"Go down to Mrs. Nunn or Miss Jones in Gowns and ask which of their girls got stuck in the lift."

While Mr. Wills was away John did something unusual. He went to the cabinet under his window. He examined the of rows of bottles inside.

"Ought to be champagne," he thought. "That's the right stuff for a celebration. But I can't celebrate alone, and I can't celebrate with David—not yet." He took out a bottle of port and poured himself out a glass. He raised it and spoke out loud.

"Here's to you, David boy. May this be the beginning of a long and successful life in the firm."

Mr. Wills knocked.

"May I come in, Mr. Babbacombe?" He came over to John. "The girl's name is Carson. She's just begun as a junior. A relation of the Carson in Hardware."

As the door shut John drew a pad towards him. On it he wrote: "Keep an eye on Miss Carson."

George liked having Beth in the same business with himself. For thirty-six years he had been hurrying off to work alone, and he had never given it a thought. Now he found the morning start quite a bit of fun. It began the first day, when he went along to Beth's room to be sure she was getting up. She had stuck her head out, laughing.

"Get along with you. D'you think you're the only one who gets up?" Then she had given his face a pat. "I'll give you a call tomorrow. Don't want you fined for being late."

That was the beginning of one of those silly little jokes that live in families. It was a race in the mornings for which of the two should knock up the other. They had all enjoyed it when on the Thursday Beth and George had met in the passage coming to call each other.

They sometimes walked home together, and George found himself looking up at the clock towards six, feeling expectant. Old Beth would be starting to put things away about now. He hoped it hadn't been a rushed day, because then she'd get out about the same time as he did. They had made a bargain, and

George stuck to it, that they would not wait for each other after a quarter past six, but he took a precious long time walking up the street after the quarter, and his head was more over his shoulder than in front of him.

He was proud of being seen with Beth. They had walked home together after Beth's first day in the shop, and they had run into Fred Grey, the buyer of Hardware, and George had introduced them. The next day Fred Grey had spoken about it.

"Nice-looking kid your daughter is, George." Then he had sighed. "Must be a bit of all right having a daughter." Then he had given George a kind of nudge. "Some men have all the luck."

George knew that Fred Grey's wife had run off and left him, and that he had never cared for anybody else, and lived on alone in the house at Harrow. He knew, too, what Fred Grey earned, and it was a lot more than his four pounds a week; but, for all that, he knew he was right. Money did not come into it at all. With his family, especially Beth, and with a person like Janet for a wife, he did have all the luck.

It was good, too, to have someone to talk to about Babbacombe's. With the years Janet had picked up quite a piece. She knew the names of all the men in George's department, and the names of people higher up, and a bit about how they carried on; but you had to belong before you really could talk about business. When Beth talked, George remembered himself thirty-six years ago. He had started as an apprentice, and things were harder then. When Beth talked about the standing and how tiring the carpet was, he liked telling her how things used to be.

"Wonderful the improvements. That comes of Mr. Babbacombe having worked himself. He doesn't need a Government inspector to tell him what's wanted. He knows."

Beth loved teasing her father.

"It's a pity there isn't a Mrs. Babbacombe, then, who's worked in the shop. I'm not grumbling, Dad, but there are improvements for the women that only a woman would know."

George pretended to be shocked.

"Listen to her. Not in the place a week and wanting to reform it. I suppose the welfare supervisor and the sister in the rest room aren't any good? Nothing will be any good till Miss Beth Carson's in charge."

That Saturday George hung about well after a quarter past one waiting for Beth, but it was a quarter to two before she got home. They were all at dinner, the leisurely Saturday midday dinner, which Janet took half the week planning.

"What kept you?" George asked.

Beth glanced at her mother and held out her hands.

"They're not really dirty. Will they do?"

Janet pretended to inspect them as she had done when she was small, and as she still did Paul's and Eve's, and sometimes, from necessity, Girda's and Edward's.

"Well, they could have stood a lick and a polish, but they'll pass."

Eve bounced on her chair.

"Say it, Mummy, say it."

Janet recited.

> "Seesaw, Marjorie Daw.
> Sold her bed and laid upon straw.
> Wasn't she a dirty slut,
> To sell her bed and lie upon dirt?"

Edward, Girda, Paul and Eve pointed at Beth. Long practice had taught them to speak well in unison.

"Wasn't she a dirty slut? Slut! slut! slut!"

Beth threw her hat, gloves and bag on a chair and sat down.

"I thought I was never going to get away. I got stuck for half an hour in the staff lift. Of course Miss Jones didn't get on at first to what had happened, and was furious, for she had a customer waiting for some ribbons. When she did hear what had happened, she was sorry, but she'd left everything for me to do, and I had to do it. I thought I'd be there till Sunday."

"We need a new lift," said George. "It's always sticking. Were you alone?"

For a moment Beth toyed with the idea of saying "yes". Some part of her was whispering, "Keep it to yourself. You don't want to discuss him with all the family." Then her real self took command. What was there to make a mystery of? Besides, they would all enjoy the story so, and it would be fun telling them. She looked round at them, her eyes twinkling. "It's a story in two halves, really. When I went to Paddington to meet her"—she nodded at Dulcie—"I was knocked over by a dachshund, and the man the dachshund belonged to picked me up."

"What was the dog's name?" asked Paul.

"Scissors." She looked at Janet. "He said he called him that because he was always missing when he wanted him."

Janet liked that.

"Scissors! What a name! Go on. What happened?"

"Well, nothing then. I met Dulcie and thought no more about him." She took a mouthful of meat to give herself time. Why had she added that last line? It was not true, and it was not like her to say things that were not true. She swallowed her mouthful. "This morning Miss Jones sent me to Ribbons, and I was just going up in the staff lift when a man came along and said, 'Wait a minute', and it was—"

They were all waiting for it. With a roar the children finished the sentence:

"The man who has Scissors."

She nodded.

"Scissors wasn't there, only the man, and we looked at each other and—"

Edward broke in, speaking in a high voice meant to be Beth's:

"Oh, fancy meeting you, Mr. Scissors!"

Everybody laughed. Beth grinned at Edward.

"It was rather like that. We both said it was odd our meeting at Babbacombe's, and I asked how Scissors was. And then the lift stuck."

Girda's eyes goggled.

"Gosh! Weren't you frightened? I would have been."

Dulcie gave a rather nasty giggle.

"What, at being alone in a lift with a man?"

There was an awkward silence. Girda was too young to see what Dulcie meant; Edward half knew and turned crimson; George looked at his niece as though she were some unpleasant slug; Janet, though she was sorry the children had heard that sort of cheap talk, felt full of pity. What an upbringing the girl must have had that the mere thought of being alone with a man made her snigger and talk like that! Beth surprised herself by seeing red. Telling the family about David had been nice—it made him feel as if he were a friend, a person that she might see again. Letting Dulcie hear about him was all right as long as she kept her thoughts to herself, but if she imagined she could break in with her sordid ideas, spoiling things, then she was wrong. She looked at her.

"You may think saying that sort of thing funny, we don't."

Dulcie winked at Janet and George.

"Hit the nail on the head, I should think, shouldn't you?"

George swallowed, then opened his mouth to speak. Janet broke in before he had time:

"I think that sort of talk is downright silly, Dulcie. Beth's just a schoolgirl, and so are you. You don't want to go repeating silly cheap things you've heard someone else say; you don't mean any harm, but it makes people forget you're only a child, and think of you as a rather nasty grown-up person." She turned to Beth. "Well, what happened, dear?"

The last thing Beth wanted was to go on with her story. With Dulcie's grins and winks in her mind, it made what had seemed rather nice, sordid. But Janet's voice was urgent. It did not just say the words that came out of her mouth, it added, "Go on, be a sport, help me out. We don't want Saturday dinner spoilt because of her." Beth gave Janet an 'all-right' smile. She had finished her meat; she leant forward and collected her family with her eyes, and gently but firmly excluded Dulcie.

"Well, there we were; and he was awfully nice, and took off his coat and we sat on the floor. We got talking about the shop, and I told him off because I didn't like his tone: I didn't think he spoke nicely of Mr. Babbacombe." She looked at George, her eyes dancing. "Who d'you think he was?"

George shook his head.

"I don't know?"

"Mr. Babbacombe's son."

George's face lit with interest.

"Mr. David?"

"Yes. D'you know him?"

George nodded.

"Been about the place since he was a nipper. I'll never forget the first time I saw him. He was about four or five—came round holding his father's hand. Never saw Mr. Babbacombe look so proud. Going to Toys to choose a present, they were. Proper caution he was. He could have had what he liked—you know, model trains or anything—but he gave one look round, so they tell me, and said: 'I don't want anything here: I don't want anything made by other people—I like things made by me.'"

Janet smiled.

"That's like you, Edward."

George shook his head.

"Been a disappointment to his father. Wouldn't work in the store—wanted to be an engineer, they say, and his father wouldn't have that; so now he does nothing."

"He told me that," said Beth, "and I told him I thought it was pretty disgusting taking money for what he didn't do."

George's face was disapproving.

"You shouldn't have said that; it wasn't your place. Mr. David knows his own business best."

Beth hated to hear David called "Mr."—it made her feel that he and she lived in different worlds—but she showed no sign of it; she was up helping her mother to gather together the plates. Picking up her father's, she gave him a kiss.

"It was all right; I said it quite nicely; I don't think he thought it cheek."

After lunch George had a smoke before going out to garden. Janet, her washing-up done, came and sat on the arm of his chair.

"What's this Mr. David like, George?"

George was surprised.

"Why?"

"Oh, I don't know. Just wondered. You can't help wondering about any man your daughter meets, can you?"

George frowned.

"Don't be so silly. You're as bad as Dulcie. He's a nice enough young man. I was always sorry for him, for I don't hold with making children work at what they don't feel fitted. But whatever he's like he's nothing to do with us: he went to Eton and Oxford."

Janet nodded.

"He was well liked in the shop? I mean he behaved himself?"

George puffed at his pipe.

"Proper old hen, you are, flapping round a chick. I never heard Mr. David spoken of anything but well; but if he had a bad reputation I'd trust Beth to look after herself. She's all right —Beth."

Janet patted his hand.

"Don't I know it?"

Up in their bedroom Dulcie sat and polished her nails; her eyes were eager.

"What's he like, Beth?"

"Who?"

"This David Babbacombe."

"Just like anyone else, I suppose."

Dulcie's eyes were lowered over her nails, her lips had a half smile. Beth might be a fool and think old Babbacombe's son looked just like anyone else, but she knew better. Babbacombe was rich, so his son was a thrill. Since she had been about ten she had planned to marry a rich man. Up to date she had never come anywhere near one. Now Beth, the poor fool, had met one, and she would meet him, too, before she was very much older, or her name was not Dulcie Carson.

"What are you smiling at?" Beth asked.

Dulcie raised innocent eyes.

"Just pleasure. I was thinking how glad I was I was starting work on Monday."

CHAPTER FIVE

IN HER second week at Babbacombe's Beth settled down. Her feet got used to the carpet, and herself used to standing. She found she had more leisure than she had believed possible in her hectic first week. There were ways of doing things, just as there had been ways of arranging her life at school—only a muddler had to be flying about all the time.

Between jobs she had time to think—more time to think, or perhaps more to think about, than she had ever had before. Babbacombe's had a news service more efficient than the African's tom-tom. It was believed that if something of interest happened on the ground floor, it had reached the farthest corner of the restaurant on the top floor in under five minutes. That David Babbacombe was working in Cooked Meats blew through the store like a blast. Beth heard the news when she was tidying a fitting-room—Jenny told her.

"I say, have you heard? David Babbacombe's working in Cooked Meats."

Beth had to stoop hurriedly to hide her scarlet cheeks, but Jenny would not have noticed. She bustled out, anxious to be the first with the news somewhere else. Beth straightened and gave herself a hug. Her heart had stood still when Jenny spoke, and then throbbed as if it were running a race. He had said: "I'm not sure it's going to be goodbye. Look out for me. I might come back to Babbacombe's. You never know."

Should she look out for him? She could easily find an excuse to walk through Cooked Meats—everybody else in Gowns would

manage to. Between hanging frocks and running messages she
gave herself up to wondering. She could not doubt that what she
had said in the lift had influenced him. He had been going up
to his father for a cheque, and here he was working. Would he
think her mean not to take any interest? He would know that she
would know where he was. Her inclination was to have a look at
him. Even the knowledge that he was under the same roof as she
was made the whole store different. It was wanting to see him
so much that kept her from going. Whatever was she coming to?
She, sensible Beth, who had only just stopped being head girl, to
get all sloppy over a man. She, who despised sloppiness.

By the Wednesday her resolutions not to see him were weak-
ening, and perhaps on Thursday she would find some reason to
go to Cooked Meats, but on the Wednesday evening she walked
home with George.

George had known the walking to and from work with Dulcie
would be a bore, but after one day he had decided it was one of
the bores he was just not going to stand. At the same time he
knew it was impossible to say he was not going to: he would be
shamed by Janet, who would say some strong things about Dulcie
being Gerald's child, and how he had neglected her. The neglect
part did not worry him. Somerset was a long way off and he had
never had the time or money to go visiting there, and he did not
suppose Miss Rosa Pole would have wanted to be bothered with
him if he had. But the bit about Gerald's child got him. He never
had been able to stand his half-brother, and every time he looked
at her, Dulcie seemed to be more like him. The very fact that she
was Gerald's child made him regret the day he had taken her in.

"Bad stock," he often thought. "It's bred in the bone." But he
was not saying too much about her to Janet. After all, it was Janet
who had said, "Do we have to have her?—I do like us being just
ourselves." And it was he—more fool him!—who had insisted.
Wonderful woman, Janet, not to have thrown that in his face
long ago. Most wives would have.

With cunning he manoeuvred for a slightly earlier start. Early rising was not one of Dulcie's virtues; and in any case she took twice as long to dress as Beth, for her curls and elaborate make-up took time.

"Think I'll get off now, girls," he said on the Wednesday morning. "You ready?"

Beth looked at the clock; it was five minutes before their usual starting time. She looked at her father; there was a come-on-be-a-sport light in his eye. With a twinkle she went for her things. Dulcie was only just down; she, too, looked at the clock.

"What's the hurry? There's no need to start yet."

"Not for you, perhaps," said George; "but I've got a big day ahead of me."

Dulcie hated doing things alone, but she wanted her breakfast. She gave an angry shrug of her shoulders.

"I think Beth might wait. It's awfully selfish of her."

George, having got his way, let that pass. Up the street he tucked his arm into Beth's and they both giggled like school children.

"Aren't you a bad old man?" said Beth.

He hugged her hand to his side.

"It's a good many years now I've been waiting to have my daughter walking to work with me. Any reason why I shouldn't?"

Beth felt a twinge of conscience. There had she been wishing that she had some nicer work to go to than Babbacombe's, and there was Dad looking forward to her coming. Lucky she had never spoken out about wanting to do something else; it would have hurt him.

"I'll try to get away sharp tonight," she said, giving his arm a squeeze. "Of course, if Dulcie's about, she has to come along too; but it's fun being just you and me."

Dulcie had, without arrangement between George and Beth, but with instinctive understanding, not been told about the wait-ing-until-a-quarter-past arrangement. As a rule the lift-girls got off pretty sharp at six o'clock, but they had to change, and there was a good deal of loitering and gossiping. It was after twenty past when she left the store.

George beamed when he saw Beth.

"Hullo! Had a good day? Let's get off."

Beth hurried beside him, there was no need to add "Before Dulcie catches us up."

"Any news?" she asked.

George did not answer until they were safely round the corner.

"No. I hear Mr. David's shaping well in Cooked Meats."

Beth felt her cheeks burning; she turned her head and pretended to look in a shop window.

"Good!"

George shook his head, puzzled.

"Funny his working there. D'you suppose what you said to him had anything to do with it?"

"Shouldn't think so—except that anybody saying right out what I said would make a person think."

"You seen him since?"

"No." They crossed the road to the bus stop.

George lowered his voice as they took their place in the queue.

"That's a good job. Of course, I know with you it would just be passing the time of day. But he doesn't want to be seen hanging around the girls."

"Why?"

George had no idea that he was breaking a dream. Anything to do with the Babbacombes was news, and was retold purely as such.

"From what I hear, Mr. Babbacombe's giving him another chance. In the canteen they were saying that they reckoned after six months Mr. Babbacombe would give him his rightful place. If that's true I would guess he'd do better to watch his step. Mr. Babbacombe has eyes in the back of his head."

Beth felt like a cat whose fur has been rubbed the wrong way.

"I don't see why Mr. Babbacombe should mind who his son talks to. After all, they didn't come from so much themselves."

The bus stopped in front of them.

Boarding the bus was an adventure, because luck figured so largely. Sometimes it was strap-hanging all the way home. Today their luck was in. The bus was not full; they got seats together. George felt in his pocket for coppers.

"What you come from isn't what makes the difference. It's what you're educated to. Mr. Babbacombe educated Mr. David right up to the top."

"Where was he educated himself?"

George chuckled.

"The same as I was—the nearest school. You know, Babbacombe's wasn't always like it is now. Why, even when I went it was half the size. When Mr. Babbacombe's father started it, it was just a grocery. He built it, you know."

"Well, if he built it, hadn't he the money to educate his son?"

George shook his head.

"Daresay he thought the board school, as we called them then, was good enough. Mr. Babbacombe was twenty-five when I came to the shop, and working twenty-three hours out of the twenty-four, and very much 'Mr. John' to everybody. But there were plenty of the older men who'd taught him all he knew, and they still called him 'Ginger'. So did we all really behind his back—'Ginger Babbacombe'."

"And then he got married?"

"Soon after I came to the shop. What a time that was! Wedding cake and a bit of cheese we all had, and drinks too. She was a sweet, pretty thing—Miss Rose Barton. Her father was a baronet. She died when Mr. David was born."

"Oh, Dad, how awful!"

He nodded.

"Yes; I can see Mr. Babbacombe's face to this day. He came in as usual, but he looked as if he'd had the heart cut right out of him and couldn't feel any more."

"Oh, poor Mr. Babbacombe! But he had the baby." George nodded.

"Mr. David. I reckon that's what kept him going. Never saw a man so wrapped up in a child."

"I suppose that's why he educated him so grandly?" George considered the question.

"No, Mr. Babbacombe's not the man to set store on that sort of thing. But, you see, Mr. David is half his mother's, and I reckon he's done all he can to keep him where she belonged: he'd think she'd like it."

"I shouldn't think, then, she'd like him to be selling cooked meats."

They were nearly at their stop. George got up.

"I daresay that's right; but maybe Mr. Babbacombe feels he needs a bit of toughening. He didn't do much good when he came in at the top, so perhaps he thinks it'll do him no harm to try the bottom."

Up in her bedroom Beth opened the window, leant on the sill and looked out into the street. She felt at cross purposes with herself, and needed straightening out before she contended with the family, and still more with Dulcie. So David's mother had been the daughter of a baronet, and David had been brought up to that world, and whatever he might do in the future, to that world he belonged. However much she hated admitting it, she'd better face the fact squarely that no good would come of seeing him.

"I can't think," she told herself angrily, "why you want to see him. I can't think why you've got so sloppy all of a sudden; you never used to be."

Dulcie came round the corner. Beth drew in her head. She combed her hair and went along to the bathroom to wash. Paul's shrill voice called to her from the attic:

"I say, Beth."

She climbed the ladder to the bedroom.

"Hullo, darling."

"Look on the window-sill."

She turned to see to what he was pointing. In a pot were three straggling green objects.

She fixed her face in an expression of admiration while she tried to solve what the things were.

"Aren't they tall? What are they?"

"Corn. At school they told us the country ought to grow more corn so we didn't have to have it come in ships. So that's mine."

Beth controlled a twitch at the corner of her lips.

"Isn't that splendid!" She came over to tuck him up. "Lie down." Paul moved carefully down the bed, avoiding a small hump. Beth looked puzzled. "Is that a hot-water bottle?"

Paul gazed up innocently.

"That? Oh no, that's just nothing."

Suspicion dawned in Beth's eyes. She pulled back the sheets, and saw a contented Penny curled up asleep.

"Oh, Paul! You know you aren't allowed to have him in bed."

"I had to have him up," Paul protested, seizing Penny in his arms. "He and me had a misunderstanding, and I've forgiven him; but he can't know I've forgiven him unless he sees me, can he?"

"What did you disagree about?"

Paul hugged Penny closer and lowered his voice.

"I don't want him to hear and think I'm telling tales about him; as a matter of fact, he's scratched up my mustard and cress."

"All of it?"

"Nearly. And seeing what he was most likely scratching for, I expect what's left won't be so good to eat."

"It can be washed."

Paul nodded.

"It can, but washed mustard and cress isn't nice—like mustard and cress with earth on it."

Beth kissed him.

"I'll bring you a new packet of it from Babbacombe's." She gently took Penny from him. "Let me have him, and I'll see he has something special for supper."

Paul let Penny go.

"All right. Goodnight, Penny darling, you lovely, gorgeous cat. Goodnight, Beth."

Beth slipped quietly into Girda's and Eve's room. Eve opened sleepy eyes.

"I was afraid I was going to sleep before you came to kiss me."

"Sorry, darling." Beth sat on the edge of the bed. "Paul called me, so I went to him first. Did you want something special?"

"No. I jus' wanted you, because I love you." She stretched up her arms, and Beth hugged her.

"Goodnight, pet."

In the kitchen, where Janet was getting supper, Girda, who was officially there to help, was arguing fiercely:

"But, Mum, it'll be my frock, so why can't I choose?"

Janet, with experience of arguers, went on quietly stirring, merely saying vaguely:

"Yes."

"But it isn't 'yes'," Girda stormed. "Everybody else at the concert will be awfully smart, and you want to make me look a fool." She heard Beth come in, and turned to her for support. "You don't think I'm too young to wear black, do you?"

Beth sat down on the table.

"What for? A funeral?"

Janet looked over her shoulder at her with a grin.

"Girda's reciting at a concert the school's giving for the Children's Country Holiday Fund, and I've said she can have a new frock for it—she'll need it in the autumn, anyway."

Girda broke in:

"And she wants it to be pink or blue, or something feeble like that."

"Not pink or blue, darling," Janet protested mildly. "Only it's got to be your party frock next winter, and black isn't suitable for parties, even if it is for reciting."

Girda, with tears in her eyes, turned to Beth.

"I'm doing 'The Little Match Girl', and it's awfully sad, and I want to wear black satin."

Beth laughed.

"I don't think black satin is awfully sad. Dulcie wears a lot of it, and she doesn't look sad at all."

"That's just it." Girda sat on the table beside Beth. "It's Dulcie wearing it made me think of it. After all, she's the only really well-dressed person I ever knew."

Janet turned round from the stove.

"Well dressed. Dulcie!"

Beth gazed at Girda in amazement.

"You don't admire her clothes, do you?"

"Of course. Please, Mum, let me have black. It won't cost any more."

Janet gave her a kiss.

"No, not black. Now take those hot plates into the dining-room. We'll go shopping on Saturday, and we'll get something you'll be ever so pleased with. You'll see."

As Girda went out, Janet looked at Beth in dismay.

"I never thought of that. Dulcie is a silly little girl, and I'm sorry for her, but something will have to be done about her if she's warping the taste of my children."

Because she did not want to think about herself, and what she felt was her silly mood, Beth flung herself even more than usual into the doings of her family. Janet's fur coat was the supper-table joke. It was a pity, George said, the summer sales had gone by and they hadn't bought it—he didn't want another winter to pass and she do without it.

"We could buy it on the never-never," Beth suggested.

Instalment paying was a sure laugh. George was dead against it, considering it the root of most trouble.

Edward giggled.

"And then, when we couldn't keep the instalments up, they'd take it away in bits—first one arm and then the other, until Mum had only the collar left."

Janet, helping them all to food, her eye raking the table to see that nobody's appetite was failing, shook her head.

"No 'never never' for me, Edward. When I'm ready for my coat I'm going to take two or three hundred pounds out of my box, walk into the smartest shop, and say 'Show me a sable with an ermine collar and mink cuffs'."

"I can't think how you can laugh about it, Aunt Janet," said Dulcie. "I couldn't laugh at the things I hadn't got." Janet looked at her with her eyebrows raised in amused pity.

"Couldn't you, Dulcie dear? It's worth learning to try, you know. Nobody can have everything they want, so it's a help to have a laugh ready."

Dulcie wriggled crossly.

"Some people can. Look at very rich people; they just buy what they like when they like."

"Oh, buying!" Janet dismissed buying with a gesture. "Do you really believe that if all the shops were open and we could all help ourselves, we'd be happy?"

Dulcie marvelled, not for the first time, at the stupid things her aunt could say.

"Of course not. It's only fun having things so that you look better than other people."

Edward always found Dulcie funny—he thought everything about her comic. Now he began to laugh. She turned on him.

"Well, what's funny in that?"

"Mum wanting a fur coat so that she could strut about lording it over the neighbours."

Janet saw that George was longing to give Dulcie a bit of his mind, and that Dulcie did not like Edward laughing; she got up.

"Come on, you three girls; give me a hand in the kitchen."

In the summer, when it was warm enough, George liked to smoke his after-supper pipe in the garden. When her washing-up was done Janet usually joined him. They did not say much, almost automatically stopping in front of their especial joys amongst the plants. Sometimes George said quietly, his voice carefully dulled to hide his pride, "Not done so badly, that delphinium"; and Janet burst out, "Oh, those lilies! I could do with a whole garden of them." But mostly it was silent, companionable walking—arm in arm, both glad of each other and the restful minutes.

Tonight Janet had a coat thrown round her, for it was cold. She stopped to sniff at a rose.

"We ought to plant some extra things this autumn," she suggested. "Dulcie's pound will make a lot of difference."

George puffed a moment in silence; then he smiled.

"That's not a bad idea. It'll be something good coming from the girl if she means a row of daffs."

Janet led him on. They came to the fence at the bottom, where the embankment grass sloped down to the railway line. Over the end of the fence a Dorothy Perkins was climbing. She nudged George.

"That Dorothy Perkins is a sight this year. I often see people in the railway carriages looking up at it."

George sucked his pipe contentedly.

"Not so bad."

Janet squeezed his arm.

"But there was a time when it was not so good. Took a bit of persuading and pruning and tying in place to get it going."

"What's this leading to?"

"Dulcie—she's like the Dorothy Perkins."

He put an arm round her.

"All right, gardener."

Outside the sitting-room they slowed down. They liked peeping in: it was fun seeing the children while they were not looking. Tonight Beth was at the table with Edward, busy with a jigsaw puzzle. Girda was lying on the floor with a book in front of her, her fingers stuffed in her ears, evidently learning something by heart. Dulcie was doing some needlework, stitching at a wisp of chiffon. Suddenly Janet felt a clutch at her heart; she pulled at George's sleeve, and dropped her voice to a whisper:

"Look at Edward."

Edward had a piece of puzzle in his hand and was peering at it. He had on his glasses, but he was straining to see clearly, his head moving from side to side, his eyes screwed.

"And he has his glasses on." George's voice was scared. That tone from George pulled Janet together; she managed the ghost of a laugh, and gave his arm a pull.

"Come on. Couple of old fusspots, aren't we? I daresay he's a bit tired, that's all. But I'll take him to the hospital—no harm in having him looked over."

In the sitting-room Janet went casually to the table and put an arm each round Edward and Beth.

"It's too dark for you two to see that: put on the light, George."

The light sprang up, and she turned away to draw the curtains. She would not look at Edward again for a minute; perhaps she was imagining things; maybe it really was too dark to see.

"I can't think why you have to make such terribly difficult puzzles, Edward," said Beth.

Edward was pleased.

"I knew it would be a beast." He looked over at Janet's back. "Come and see, Mum. It's the new one I made last week."

"The most awful bunch of sweet peas," Beth groaned. "Every petal alike, and the same bits fit anywhere."

Janet turned her eyes to Edward. No, the light made no difference: there he was peering at a piece as if he saw it through a fog.

"What d'you want to make such difficult ones for?" She came over and stood by him.

"It's more fun."

"You look as though you found it pretty difficult yourself." Her voice was carefully casual. "You're squinting at that bit."

Edward grinned at her.

"Was I? Matter of fact I don't go by the colours, I go by the shape. Colours get so blurred if you stare at them."

George, leaning against the mantelpiece, gazed at his son; his face seemed to age when he looked.

"Reckon you shouldn't be doing too much of that, boy, if it tires your eyes," he suggested gently.

Edward was quite unaware of his parents' glances.

"Rot."

Girda got up from the floor, tears streaming down her cheeks.

"Oh, gosh!" she gulped. "I don't know how I'm ever going to recite it—it's so terribly sad."

Edward came over to her.

"Imitation," he announced "of Miss Girda Carson reciting 'The Little Match Girl', by Hans Christian Andersen."

With terrific imitation sobs he gave a garbled version of the end of the story. Everybody, except Girda, laughed; she mopped her eyes.

"I don't know how you can laugh about it," she said. "Don't you see she died of co-co-cold? I'm going to bed. But I shan't sleep a wink—I shall cry all night."

Janet fetched her darning basket and drew up a chair to the table.

"I'll be up to tuck you up in a quarter of an hour, darling," she called after her.

Beth looked at Dulcie.

"I say, Dulcie, that's Mum's chair."

Dulcie raised her eyes from her sewing.

"D'you want it, Aunt Janet?" she enquired ungraciously.

Janet shook her head.

"No, dear."

Dulcie made a face at Beth.

"Anything else, Miss Interference?"

Beth flushed. Always her mother had sat in that armchair with her sewing. Dulcie had not been in the house long, but even she must have known it was more or less her property. She wanted to say something cutting, but she controlled herself. Dulcie was an orphan, she had never had a chance. She was insufferable, but she might improve. In any case squabbling with her would not help. After a moment she said to Edward:

"What an awful lot of mauve bits there are!"

She was rewarded. Janet appreciated her effort and gave her an enchanting smile.

It was always with a conscious throwing back of her shoulders and stiffening of her jaw that Beth went into her bedroom. A long *tête-à-tête* with Dulcie meant a constant guarding of her tongue. It would be so desperately easy to start a quarrel, and, having started it, so hopeless to get back to a semblance of good terms; and, if there were a quarrel, impossible to keep it from her father and mother, who would be made wretched by it.

Dulcie had gone up first, and was at the dressing table putting her hair in curlers when Beth came in. She looked round.

"I do think it's a bit of a shame your mother won't let Girda have the frock she wants for her concert."

Beth took her dressing gown off its hook.

"She's too young for black satin."

"I don't see why. I wore a little black satin frock when I was younger than her. I had my hair in ringlets and a big black bow. Everybody said I looked sweet."

Beth could just imagine the vision.

"I daresay you were more the type."

Dulcie took that as a compliment.

"Well, I was a pretty little thing, and paid to dress. All the same, I'm sure I could do something with Girda if I was given a free hand."

The thought of what a free hand of Dulcie's might do made Beth loosen her hold on herself. "I'm sure Mum would rather see to her herself."

Dulcie gave an angry shrug of her shoulders.

"You're all so pleased with yourselves in this house. So certain everything you all do is perfect. There are a few things even I could teach you, you know."

"Are there?" Beth did not mean to sound surprised, she did not mean to do more than just say something to fill in, but even as the words came out she knew they were rude. At once she was all contrition. "I'm so sorry. That sounded rude. I never meant it like that."

Dulcie eyed her cousin stonily.

"You meant it rudely. You hate me, don't you, Beth Carson? But not a bit more than I hate you. I'll show you a few things I can teach you before I'm through."

CHAPTER SIX

IT WAS after half-past five. The assistants in Gowns were getting dust-covers ready to put over the things. All the clearing up that could be done was finished. Already mentally the girls were shaking Babbacombe's off them, and they were seeing themselves changed and outside meeting their men friends, or on their buses and tubes halfway to their swimming, tennis, or perhaps to a quiet evening at home. Then suddenly into the department came a customer.

The salesgirls looked at each other. The customer did not seem to be rich, but she was very young, and would be likely to be slow. In other words, they would be kept late without a sufficiently compensating percentage. Then one of them happened to think of Beth. Sales were open in Babbacombe's—even a junior might sell if she could.

"Go on, Beth," said one of them. "You'll get a percentage on whatever you sell her."

"Quite threepence," one of the others added.

"Me!" Beth's eyes opened.

"Yes. Go on."

Beth stepped forward.

"Good evening, Madam."

The girl was looking round with nervous, anxious eyes.

"I hope I'm not late."

"Oh no, Madam."

"Well, look. I'm going to stay with an aunt for a week. I've never been asked before, and I was a little worried, for she knows such smart people, and I've absolutely nothing for that sort of house. And then today she sent me thirty pounds to fit myself out. Imagine! I never had so much before."

Beth looked at the little sandy-haired person in front of her. Just now she was wearing a rather baggy brown coat and skirt, and a hat which appeared to have been bought because it would pack easily. She stretched her imagination and tried to think of the right colours for her.

"Where is the house? What sort of things will you want?"

"It's in Sussex. My mother went there once, and she says it's a castle, really. What do you think?"

Beth tried to look like a person who was used to castles.

"We've got some awfully nice flannel frocks. Do you think you'd like something like that?" She led the way to where they were hung. "They look summery and yet they're warm."

The assistants nodded to each other.

"Just a flannel. I guessed as much."

"And she'll take all night choosing it."

"Still, it's good experience for Beth."

Beth, her arms full of frocks, led the way to a fitting-room.

"In here, Madam. Can I help you undo that?"

The girl looked quite different without her coat and skirt and the ugly hat. In her slip she seemed pretty in a rather mouselike way. Beth lifted a soft blue flannel over her head.

The blue flannel was a success, and so was a grey with a scarlet belt. For the afternoon, in case there were a flower show or anything like that, Beth persuaded the girl into a most becoming patterned crêpe-de-Chine, with a coat to tone. For the evening she wanted a bright yellow taffeta, but Beth urged against it. The taffeta was cheap, and she thought it looked it. Instead she pushed the claims of a very simple black chiffon which had been expensive but was now marked down.

"That dress looks so good," she explained. "And that will be so important in that sort of house."

The girl nodded.

"All right. I ought to have another, though. What about the yellow for my second?"

Beth shook her head.

"You can't, Madam." She made a lightning calculation on a slip of paper. "Two flannel dresses three pounds sixteen shillings each. The afternoon dress five pounds ten shillings, and the black four pounds eighteen shillings. That comes to eighteen pounds. Say five pounds for another evening dress. That's twenty-three pounds. That leaves you with seven pounds for shoes, bags, and two hats. Or have you any that will do?"

The girl looked doubtfully at her battered felt.

"D'you think—?" She caught Beth's eye, and they both began to laugh. "You are right—I know you are. I am lucky I had you to serve me. You feel as though you are really interested."

"But I am," said Beth sincerely. "I should like to think you absolutely startled the rich aunt. But to do that you'll have to be careful. The same bag and shoes must do for both evening dresses."

In the end a charming brown net was discovered. Beth made notes on a sheet of paper.

"Look. For the two flannels you want white suede shoes." She looked at the customer's brown, laced, flat-heeled pair in which she had arrived. "Those are more comfortable, but I think I'd get court with high heels. You can get them for about thirty shillings. For the afternoon very fine black ones—better say two pounds. For the evening gold sandals, eighteen and six. I think you could get a white hat to go with the morning frocks for about ten and six, and have two hatbands for it, one grey and the other blue. Then there's a black one for the afternoon. Better say a pound for that. Then there's the gold bag. You might get that for twelve and six. That only comes to just over the seven pounds, and you might get some of the things cheaper."

The girl looked at Beth with the eyes of an affectionate puppy.

"I can't thank you enough. What's your name?"

"Beth—Beth Carson."

"Mine's Barbara Allan. I'll send you a postcard to say how I get on."

Barbara wanted to take the frocks with her. It was twenty past six, everyone had gone, so Beth packed everything herself.

"You'd better hang them up directly you get in. I'm new here, and I haven't learnt to pack."

Beth left Babbacombe's with her eyes shining. This had been fun. Selling clothes became a very different affair when people turned up who needed helping. She hoped—oh, how she hoped!—Barbara Allan had a lovely time.

She was pulled back to the moment by a sharp, hoarse little bark, and there was Scissors tearing towards her, dragging David at the end of his lead.

Beth was so frightfully pleased to see David she was certain it showed on her face. To hide this she knelt down and made a tremendous fuss of Scissors, who made a great fuss back, wagging and licking and wriggling like a performing seal.

"Darling," she said ecstatically.

"Me or Scissors?"

Beth looked up, laughing.

"Aren't you silly! How's Cooked Meats?"

"Splendid! I wear a white coat and chef's hat and look a proper kingpin."

She got up, her face showing distaste.

"Why do they dress you up like that?"

"To cut the meat. Must look a proper chef."

Beth was shocked at the thought of him dressed like that.

"I think it's hateful of your father to put you into a job of that sort. He could easily have given you something else."

"Hark at her!" David said to Scissors. "And this, my boy, is the lady I told you about. The one who drove us to our present lowly post. The one who said 'You might as well be a cabbage.'"

Beth's eyes twinkled.

"I'm not a bit sorry I said it, but I am sorry you didn't get a better job."

They sauntered up the road, Scissors tugging from the end of his lead as if to say to David, "She may be nice, but that's no reason why we shouldn't walk briskly, is it?"

David defended Cooked Meats.

"It's a useful department. 'Yes, Madam. Good morning, Madam. Scotch beef? Yes, Madam; very underdone. Prime English lamb. Galantine chicken and ham, chicken and tongue. Oh yes, Madam, all cooked by our own staff.'"

Beth did not laugh. Somehow, though she did not care a bit where she worked herself, and was quite happy her father should be in Hardware, she did not like to think of David selling slices of cold meat. She changed the subject.

"Any news of your seaplane?"

"No; nor will be for months. You know what Government departments are."

They came to the corner. She stopped.

"Which way do you go?"

He raised an eyebrow at Scissors.

"She thinks we're here by accident. She doesn't realise we've been hanging about for nearly half an hour to see her."

"To see me!"

"Yes. It's Scissors' fault. He said every day, 'I wish we could see that girl I knocked over at Paddington Station.'"

She laughed.

"Does he wait in the shop all day while you're working?"

"He should, but actually he's got round one of the van men, and he goes out with him delivering parcels. He's seeing life, is Scissors."

She stood looking down at Scissors, not knowing what to say next. It had thrown her right off her balance to know he was waiting for her. It was so much what she would like to have happen that it gave her a detached feeling, as if she were dreaming. All the same, though this meeting was a lovely thing, and she would be glad about it in her heart, she kept her head. Here he was hanging about outside Babbacombe's talking to one of the girls.

Just the very thing her father had said he ought not to do. "You mustn't be seen here talking to me."

That surprised him.

"Why on earth not?"

"Your father might see you, or somebody will tell him. He wouldn't like it, I'm sure."

He took her by the elbow.

"Come along and have a drink somewhere. You've got a bee in your bonnet, and it wants getting out."

She refused to move.

"I haven't, and I don't drink, anyway."

"You can have a tomato juice or something." He saw she was going to refuse. He dropped his light tone. "Come on. Fair is fair. You can't just take up this attitude and give me no chance to get a word in."

She tried to think clearly. Would it be all right just for once? Surprising though it was, he wanted to see her, and had taken it for granted that he could. It did seem as if it would be better to talk things out and explain exactly what she meant.

"Very well; but we must be quick, or my family will worry."

David had a club near by. Not one of his solid men's clubs, but a frivolous one where, he told her, in his beachcombing days he had played poker. He led her down to the bar. It was in a fumed-oak room, a chromium-and-jade affair, surrounded by long-legged chromium stools with jade-leather seats. Most of the seats were taken: smart, over-made-up women and girls and their males whispered together, or howled at each other like parrots at the Zoo.

Beth felt shy. She was conscious that except for a little powder and the merest touch of lipstick her face was her own. She was conscious that it was a summer day, and light gay frocks and silly hats were right, and that she had on her dark green working frock, and since it had to be kept clean, a navy blue overcoat. She knew her navy straw hat was harmless, but it was a very poor relation of the other hats in the room. What she did not know was that shyness made her flush a little and was becoming to her, that her hair was curling charmingly round her hat, and that not only David was looking at her, but most of the men present had given not a thought to what she wore, but had merely registered that she was easy to look at.

David was evidently well known. He was greeted by everyone with nods and "Hullo, David." David returned the nods and found two vacant stools. He beckoned to the barman.

"What's a good drink for someone who doesn't drink?"

The barman leant on the bar and studied Beth as though by looking at her he could gauge what liquid would suit her.

"How about one of my specials? Made with fresh pineapple. It's got a little gin, but not so you'd notice it."

David turned to Beth.

"That do?"

She nodded.

"Very well. One of those and a gin-and-french for me."

Their stools were at the end of the bar. When the drinks had arrived and David had given Scissors some cocktail biscuits, he swung round to face Beth. This turned his back to everybody else, and, talking quietly, it was as if they were alone. He lifted his glass.

"Here's to our many meetings. Now what is all this snob nonsense?"

Beth sipped her drink.

"There won't be meetings. It's not snob nonsense. You are Mr. Babbacombe and—"

He laid a hand on her knee.

"I'm not Mr. Babbacombe—I'm David to you. Who are you? I've always thought of you as Miss Paddington Station."

"I'm Beth—Beth Carson."

"Beth." He tried the word over. "It's a nice name. Well, Beth, to get down to our muttons, what is this you-must-not-be-seen-talking-to-me stuff?"

She leant forward. Her face, he thought, was even more charming when she was being earnest.

"It's true. Dad was telling me about you—where you went to school and everything, and how you were brought up; and everybody thinks that in six months, if you do all right, you'll take your proper place in Babbacombe's."

He lit a cigarette.

"With any luck in six months' time I won't want to be in Babbacombe's."

"But you mustn't think that. You must work and try to please your father, as if there wasn't your seaplane. After all, it's not certain about that."

"I don't mind working, but I'm not going to have my father dictating who I know outside business."

"But I'm not outside. I'm in."

"I'm meeting you outside. Nor do I see any likelihood of his minding. After all, who are we? You talk as if we were royalty."

Beth hesitated, then she said gently:

"He'd mind because of your mother."

"Rot!"

Beth shook her head.

"It's not rot. He mightn't say anything but he would mind just the same. I should feel simply awful if after six months you didn't get moved and it was my fault."

He put down his cocktail and signalled to the barman for another.

"There is my side. You were quite right when you told me I ought to be working. All the same, I think I ought to have a little jam with my powder."

That sort of talk only stiffened Beth.

"What rubbish! You've still got your own friends. All these." She nodded at the other drinkers.

"Not these. Spare me. Poker acquaintances aren't friends. As a matter of fact, I'm living now on the two pounds a week I'm paid, and that more or less cuts me off from my old crowd; but it would run to a cinema and a bite now and again if you'd come."

Never was Beth so tempted. A cinema! And she loved cinemas! And a cinema with him would be quite perfect. But she shook her head.

"No. You won't persuade me. I know it would be a mistake."

"Stubborn, aren't you?" He called to the barman to know how much. "But I can be stubborn too. You can't stop me meeting you outside the staff entrance."

"I'm hardly ever alone."

"Don't I know it! Scissors and I have snooped around waiting for you every night this week. This is the first time we've had any luck."

She got off her stool.

"I must go."

Outside he waited beside her at her bus stop.

"She may think," he said to Scissors, "that this is our last meeting, but fortunately you and I have second sight. We know differently." The bus swung round the corner. He took off his hat. "Au revoir, Beth."

She climbed onto the platform and looked down smiling.

"Goodbye, David. Goodbye, Scissors."

The family were at supper—in fact, they had nearly finished. George was so anxious he sounded cross.

"Where have you been?"

It was on the tip of Beth's tongue to tell them; then her eye caught Dulcie's eager look.

"I was kept late." She sat down and unfolded her napkin. She turned to her mother. "Imagine, Mum—" In a moment she was deep in the story of Miss Barbara Allan and her clothes.

The family, especially the children, were entertained; but Beth felt horrid. She had never deceived her father and mother, and she did not want to start, but she really could not explain in front of Dulcie. She would tell them all about it directly they finished eating, and they would be sure to understand.

Because Janet was likely to be the most sympathetic, Beth manoeuvred to get her alone in the kitchen.

"Don't you help tonight," she said to Girda. "You get on with your Match-Girl. I'll help Mum dry."

In the kitchen she shut the door. Janet was over by the sink. Eager to get her story told, Beth burst out:

"I say, Mum." Janet turned round, and Beth was shocked at how ill she looked. She had been sideways to her at supper, and had not seen her face. "Mum, what is it?"

Janet opened her lips twice to speak, then suddenly she turned and buried her face in the roller-towel, her body shaken with harsh, dry sobs.

"Lock the door," she gulped.

Beth locked it, and ran to her mother and put her arms round her. "What is it, Mumsy?"

After a moment Janet got some sort of grip on her voice.

"It's Edward. I took him to the hospital today. There's something bad wrong with his eyes. Later on they'll operate, and then they'll know."

Beth's voice was a whisper:

"Know what?"

Janet choked back some sobs.

"If he'll be blind."

There was an appalled silence while the word "blind" seemed to echo and re-echo in the kitchen, then Janet went on in a dull voice:

"He's not to know. He's just to be told his eyes need resting and he's not to do close work. It's a slow thing he's got—it'll get worse gradually. I hadn't meant to tell you, but I couldn't help myself."

Beth squared herself to bear her share of the weight of sorrow.

"Of course I've got to know. I can help."

Janet for a moment rested against her as if she were the child and Beth the mother.

"I don't know what I'd do without you."

"Does Dad know?"

"Not yet. I'm telling him tonight." She gave Beth a little push. "Go on in to them; and, mind you, Edward's not to feel you're different. None of them are to know. I'll finish here. It'll give me time to get my face straight."

In the passage Beth paused a moment, gathering strength. How quickly your world could turn upside down! A few minutes ago she had been certain that her mother would want to hear about David—a silly, sloppy little story. As if she and he mattered now!

Edward was lolling over the table, flipping a marble to and fro in an aimless way. He looked up as Beth came in.

"Like to finish my jigsaw?" She agreed, and he fetched the half-done puzzle on its tray and put it on the table. "I went to the hospital today," he said, tipping the rest of the puzzle out of its box. "The doctor says I'm not to make any more for a bit, as I've strained my eyes a little. He said I shouldn't use them more than I can help. I'm going to train Penny to take me about on a lead like blind people do dogs." He looked at Beth to share the joke. "Can you see old Penny at it?"

Beth blinked her eyes. There was a mist between her and the sweet peas.

"You do talk a lot of rot, you old silly!"

CHAPTER SEVEN

DULCIE's lift worked from the food department. The lift girls, with their tricorne hats, many-collared coats, breeches, and top boots, represented glamour in Babbacombe's. All the younger men knew the lift girls by their Christian names, and snatched at chances of a word with them. The arrival of Dulcie caused a flutter. The food department bragged.

"Seen what we've won in the sweep."

"Quite a peach."

"Looks a hot little bit, our lift girl."

Dulcie was perfectly conscious of the feelings she aroused. There were nearly all men working in the food department—which was lucky, she thought, for she seemed to spend more time there than anywhere else. She liked the slack moments when she had time on her hands and could stand about calling out, "Going up, please?" She liked pretending that she did not know the men were nudging each other, and not understanding what they meant when they said, "If I come up with you will you promise a breakdown halfway?" She adored the dress, which suited her. She knew that its concealing capes and the ridiculous boots seemed to excite people, and she did not see how there could be a more amusing sensation than people being excited. The feel of the eyes of the male employees, and, better still, of the male customers, kept her in a constant glow.

The other lift girls despised Dulcie, and she despised them.

"Common lot," she told Beth. "No education. It drives me mad having to talk to them."

"I expect they're quite nice really when you get to know them," Beth soothed.

Dulcie sniffed.

"They never talk about anything but knitting patterns." Beth saw no harm in that.

"Well, what d'you want to talk about?"

Dulcie lowered her eyes.

"Oh, things."

"What things?"

Dulcie's lips curled at the corners.

"Things that have happened to us."

The lift girls often left their discussion of knitting patterns when Dulcie was not there.

"She's got a dirty mind, that girl."

"I wish she hadn't come on the lifts. One of us giving eyes all round the place makes the men think they can act anyhow."

"If that's what comes of going to a boarding school, I'm glad I never had the chance."

One of them, a fair girl, called Ann, was sorry for Dulcie, and tried to understand her.

"Is it nice living with your uncle and aunt?"

Dulcie shrugged her shoulders.

"It's cheap. I have private means which I pay to them, so what I earn here is just pocket money."

Ann looked round to see they were not overheard.

"I wouldn't talk like that to the others if I were you. We don't earn much on 'lifts', and for most of us it's a bit of a squeeze to get along. It'll make them feel you're different if you call Friday's envelope pocket money."

"Well, I am different."

Ann sighed. This being kind was uphill work. She changed the subject.

"I'm trying to buy my trousseau bit by bit. I'm making most of it, of course; but it's slow going."

Dulcie opened her eyes.

"Are you getting married?"

"Yes. He a waiter at 'The Magnificent'."

Dulcie eyed Ann thoughtfully.

"You're pretty: I should think you could do better than that."

Ann flushed.

"I couldn't do better than John. You see, I love him."

Dulcie was puzzled. Surely love was not a disease. At any rate you could fight it. It was an awful outlook if you could make a muck of your life by falling in love with a waiter in an hotel.

"I shan't let myself fall in love," she said firmly.

Ann's eyes were amused.

"I shouldn't think you ever will."

A couple of counters from the lift was the cooked meat department. It was Dulcie's focal point. From where she stood in her lift entrance calling, "Going up: boyswear, menswear, inexpensive millinery, perfumery, gloves, post office, library, restroom," she could see him, and, better still, he could see her. Even her practically unshakable egotism could not blind her to the fact that he was not, up to date, especially interested in her. She knew the whole department whispered about her, and that these whispers reached David; for she had seen the other men nudge him, and say something, and had seen him look in her direction and grin. Of course that sort of recognition from him was not what she really wanted. Still, she comforted herself, any notice was better than none; and when he had got her well fixed in his mind she would see he got a chance to speak to her. From there her dreams had no boundary. The affair would start with little dinners and theatres, and finish at St. Margaret's, Westminster. Sometimes she had a pang at the slowness of his awakening interest, and sometimes she wondered if he was getting a wrong idea of her from the cheap way the other men talked. On the whole she dismissed this latter worry. A real gentleman like David Babbacombe would be sure to recognise a real lady when he saw one.

David, slicing meat, never gave a thought to Dulcie. She was one with the fruity stories which sometimes enlivened the department, and of no more account. His mind was fixed, with a tenacity which amazed him, on seeing Beth. Since the age of fourteen, when he had fallen violently for a housemaid to whom he never declared his passion, he had been off and on in what he had supposed was love. Now he knew it had been nothing of the sort. Love was not a blinding, searing, hot-and-cold-all-over, lasting a-few-weeks affair. Love was simple, really. You could meet it on even so unlikely a spot as Paddington Station. It was not blinding or searing: it was so gently absorbing that at first you did not know what had happened to you. It could creep through you so insidiously that it was only when you met the girl a second time that you noticed it. After that it had you. Only Scissors knew it had David, and he heard a lot about it. The evenings which before were spent in his basket were now spent with his master, and very wakeful evenings they were. A dog does like his sleep, but no decent dog sleeps when he is being spoken to. Scissors exhaustedly forced open his eyes and listened.

"She's wonderful, old man. You must have noticed that yourself when you knocked her down. Did you ever see such eyes? Like looking into a loch, aren't they?" In a pause like that Scissors did what he could. Usually he thumped his tail on the floor. David liked that. "Glad you agree? Do you remember she said at once it wasn't your fault? There's a girl for you! Not many of them would take that view when they'd been sent sprawling on a platform." Scissors gave another encouraging thump. "She was wonderful in the lift. You missed that. I'd gone to the old man for a cheque, and she said, 'I'd rather do anything than take money I didn't earn.'" Scissors had heard all this so often that he sometimes forgot himself and yawned. David was reproachful. "Sorry if I'm boring you, old man, but you ought to be interested. It was you who found her, you know. Come here." Scissors, in squirming delight, jumped up on David's knee. "We told her it was only au revoir, didn't we? We could, of course, try to meet her outside the staff door, but she doesn't like it. Can't you think of a better way, Scissors? There must be a way, old man; there must."

One of John Babbacombe's firmest beliefs was that all bad health came from teeth. To instil this into his people's minds he had the staff rooms plastered with posters showing in illustration the horrifying evils which came from decayed teeth. He also paid lecturers to talk to his staff in the canteen on "Teeth Welfare". He went further. He kept a staff dentist. His older workers could get their teeth attended to through their societies, but the younger ones who had not been insured for sufficiently long to cover dentist's bills were, he felt sure, bound to neglect theirs. To avoid this it was a rule that every new employee must be seen by the dentist, who would give them the treatment necessary, and also, if he thought fit, call them up again in a few months' time. This rule was unalterable for anybody, and so David, though he had quite recently seen his own man, was ordered by his buyer to report.

The dentist—a Mr. Piper—had been with the firm for years, and had off and on dined with John Babbacombe, and had known David since he had been a schoolboy. He gave his teeth a look over, then put down his instruments.

"You're all right."

David rinsed his mouth.

"Good! I was afraid you might want to whip the whole lot out."

Mr. Piper laughed.

"So you're really working, are you?" He picked up his appointment book and read "Babbacombe, D. Number 9754. (Cooked Meats.)"

David unconsciously eyed the page. Suddenly he stiffened.

"I say, may I have that a minute?" He read in silence, then he raised his head, his face radiant. "It's fate. Look." Mr. Piper looked and shook his head.

"Can't see anything in that. It says Twelve o'clock. Carson, Miss B. Number 7941. (Gowns.)'"

"Twelve o'clock tomorrow," said David happily. "Piper, old man, you're a wonderful dentist, but you've made a mistake. There are at least three molars badly in need of attention. In fact, so badly that I'll have to come back tomorrow."

Mr. Piper clicked his tongue.

"Is that so? Have to come back about twelve, will you?" David got up.

"Piper, you're a sportsman."

Mr. Piper held up a finger.

"Not so fast. Who is she?"

"She's divine."

Mr. Piper sniffed.

"Like that, is it? Haven't you anywhere else to meet but in my surgery?"

"No. She won't meet me. She says I'm a Babbacombe, and should look higher."

"A girl of sense." Mr. Piper turned back to his book. "I shouldn't be doing this, you rascal." He scratched his nose. "Can't have two of you coming at the same time. I'll send a card to your buyer calling you at 11.45."

"And you won't be able to squeeze in my appointment, and will have to see me again."

Mr. Piper closed the book.

"No, once is enough. The girl's probably got perfectly healthy teeth."

"But if she hasn't—or if your hard heart melted."

Mr. Piper gave him a pat on the shoulder.

"Get along with you."

Mr. Piper's consulting-room was full of aged copies of *Punch*. Beth, with the sinking feeling inside that most people get while they're waiting for the dentist, tried to be entertained by topical jokes of the year 1904. She heard the door open, and raised her eyes, expecting to see the nurse. She had no chance to control her face or her voice. She was glad to see David, and every bit of her showed it. With shining eyes she exclaimed:

"You!"

David, with Scissors under his arm, sat on the table beside her.

"Yes, it's me. You got an appointment?"

"Yes. Twelve."

David looked at his watch and shook his head. He showed it to Scissors.

"Our luck's out, old man. Quarter to. He won't see us today."

"Hadn't you an appointment?"

"Not exactly. I saw him yesterday, and he said, as my case was urgent, I could be here at a quarter to twelve, and he'd do what he could."

Beth's face was concerned.

"Have you got toothache?"

David patted his face.

"Nothing I can't bear. I daresay he'll see me again soon—at least, I hope so."

"Fancy hoping to see the dentist," said Beth. "I could never hope that."

"You wouldn't mind if he didn't hurt you."

She looked round.

"I wouldn't like it. Dentists' rooms make me think of drills, even if they're not going to use one. Have you heard from the Admiralty?"

"No." He eyed her. "You look paler than when we drank together. Is Babbacombe's getting you down?"

"Oh no. I love it."

"Extraordinary. I should think selling clothes to other women would be absolute hell."

"Oh no. Sometimes it's awfully interesting. Look." She opened her bag and brought out a postcard, with a picture on it of a stately home. "That's from a customer. Read it." He took the card and read:

> "'Every minute has been too heavenly. My aunt has been so very kind, and says my clothes are just right. I have to thank you for this.
>
> (Signed) Barbara Allan.'"

He laughed. "They might have missed calling her Barbara, with that surname." He turned the card over. "Ribstall Castle. Why, that's Maggie Wentwood's place."

"Who's she?"

"Frightful old trollop. Oozing with money. Married Lord Wentwood—you know, Wentwood's soaps." He gave her back the card. "You seem to be a bit of all right as a saleswoman." His voice was gentle. "If it isn't Babbacombe's, why the pale cheeks? You are paler, you know."

Beth put the card back in her bag. She had a sudden feeling she would like to tell him—that his knowing would help.

"It's a worry at home. I've a brother called Edward. He's fifteen. His eyes are bad—it's something growing. Nothing can be done until it's worse; then they'll operate. After that they'll know what chance he has. He might be blind."

David was appalled. He had never known tragedy—his life had been one long laugh. A short while ago he would have shoved Beth's story out of his mind with a "God, how awful! Let's have a drink!" Now it touched him. This Edward he had never met was Beth's brother. His feeling for her seemed to have brought other senses alive. He minded about Edward's eyes—minded as if he knew him. His imagination, often dormant, threw up a picture. He could feel what it might be like to be facing everlasting night.

"My dear! Can't I help?"

George, Janet, and Beth could only keep up the fiction that nothing was wrong by scarcely mentioning Edward's eyes, or, if they mentioned them, only doing so in a dispassionate way, as if it were not Edward they were talking about, but a stranger. David's sympathy broke Beth's control. Her eyes flooded with tears.

"There's nothing anyone can do. He's being seen by the best people at the hospital. He doesn't know."

He picked up one of her hands and patted it.

"But he will, of course. Can he use his eyes much?"

"No. He's having stronger glasses to help, but he's to come off reading and close work. He thinks it's temporary."

"Is he the sort of boy who minds that?"

"Awfully. You see, carpentry is his hobby: he loves making things. He's still doing that but—"

He squeezed her hand.

"The operation may be a success."

She nodded. There was no time for more: the nurse opened the door.

"Miss Carson, please."

Mr. Piper looked at Beth with interest. So this was young Babbacombe's 'divine' girl. She was a good choice—pretty; but something much more than that. She looked as if something had upset her, though. Whatever could that young fool have been saying?

David pulled Scissors' ears.

"That's a pretty blood-stained story. Can't we do something, Scissors—something that would help? What would we do if we couldn't see? We'd talk to each other, of course, and—Jove, that's got it!"

In the consulting-room Mr. Piper went to a drawer and selected an instrument.

"There's a small hole at the back here. I'll clean it up and put in a temporary stopping. You'll have to come back next week."

Beth gripped the velvet arms of the chair and held her mouth wide open and prepared herself to endure.

"There," said Mr. Piper, after a few minutes' drilling.

"That wasn't so bad, was it? Now for the stopping." He picked up his mortar. "Was young Mr. Babbacombe waiting outside?"

"Yes."

Mr. Piper went on with his mixing.

"You might give him a message as you go out. Tell him I couldn't squeeze him in today, but I'll send an appointment for next week."

Beth sat up.

"Not till next week. But he's got toothache."

Mr. Piper disguised a smile. He brought the stopping over to her.

"Open wide. Sorry about his ache, but if you give him that message he'll know I'm doing all I can."

Beth hesitated outside the waiting-room door. If she went in and gave David Mr. Piper's message they would obviously walk back to Babbacombe's together. That was exactly the sort of thing she did not think he ought to do. On the other hand, she would like the walk very much; and it would not hurt, just for once. And she had been asked to give the message. And Mr. Piper would think it odd if she did not.

David slid off the table at sight of her.

"Did he hurt you?"

"Not too bad." She gave the message, her face full of sympathy. "I told him you'd got toothache."

David nearly laughed.

"What did he say to that?"

"Oh, he said he was sorry, but you'd know he was doing all he could. I didn't say anything, but I thought that was rather mean. Does it keep you awake at night?"

David thought of the amount of tossing and turning and think-ing of her which he was indulging in.

"I don't sleep too well."

"I should make a row about it. I mean there must be some way he can fit you in earlier."

David felt poor Mr. Piper was being unfairly treated.

"He knows he can't help the ache." He picked up Scissors. "Come on. It's no good you saying we go different ways, because I know we don't."

Walking back to the shop, David said:

"While you were being tortured I had an idea. How would your brother like a dog?"

Beth stood still.

"A dog! Like Scissors?"

"That's what I thought."

"Where would you get one? Wouldn't he be awfully expensive?"

"There's a place I know in Sussex, and I intend to get one as a present. Will you come with me on Saturday afternoon and choose one?"

Beth frowned.

"That's bribery. I mean, you know I'd love Edward to have a dog. If he's as nice as Scissors he will be an awful help. But going out with you is what I said I wouldn't do."

He was horrified.

"It wasn't meant as bribery, though I see it looks like it. Matter of fact, there's an awful lot of difference in dogs. You ought to choose him."

They were crossing the road. Babbacombe's was in sight. Beth thought of Sussex. She knew it only from their yearly fortnight at Bexhill. Even seen like that it had always been her idea of perfec-tion. But how far more lovely it would be with David!

"How would we go?" she asked weakly.

"By car. I've still got mine. The chauffeur keeps it filled with petrol, so it doesn't cost me much to run."

She had a vision of them. Sussex would be very green and flowery now—it was yellowing a little always in September. She would wear the blue linen Mum had bought in a sale last year. She had hardly had it on. She could not help her face glowing.

"All right, I'll come. It's awfully nice of you. I wouldn't take the puppy for me, but for Edward it's different. Only you do see, don't you, that I haven't changed my mind? I mean about going out with you."

He nodded gravely.

"Of course; one swallow doesn't make a summer and all that sort of thing. Where shall we meet? Here, or may I call for you?"

Beth considered. Could she tell the family where she was going? It would be nice to confide in them. Then she thought of Dulcie. It would be no good telling Dulcie not to talk: if Dulcie saw her going off with David, all the shop would know of it before ten o'clock on Monday morning.

"No, I'll meet you after lunch. Would Victoria Station be all right? I'll be outside the newsreel cinema."

He gave Scissors' lead a pull.

"Hear that, Scissors. We're going to see the home where you were born, with the little lattice window and all that." They were in the street leading to the staff entrance. He gave her arm a quick squeeze. "Saturday, the newsreel cinema. Two o'clock?"

That evening Beth and George got out at the same time. For all his efforts to hide it, Edward's trouble had upset George as if he had been through an illness. His back had bent a little, and there were quite a few extra grey hairs over his ears. Beth felt such pity that it hurt.

"I wish it was September, Dad," she said gently. "You can do with your holiday."

He gave her a would-be cheery smile.

"Bexhill won't be Bexhill with you not there."

She put her arm through his.

"I'll be all right here with Dulcie. You'll have to make Bexhill extra nice this year, because of Edward. He can do all the things there the same as usual."

George did not answer for a moment.

"I think I'm going to tell him how things are," he said at last. "You see, with this cataract he's got to be near stone blind before they can operate, and I think he ought to know."

"Must he know yet?"

George nodded.

"I was talking it over with your mother last night. He's a brave boy. I think he should have a chance to adjust his own life. You see, none of us can help him in that; we can do what we can, but it's how he faces up to the business himself that will count."

"When are you going to tell him?"

"He wants to go to a cricket match on Saturday. I reckon to tell him coming back."

"Saturday!" Beth looked up. "If it's Saturday I'm getting a present for him. It might help."

"What sort of present?"

Beth was annoyed with herself to feel her cheeks getting red. What a fool she was! Just as if she had done something wrong. She gave herself a mental shake and told her father about David.

George listened without interrupting. Beth's story was short. He heard about the drink at the club and how David had asked her to come to a cinema sometime; of how she had refused; and of today's accidental meeting at the dentist's. But he did not hear how Beth felt about the meetings, and there was nothing in her calm recital to give even a hint.

In the bus they were separated: Beth in a seat, George standing. It gave him time to think. Walking home he said nothing for a time. Beth eyed him affectionately out of the corner of her eye, knowing his habit of turning over his thoughts and not producing them until they were certain. At last he cleared his throat.

"It's good of Mr. David to think of the dog. I was wondering about one myself—planning to step along to the Battersea place and see if they'd a nice stray. But one of those dachshunds will be better. I don't see any harm in you going just this once. Even if Mr. Babbacombe heard he wouldn't mind if he knew the whys and wherefores. But, mind you, it must be mum's-the-word at home. If Dulcie got on to it she couldn't run quick enough to tell the tale. You tell your mother, of course, but for the rest just say someone at the shop's giving the dog. No need to say who."

"It wouldn't do any harm if I saw him now and again, would it?" Beth managed to sound as if she did not care one way or the other.

George deliberated the question until they were nearly home, then he shook his head.

"Better not. They're not our sort, and we're not theirs. No, you go to Sussex on Saturday, and after that cut him out. No good can come of meeting him."

Beth had expected just that answer—it was only backing what she had said herself; but she hated to hear it put in words. She longed to argue, to say, "Can't we be friends even if he was differently brought up from me?" But obedience was strong in her, and her commonsense told her George was right. In a rather small voice she agreed with him.

"No, no good can come of meeting him."

CHAPTER EIGHT

JANET came up to help Beth change. The blue linen was lying ready on the bed.

"I left ironing it until this morning," Janet said, lifting the frock over Beth's head. "I was afraid the sight of a bit of linen in one of our summers would bring the rain."

Beth looked out of the window at the sky, which was blue and cloudless.

"Aren't I lucky in my day? I hope you get weather like this at Bexhill."

Janet picked up the comb and twisted a strand of Beth's hair over her finger.

"So do I." She peered at Beth's reflection in the glass. Then suddenly she took hold of her shoulders and turned her round. "You're excited, aren't you? You won't be silly, will you? I can see this afternoon means quite a bit to you—I could see that when you were telling me you were going. But you know his sort are only out for fun. Don't let yourself get fond of him. He'll be a bit different from others you'll meet, and he'll spoil you for Mr. Right when he comes along."

Beth hugged her mother.

"Aren't you an old silly? I'm not seeing him after today. I shouldn't see him today if it wasn't for Edward's dog."

Janet gave her a kiss.

"All right, as long as you're warned. Now turn round. If you're going without a hat I must do something about these curls."

Beth told Edward about the coming day over luncheon. "Where d'you think I'm going this afternoon?"

Edward helped himself to potatoes.

"Buckingham Palace."

She dug her elbow into him.

"Shut up, silly. No, I'm getting you a present."

"What!" His ears grew red with excitement.

"Well, I was telling someone at Babbacombe's about you not being allowed to use your eyes much, and they said 'Would you like a puppy?'"

There was a scream from Edward, Girda and Eve.

"A puppy!"

"What sort?"

"What's his name?"

Paul glowered at Beth.

"That's a fine thing to do. Bring a dog to the house knowing that Penny simply hates dogs."

"What sort, Beth?" Edward repeated.

"A dachshund."

Edward's pleasure brought a lump to three throats.

"A dachshund! The sort of dog I've wanted most. Is he to be absolutely mine? I mean not family, like Penny."

"Absolutely yours," said Beth.

Paul looked proud.

"As a matter of fact nobody else was wanting him. Myself, I shan't speak to him. I'm on Penny's side."

"Where are you going to get him, Beth?" asked Dulcie. Unthinking Beth answered:

"Sussex somewhere."

"Sussex!" exclaimed the children.

"That's where Bexhill is."

"Are you going on the green line bus?"

"Are you going by train?"

Beth extricated herself from the questions as best she could.

"No, as a matter of fact, I think by car."

"A car." Dulcie was annoyed. If a car was going, it should be she who was to travel in it, not Beth, who hardly looked as if she had left school. "Is it coming here?" Janet looked at the clock.

"It isn't, and you'd better be off, Beth, if you're to meet—" There was so faint a pause before the "it" that it would seem unnoticeable, but Dulcie noticed. Janet had been going to say something else. What else? It must be "him" or "her". If it was her she would surely have said so. Then it was a "him". Beth was going with a man, and a man who had a car. Jealousy flooded over her to such an extent that she felt physically sick.

The dachshunds lived in a part of Sussex Beth did not know. They were near Amberley. In her one fortnight in the year she had always travelled by train. She had thought Sussex lovely, though her knowledge of it was mostly confined to the views from the Southern Railway; but nothing in her previous knowledge had prepared her for the exquisite view above Arundel. The sun shone blue, the green distance, picked out with great trees, looked to her like a fairy tale. All the way down David had talked nonsense.

Now that he had stopped the car at her gasped "Oh, look!" his voice dropped as if he were going into a church.

"Would you like to get out a minute? There's plenty of time, and Scissors would be glad."

They climbed up a bank and sat under a tree. Scissors, with wild, shrill barks, hung over a rabbit hole.

"It's perfect," said Beth.

He lit a cigarette.

"Funny, I've passed here hundreds of times and thought it looked a bit of all right, but I never thought of it as something special until today. That must be you."

She turned to him.

"You know, I do think who you're with must make a difference." She was afraid that she had said too much, so she qualified her statement, "I mean if you saw the same thing with somebody you liked awfully, and then with somebody you simply hated, I'm sure it would look different."

"Of course it would. This afternoon everything has looked grand."

Her heart throbbed, but she dared not say anything. It was as if they were both leaning against a door: if either pressed too hard it would give and they would tumble through. It was her business to keep that door shut. That was what Mum had meant when she said "Don't be silly." Just for the moment David was liking her. It was enough to know that. She was not such an idiot as to think he really cared.

David was in torture. Every pulse in his body hammered. Her nearness, the sun on her hair, made it agony not to take her in his arms. But something in her held him back. She would hate it, he was sure. She was so young, and probably intolerant; she might be disgusted.

Because he could not bear himself another second he got up and went over to Scissors, and to work the excitement out of his system urged him on to battle.

"Go on! Good dog! Fetch it out."

Scissors thought the game entrancing. He knew, and master knew, he had never as much as touched a rabbit, but it was grand pretending.

Beth was hurt. She had been so happy sitting beside him, she had hoped he was liking it too. Then she gave herself a mental punch in the ribs. Here she was being silly. Why should he like it? She had been terribly dull—she hadn't said a word. To show she did not care, she got up and joined in the game.

"Go on, Scissors! Good dog! Fetch him out."

In a series of large wire kennels forty-three dachshunds were leaping and barking.

"Go round, duckie, and pick your fancy," said David.

Lydia Neal, who owned the kennels, raised an enquiring eyebrow at David.

"Who is the child?"

David offered her a cigarette.

"Nothing to raise an eyebrow over. She's a nice person. The puppy is for her brother, who's got eye trouble."

Lydia tapped her cigarette on her hand.

"She looks nice—too nice to hurt."

David lit a cigarette.

"Who said anything about hurting?"

Lydia gave his face a pat.

"Nobody, but if we waited for you men to use the word it would never be said."

There was a cry from Beth.

"Oh, look! That's the one."

Lydia went over and opened the kennels. Amongst the mass of puppies one was sitting apart, apparently deep in thought. He was golden brown; still so young that his coat fell in bracelets over his feet. His nose had still a puppy's roundness, but in spite of his youthful look he seemed a dog of purpose. He had his gay moments in a busy life, but in all he did he appeared to say, "You fellows can do what you fancy; but I've no time to waste—I'm a working dog." Lydia picked him up and brought him to Beth.

"You've chosen the best."

Beth took the hide fellow in her arms.

"What's his name?"

Lydia laughed.

"Well, he's really Newton King—that's his stud name—but he doesn't know it. If you have him I should give him something more friendly."

David drew Lydia to one side.

"You aren't getting paid for that dog for a while: I'm doing a bit of life-is-real-life-is-earnest working in the shop for two pounds a week."

Lydia nodded.

"If half my clients were as sure to pay as you are I'd be a rich woman."

David came back to Beth.

"Settled on that one?"

She raised an ecstatic face.

"Yes. He's lovely. Edward will adore him. Let's take him and show him to Scissors."

Scissors had been left in the car during the dog-buying, as the sight of him walking aloof and free while they were behind wire caused hysteria in the other dogs. Now as the car door opened he came bounding out, and then stopped short at sight of the puppy.

Beth sat on the ground, and the puppy promptly stumbled up and sat on her lap.

"There's his name for you," said David. "Keith Prowse, 'You want the best seat, we have it'."

Lydia was delighted.

"Perfect."

Beth held out a hand to Scissors.

"Come and meet Keith Prowse. Don't be jealous: he's not going home with you."

Scissors seemed to take this in. He gave two sharp barks at Keith Prowse as if to say, "Let's have no nonsense from you," and then seemed to forget him in a sudden burst of joy at seeing Lydia. They set off homewards with Scissors sitting between them and Keith Prowse asleep on Beth's knee.

"It would be pleasant to have some tea," said David. "Shall I stop if I see a harmless place that doesn't say it's 'Olde Worlde'?"

Beth thought that would be nice, and presently they drew up outside a cottage which said "Teas" and which had obviously got a garden to eat them in.

They were a little late, and had the place to themselves.

It was a real cottage garden, full of sweet williams and pinks and marigolds. They settled down at a round green iron table on two green iron chairs and drank very black Indian tea, and ate slabs of bread and butter and jam, and thought it perfect. Scissors and Keith Prowse explored the garden.

Suddenly they heard a car stop outside and voices.

David made a face.

"Vile trippers."

Beth laughed.

"Just like us."

Another man and another girl came out of the cottage and sat down at another green iron table on two more green iron chairs. The girl's back was to Beth, but she noticed that she was wearing what she was sure was a Babbacombe's flannel frock—a grey one with a red belt like she had sold Miss Allan.

"Can we have some tea and whatever you have?" the man said to the waitress.

David swung round.

"'Tis the voice of the Sluggard."

The other man looked up.

"Good Lord! David Babbacombe!"

David put his hand on Beth's arm.

"Beth, this is Lord Pern. Better known as 'Slug'. This is Miss Beth Carson."

Lord Pern said how do you do to Beth and turned to introduce his companion, but the two girls had already recognised each other.

"Beth Carson."

"Miss Allan." Beth could not stop there. "Did you have a nice time?"

Barbara flushed.

"Heavenly! I'm still there. You see, John"—she nodded towards Lord Pern—"was there too, and—and—"

Lord Pern put his arm round her and turned to David.

"Congratulate us. We're engaged. It happened this afternoon."

After that the tea party became a foursome. Scissors and Keith Prowse were introduced, and David and John fell into a conversation about a golf club that they were interested in, and Barbara, trembling with happiness, whispered to Beth:

"You can't think what it's been like. You know my aunt meant to be kind, but she wanted me to be useful. Well, of course, with a big place there's a lot to do, and just at first it wasn't very interesting. I was always busy, and nobody knew who I was exactly. They were nice, but never knew my name or anything. And then John came." She paused. "I was cutting roses for the dinner table. He came and helped. After that everything was different. My aunt was awfully nice, and said I mustn't do any more odd jobs—I was there to enjoy myself. And then when my week was up she said I was to stay on; and John kept coming down; and then today—"

Because Barbara felt a great need to confide and could not do it properly in front of John, the two girls went into the cottage ostensibly for the usual powder. In the cramped little bedroom into which they were shown, Barbara clasped Beth's hands.

"You can't imagine how nice he is. It seems as if it couldn't be true he loves me. I'm so uninteresting, and not a bit pretty. Have you ever been in love?"

Beth hesitated.

"I'm not sure. I mean—"

Barbara jumped to it.

"Oh, is it that man outside? I'm sure it is. He looks awfully nice."

Beth's face was scarlet.

"Oh no, of course not. That's Mr. Babbacombe—the son of Mr. Babbacombe who's chairman of the store."

Barbara gave her a shrewd look.

"What on earth has who he is got to do with it? If it comes to that, John is one of the richest peers in England, and I'm my aunt's poor niece who was being trained to be a secretary. Nothing matters except loving each other." Beth was thoroughly embarrassed.

"But I didn't say it was him, or anybody. I only said—" Barbara nodded.

"All right. Keep your secret. But I hope it's him, because he looks nice."

In the garden David gave John a cigarette. "Congratulations and all that. Where'd you meet?"

"At Ribstall. She's Maggie Wentwood's niece. She was staying there. She looked like a primrose in a greenhouse." He grinned. "Sorry if I'm poetical."

"That's all right." David gave a puff at his cigarette. "You're a lucky devil, Slug. I wish *she'd* got a rich aunt in whose house we could meet." He nodded towards the cottage to indicate Beth.

John looked enquiring.

"Who is she?"

"Works in Babbacombe's. She's a winner."

John had liked the look of Beth.

"Poor old David! You have got it badly. Is your father being difficult?"

"Doesn't know. It's she who's difficult. She won't let me see her: she's got ideas about class. Today's an exception. We came to choose the dog for a brother whose eyes are bad."

John, full of his own happiness, could not bear to see somebody else out of luck.

"Can I help in any way?"

David shook his head, then suddenly his face lit up.

"Not unless that girl of yours could. Of course, if she happened to ask Beth to something, and you happened to ask me and—"

John gave him a dig in the ribs.

"All right, old horse. Hold everything. A plan shall be planned."

Leaving the cottage, Beth felt suddenly wretched. With the shutting of its gate the day would be nearly over—there was only the drive back to town. David was ahead, seeing off Barbara and John. She turned suddenly to the cottage owner.

"Might I take one flower?"

The woman smiled.

"Yes, Miss, I'll pick you a rose."

She went into the house and reappeared with some scissors. In the front lawn was a bed of roses. She looked at Beth enquiringly.

"What colour will you have?"

Beth saw the scissors hovering between a magnificent great white bloom and a flame-coloured one.

"Oh, please, a bud; it will last longer."

The woman snipped off a deep crimson bud and gave it to Beth.

"Clip its stem up and it'll stay quite a while."

Beth ran to the car holding her treasure. She knew herself for a sentimental fool, but she did like to think that back in number ten Penruddock Road something of today would live quite a while.

They did not say much driving home. They were in a state of contentment with each other's company which words seemed to break. As they neared Victoria, David asked where he should take her, and was directed to the turning before Penruddock Road. He slowed the car and then looked down at her.

"Are you still sticking to this no-meeting business?"

She raised her eyes.

"Yes. I asked Dad's advice, and he said it was better not. I'm sure he's right."

"How about my going to my father? I never have asked the old man about my friends, but I will to please you."

Beth was certain what the result of that would be. It was bad enough not seeing him because she would not allow the meetings, but not seeing him because his father had forbidden it would be much worse.

"Oh no, don't. Promise you won't do that."

He took a hand off the wheel and patted her knee.

"All right. But don't think I'm agreeing with you. I shall be working underground like a worm, and suddenly, when you're least expecting it, there I'll be popping up under your feet." He stopped the car. "Goodnight, my sweet. It's been a grand day: I never remember a better."

She got out, Keith Prowse under her arm, her rose in her hand.

"Goodbye, and thank you for everything, Keith Prowse and—"

He leant out of the window.

"Next time we'll go to the sea. Do you like the sea?"

"But there isn't going to be a next time."

He smiled.

"No? Well, watch for the worm. So long."

Edward was hanging about in the front of the house. He gave a whoop when he saw Beth and dashed to meet her. He seized Keith Prowse.

"Beth, I say, isn't he grand!"

For one second Beth felt a pang. She had chosen Keith Prowse; he was a present from David; she didn't want to give him away. Then she looked at Edward's face. It looked greenish. He had not been crying—he never did cry—but she was sure George had told him. She burst into a description of how she had picked the puppy.

"And I knew at once he was the one for you—he'd got such a busy face."

Edward put Keith Prowse down, who yawned and gave himself a small stretch before he hurried off to investigate the street smells.

"What's his name?"

Beth tucked her arm into his.

"Keith Prowse. Da—I mean someone—christened him that because he at once chose the best seat. You know the advertisement: 'You want the best seats; we have them.'"

Edward looked up at her enquiringly.

"Who were you with?"

Beth gave him a friendly dig with her elbow.

"Ssh. I'll tell you, only you mustn't tell Dulcie. It was David Babbacombe—Mr. Babbacombe's son."

"Strewth! You a friend of his?"

His amazement hurt her.

"No, you fool. I shan't see him again. He works in the shop, that's all, and—oh, well, he happened to hear about you."

Edward called Keith Prowse, who did not know his name but was willing to answer to any friendly sound. He trotted obediently in at the gate. Edward kicked a stone off the path in an embarrassed way.

"Dad told me today that I've got to have something done to my eyes presently. He said I'd not be able to see for a bit before they're done."

Beth saw Edward's ears growing red; she was suddenly inspired.

"I know, but it won't be long; and, anyway, it's nothing to get your ears red about."

This was exactly the treatment Edward needed. George's gentle but over-laborious explanation had scared him, so had Janet's extra kindness when he got in. With Beth behaving just as usual, and a puppy of his own, his spirits suddenly soared back to normal. He gave a howl and threw open the front door.

"Hi! All of you. Come and see my dog."

Beth ran upstairs to say goodnight to Paul and Eve. She found them together in Eve's room.

"Hullo, darlings. What are you doing down here, Paul?"

Paul put his hands behind his back.

"Just gettin' something."

"What? Anything I can lend?"

Paul looked at Eve.

"Shall we show her?"

Eve nodded.

He lifted Eve's eiderdown.

"Look under the bed."

Under the bed was Eve's doll's bed—a magnificent affair given her last Christmas by Janet. It was a study in blue and white, and everything had been made by hand. Now the doll that usually lived there was gone, and in its place lay Penny, his orange face on the frilled pillows, one orange paw stretched over the quilt. Beth gave him a pat.

"Hullo, Penny. You've gone to bed early tonight."

"He had to," said Paul. "His heart is nearly broken over that dog."

Beth kept a grave face.

"Poor Penny! What's that you've got in your hand? Something else for him?"

"It's my baby doll's nightdress," said Eve, snatching it from Paul. "I said if Penny slept in a bed he ought to wear it, but he doesn't like it much: he scratched Paul when he tried to put it on."

"He didn't mean to," Paul burst out. "But he's naturally upset."

Beth wondered what would be the best way to handle the situation.

"Don't you think," she suggested, "that it would be a good thing to let them meet just for a moment? He's such a little dog: perhaps Penny wouldn't mind."

"Oh, Paul, do let him see him!" Eva gasped. "Then we could see him too."

"He's only a puppy," Beth went on. "And probably a bit shy. If Penny were nice to him it would be a help."

Paul looked grave, as if the fate of empires hung on his decision, then he nodded.

"Very well. Bring him up."

Edward brought Keith Prowse in. Penny at first sight of him spat and jumped out of his bed, but Keith Prowse had never seen a cat before, and, full of admiration, trotted after him. No cat can go on spitting at a dog who has never heard that cats are his enemies. With dignity Penny strolled back into the middle of the room, trying to look unconscious of the fact that Keith Prowse, dancing with pleasure, was at his side.

Beth, seeing that all would now be well, went to her room. On the mantelpiece was a blue vase. She filled it with water and put her rose in it, and placed it on the table by her bed. Looking at it, the day flooded back in all its loveliness: the drive, the view over Arundel, the kennels, the tea place, and above all David, his friendliness, his taking it for granted they liked each other. She stooped and kissed the rose.

Dulcie had spent a dull afternoon. There were heaps of things she might have done, but she had done none of them. Any amusement had the spice taken out of it when she thought of Beth. Where was she? Was she with a man?

The bathroom was opposite Beth's and Dulcie's room. Dulcie, coming out, saw the light, and moved across, meaning to question Beth; instead something stopped her, and she peeped through the side of the door. She looked just at the moment when Beth kissed her rose. At the sight of that kiss all the day's fears welled up in her. Beth had been out with a man. Plain schoolgirlish Beth was having a better time then she was. She flung open the door.

"Who's been giving you a rose, Beth?"

Beth answered casually: "I got it today in the country."

"Given you by one of the girls at the shop, I suppose?"

"No. If you want to know, by the woman at the place we had tea."

"And who's 'we'?"

Beth flushed.

"What on earth's it got to do with you?"

Dulcie saw red.

"I suppose I can ask you a question? You pretend to be so superior, and then go sneaking off into the country with a man doing goodness knows what, and then come back slobbering over his rose. It's—"

Beth walked over to her. Her voice was very quiet:

"How dare you talk like that! Where I go and who I go with are my business. But if I'd been with a hundred men it's not your business to go saying filthy things, making everything beastly."

Dulcie gave her a push.

"Oh, get away, you and your psalm-singing."

She snatched up the rose and jumped on the bed and pulled off its petals one by one.

"He loves me. He loves me not."

Beth watched the petals fall. For a moment she was blind with anger, then she turned to the door.

"Wait a minute," said Dulcie. "Don't you want to know if he loves you or not?"

Beth shut the door. She was surprised to find that she was trembling. She longed to go to Janet and tell her what had happened; then she took a grip on herself.

"Idiot!" she thought. "You can't go complaining of squabbles as if you were a kid. And even if she has taken the rise, she shan't spoil your day."

Dulcie looked at the bud, where one petal remained.

"He loves me." She threw the stalk away. "Oh, well, it's only a game, and of course it isn't true."

Mr. Piper was just finishing his glass of after-dinner port when he remembered his half-promise to David. He went through to his study, where the nurse had left the appointments book.

"Carson," he murmured—that was the girl's name—"Carson. Ah, here we are. Wednesday. Miss D. Carson. (Lifts.) Funny I didn't remember she was Lifts."

He took an appointment card out of a box and addressed it to the buyer of Cooked Meats. On the other side he filled in "Babbacombe, David. Wednesday. 2.15."

CHAPTER NINE

DAVID had counted the minutes until Wednesday. He had been startled at how slowly time can go. Scissors had been surprised to find himself taken for long walks late at night, during which master had strode along faster and faster, for all the world as if he were after a rabbit. Even when they got in from these walks and he, Scissors, energetic though he was, could think of nothing but his basket, master astoundingly was still wide awake and wanted to talk. Scissors tried to be sympathetic, and honestly had liked what he had seen of Beth, but there were moments when he felt he had heard enough of the girl and how master felt about her.

"If that puppy we bought the other day," he thought, "is hearing this same sort of stuff from her about master I'm sorry for him."

On Wednesday David woke up in wild spirits and went singing to his bath. He sang to the tune of "Praise to the Holiest in the Height".

> "Praise to old Piper's surgery.
> May all his work be good.
> Be all his stoppings wonderful,
> May he win his Littlewood."

He went off to work still humming, and startled his next-door neighbour at the meat counter by saying:

"I don't know a more beautiful sight than a nice piece of under-done beef waiting to be cut, do you, Smithson?"

Smithson, who had indulged in a late and thick night, looked at the joint gloomily.

"I can think of a lot of things I'd rather see. Including a hair of the dog that bit me last night. What's made you so cheerful?"

David straightened his chef's cap.

"I'm going to the dentist, and if there is one thing more than another that we Babbacombes dote on it is going to the dentist. Haven't you noticed how my father feels about dentists? Well, I take after him."

Smithson turned away.

"You're mad," he said sourly. "The dentist! Strewth!"

David, with Scissors under his arm, arrived in the consulting-room at two five.

"I'm afraid it's very doubtful if Mr. Piper will be able to see you," said the nurse. "I don't know why he sent you this card. He's got an appointment now, and another at two-thirty. He may be able to squeeze you in before the two-thirty if she's late, but that's the only chance."

David sat down.

"Don't let it upset you, nurse. Taking other people's teeth to heart is what brings on angina. Didn't you know?"

The nurse, who was only a secretary in a white linen coat, and called nurse by courtesy, giggled:

"Silly, aren't you?" and went out.

At two twenty there were steps in the passage.

"I suppose we are wrong," David whispered to Scissors, "but it feels as though we might burst."

The door opened. David half got up. Then he sat down, quite cold with disappointment; but Dulcie, who had crept gloomily along the street, was suddenly aflame. Her eyes shone.

"You!" she said and added, "Well, it is a small world, isn't it?"

David blinked.

"One takes it that you work in Babbacombe's too?"

Dulcie's face fell.

"Don't you know me?"

He felt that her face was familiar, then he jumped to it.

"Why, it's Dulcie, the pride of the lifts."

Dulcie was pleased.

"Saucy, aren't you! Dulcie indeed! Miss Carson to you."

David, looking back, never knew how he kept his face, but somehow he did, even as in a flash he guessed what had happened, and cursed Piper for a muddler.

"Sorry, I didn't know your surname."

"No?" There was a definite query in her voice. "Knew it better as my cousin's, I suppose—Beth Carson. She was shut in the lift with you. All right, don't blush. Boys will be boys."

David was nearly sick.

"Your cousin!"

"Yes." Dulcie misread his stunned amazement. "We are a bit different, aren't we? But of course I've been brought up differently. I went to a boarding-school, and I've money of my own."

He looked at her gravely.

"Yes, I can see a great deal of difference."

Dulcie winked.

"I know my way about a bit more. She's like a school kid, isn't she? Now, if you and I got stuck in a lift—"

David, to keep her good-tempered, paid her back in her own coin.

"Here's hoping. How is your cousin?"

"Oh, she's all right. She's got a cold, but I say—"

"A cold! Is she bad?"

All David's careful control was gone. Dulcie's eyes ran over him, and at that moment Scissors raised his head and looked over the table. In a second she was on to the truth. The present of a dachshund, his voice, her rose.

"But you saw her on Saturday."

It was not a question, but what seemed a casual statement.

David was surprised she had been told.

"She hadn't a cold then."

Dulcie was for once at a loss. The knowledge that her worst fears were more than realised deprived her of her usual sharp thinking. She was not sure what her next step should be. He could not really be interested in Beth—no man could—but that did not say she had planned how to switch his interest over to herself. The nurse came to her aid: she opened the door.

"Miss Carson, please."

"So long," said Dulcie. "I'll be seeing you in the shop."

David stood up.

"I shall count the minutes."

David looked down at Scissors.

"That nasty bit of work is her cousin. Would you believe it?"

Scissors, hoping this boring hanging about in a dull room was over, gave a half bark. David closed his mouth with his hand.

"You mustn't bark here. But I know just what you mean; you have several long-legged, short-bodied, unstanding-eared mongrel cousins that you can't account for. It's true, old boy. So've I. But she's certainly a blot." David slipped quietly into the passage and went to look for the nurse. He found her in the study, filling in appointment cards. She looked at him severely.

"It's no good you coming in here: you may as well go home. The two thirty was punctual; he won't see you now."

He glanced over her shoulder at the appointment book. "Is that your handwriting? Don't you write neatly!"

She looked pleased.

"Oh, it's all practice, you know."

"Isn't he busy?" said David, rapidly running his eyes over the engagements. He reached Friday afternoon, and saw, "4 o'clock. Carson, Miss B. (Gowns.)"

"It's lucky he has you to keep his book in order."

She nodded complacently.

"There's never any muddle when I see to things; it's only when he interferes that they get in a mess. He sent your card. I never would have."

He sat on the edge of her desk.

"Does this firm run to a piece of notepaper and an envelope? I want to leave Mr. Piper a note."

"I can give a message."

He shook his head.

"No, beautiful—it's a private matter, a low masculine affair."

She handed him a sheet of paper and an envelope.

"Know what you want, don't you?"

"Always."

"DEAR PIPER" [he wrote]

"You've now realised that the nasty bit of work with you is the wrong one. (I should think half an hour's sharp work with a drill on a particularly sensitive tooth would do her good.) The right one will be with you at four o'clock on Friday, and a card to my buyer ordering me to attend there or thereabouts is the least you can do for having made a dirty muddle of today.

Yours,

D. B."

He sealed the envelope and addressed it and propped it up in front of the nurse.

"There you are, my lovely. Goodbye."

She looked over her shoulder at him as he went out, then she returned to her cards with a sigh. She had a more or less attached young man called Herbert, who was quite nice; but he hadn't the way with him young Mr. Babbacombe had—not by a long chalk he hadn't.

Dulcie, released from the dentist's chair, walked thoughtfully back to Babbacombe's. She had a shrewd mind which was naturally adapted for sorting facts. In this case the facts were simple. Beth certainly on Saturday, and presumably at some other time, had seen David Babbacombe. Why was he taking this trouble with Beth? Why had he cared whether Beth had a cold or not? Why had he given her that puppy for Edward? He couldn't admire her. He couldn't! She was so simple looking—like a schoolgirl—and not pretty—at least, not what *she* would call pretty. Of course, her hair curled naturally, but it wasn't much of a colour. The more she thought about it, the more she was muddled. Nobody could suppose he was fond of Beth, but that was what it looked like. One thing was certain: if he was liking her it wouldn't last long—she wouldn't know the tricks to hold a man. Taking things by and large, Dulcie was not sure the afternoon had not been useful. She had at least had a talk with David and let him know who she was, and that she was differently educated and all that from the other girls in Babbacombe's. A man of his sort was likely to get tired of a girl of Beth's kind pretty quickly, and then he'd be looking round for someone else, and the sort of person he would look for would be one of his own sort, and that would be her. Who else?

She wondered if she should spread the news about Saturday. She thought, on the whole, no. At present the girls in the store thought David was keeping himself to himself. Pity to let them know he wasn't. Didn't want all those common cats barging in. Just now he might have his eye on Beth, but she was taking the long view, thinking of the future. Somehow she would find a way to be Mrs. Babbacombe. If there wasn't a straight way, most likely there was a crooked.

She went humming down to change into her lift things, and spent a long time fixing her face and hair. After all, hadn't he said he would be counting the minutes till he saw her again? Of course, he was only joking; but this wouldn't be the first joke turned to reality. All her life she had known that if you went all out for a thing you could have it. As she dabbed on the powder, and curled her hair round her finger, she thought; This is the beginning, and from now on you never let up.

Beth felt like Job, one trial descending on her head after another. It was hard enough to go to work knowing David was under the same roof and never seeing a glimpse of him. Every time she was sent on an errand she started off full of hope: this time Fate would be kind, she would meet him in a staff passage or in the lift. Every time anyone started to give her a message to take, her heart lifted in the hope that this time she would have to go through Cooked Meats—it would be the quickest way. Monday and Tuesday seemed to her the longest days she had known since she had been in the shop. Then on Tuesday night she started a cold—not a bad cold, but a nasty snivelling affair that made her feel stupid. On Wednesday morning she went to work with a heart like a stone. It was grey and cold, and she could not imagine anything happening to light her gloom. All the morning, just because she was feeling heavy and dull, there seemed a peculiar lot of odd jobs to do, and than after lunch came her tragedy.

She had been given a word of praise from the buyer over her sales to Barbara, and had glowed at the extra in her Friday envelope. It had been a big laugh at home—her first commission. Edward had wanted to make a case for the coins, and Janet had been as pleased as anything when most of it had gone in the fur coat box. Beth had been looking forward to making another sale. It would be Eve's birthday in August, and she would like to get her something pretty to wear at Bexhill—one of those little sun-suits, perhaps. Of course, although sales were open, they did not often come her way—she was only a junior, and there were plenty of real saleswomen about. But after lunch on Wednesday a customer came to her of her own accord.

Beth was re-hanging a pile of frocks on one of the runners, and taking the opportunity for a good nose-blow, when she heard a voice behind her.

"Are you serving?"

Beth started, and saw a smart woman in black crêpe-de-Chine and pearls.

"No." She looked round to see if anyone else was about, but the woman shook her head.

"No, please, you serve me. I'm in rather a hurry. I want something for a wedding—simple but smart."

Beth led the way to the glass-fronted cupboard which held the model afternoon frocks. "Any special colour?"

"I'd like black, but it doesn't matter awfully."

With a pile of frocks over one arm, Beth led the way to a fitting-room. The customer was quite a different proposition from Barbara Allan. She knew exactly what she wanted, and needed no advice. One after the other the frocks were put on, but there was something a little wrong with each of them. This was too fussy; the navy would crease; that brown had an ugly neck.

"Really I like this little black face cloth the best. It's funny, because it's the cheapest." The customer gave Beth a woman-to-woman smile. "And it's very unlike me to like anything that's cheap. Have you got something like it without this white collar?"

Beth ran an inward eye over the model cupboard.

"I don't think so, madam, but I'll go and look."

She was gone three or four minutes. When she came back the customer was still in the black face cloth frock. She accepted Beth's regret that they had nothing else like it with a friendly nod.

"Never mind. I'll stick to this. In fact, I think I'll wear it. I'm sick of the thing I came in." She nodded at her own black crêpe-de-Chine lying on a chair. "Would you pack it for me? I'll take it with me. I have my car."

Beth glowed. She had begun to despair of making a sale, and it had been quite simple in the end. She almost forgot her cold, as with a feeling of achievement, she opened her book.

"On account, madam?"

The customer shook her head.

"No, cash." She opened her purse and paid in five-pound notes.

"Made another sale, have you?" asked Jenny, as Beth returned from seeing off her customer.

Beth beamed.

"Yes. Fifteen guineas."

"My! Aren't you lucky?" said Jenny. "Your first two spending quite a bit."

Beth pressed her lip to stop a sneeze.

"Of course I might have done better. Some of the models I was showing her were twenty-five pounds, and that new one from Moulin of Paris is marked forty, though Mrs. Nunn will let it go for less."

Jenny looked at her sympathetically.

"You have got a cold. I'm doing nothing. Shall I help you re-hang your dresses?"

Beth had always thought Jenny a dear.

"That's awfully nice of you. It isn't really as bad a cold as it sounds and looks, but I've a nose that goes red easily."

The two girls went into the fitting-room and collected the frocks. Suddenly Beth looked round.

"Have you got the Moulin?"

Jenny examined the frocks over her arm.

"No."

Beth was puzzled.

"That's funny. I had it. One of the others must have come for it."

Jenny gazed at her with her mouth dropping.

"They haven't. There isn't a customer in just now. Goodness, Beth, *she* must have taken it."

"Taken it!" Beth felt herself going cold all over. "Do you mean she was a shoplifter?"

Jenny, almost deprived of speech, nodded.

"Yes. Run to Mrs. Nunn and she'll get the floor detective." She snatched the other dresses from Beth. "Quick."

Mrs. Nunn was just back from her lunch. Her mind was busy with her coming trip abroad in search of autumn models. She was wondering if she would take Fred, her husband, with her. He seemed to run up an astounding number of debts when she was out of sight—Satan unrestrained finding mischief for idle hands to do, she supposed. The thought of Fred sent prickles up her spine. Often when he wasn't there she felt like this, longing to have the strength to thrash him. Face to face with his easy, good-humoured smile her willpower died. Irritated already, she looked up in annoyance at the sight of one of her girls running across the showroom. She got up, looking freezing.

"Mrs. Nunn—"

Mrs. Nunn held up her hand.

"Compose yourself. Surely even in the short time you have been here you have learnt that we don't run."

Beth clasped her hands.

"I had to. I'm sorry, but I think I've let a customer steal a frock."

"What! Which one?"

"The new Moulin."

Mrs. Nunn gave Beth a gentle push and marched across to Miss Jones.

"Get the floor detective."

The floor detective was a woman—a Miss Binks. She was a slim, smart creature, who walked about the place all day looking like a customer, only now and then diving into her sanctum to change. Her changes included hair and make-up, so that though she had been pointed out to Beth, she was never quite sure she knew her by sight. Just now she was in a coat and skirt, with a small smart hat set on one side of a neatly shingled red wig. She was a competent person, and in a very few moments had those who could help sorted out and collected in her room. These were Mrs. Nunn, Miss Jones, Beth and Jenny. She looked at Beth. In spite of the hardness of her appearance her voice was gentle:

"Now, my dear, what was she like?"

At school and at home Beth had been taught to give a straight answer to a straight question. She focussed her memory on her customer.

"She was quite a bit taller than me, and absolutely stock size. None of the models would have needed any real black hair with a wave. It was in flat curls on her neck, beautifully done. She wasn't young—somewhere between thirty and forty." Miss Jones, who was nearly thirty, wriggled uncomfortably.

"Did you find her, or she you?" asked Miss Binks.

"She found me." Beth glanced at Miss Jones. "I was rehanging those washing silks as you told me. She said, Was I serving? and when I looked round for somebody she said she wanted me, as she was in a hurry. Something simple but smart, for a wedding."

Miss Binks was writing in a notebook.

"Did you leave her alone in the fitting-room?"

"Yes. She liked the black face cloth, but she wanted something without white on it. I went to look."

Miss Binks nodded.

"And when you came back she was still in the black face cloth, and she said she would keep it, and that she would pay in cash?"

"Yes, she did—five-pound notes, and five shillings, and a ten-shilling note. I had her own frock put in a box. She said her car was outside and she would take it with her."

Miss Binks looked at Mrs. Nunn.

"The usual trick. She had the Moulin underneath, of course. There's only one thing which sticks out. It seems as if she knew the department." She turned to Jenny. "You saw the woman arrive?"

"Yes. She came in through Juvenile. She just went straight across to Beth."

Miss Binks gave Mrs. Nunn another look.

"Knew she was new, and chose a time when half the staff were at lunch. Sounds as though she might be known to some of you." She turned back to Jenny. "Did you notice anything about her that this girl"—she indicated Beth—"hasn't told us?"

"No. She was across the department, and I didn't notice her especially."

Miss Binks looked at Miss Jones.

"You were on the floor. What did you see?"

Miss Jones' eyes shifted nervously. She felt Mrs. Nunn was blaming her—which she was. How unlucky she had chosen that minute to write to her Tom; but it was a wonderful offer of her aunt's to put them both up for their holiday, and it was important he should know at once.

"I didn't see the woman until she was going out." She searched her mind for an excuse. "I never imagined a junior could be so foolish as to handle a big sale without coming to me."

Mrs. Nunn gave a nod to Beth and Jenny.

"You two can go. I shall want to see you, Beth, later on." As the door shut on the girls she got up. "It's no good blaming Beth, Miss Jones. You were doing something else, I suppose. I'm not finding fault with that. None of us can have eyes all over the place."

Miss Jones blinked to keep back the tears.

"It's so bad for the department—I know that without you telling me."

Mrs. Nunn gave her a kindly nod.

"Don't be upset. You go back and take charge, will you?"

Miss Binks and Mrs. Nunn gave each other an expressive look which said clearly "Poor fool!" then Mrs. Nunn added in words:

"But so well-meaning. She's going to get married soon; and thank goodness her Tom wants her to give up work. He doesn't approve of wives in business."

Miss Binks looked through her notes.

"That new kid who let that dress be stolen is a nice child. A good, straightforward way of saying what happened. No beating about the bush."

Mrs. Nunn nodded.

"That's what I thought. She reminds me a little of my Ruth. Of course Ruth's younger, but that girl is very much the kind of person that I'm hoping she will grow up into."

Back in the showroom, Beth found her cold felt ten times worse, and she wanted to cry. How awful! A forty-guinea model, and all her fault. Mrs. Nunn had said she would see her presently. That would be to give her notice, she supposed. It wasn't likely the firm would overlook a blunder of that sort. How miserable for Dad! He'd be so ashamed! How wretched for herself! Apart from the horror of being given notice and perhaps being out of work, she would be away from Babbacombe's, with less chance than ever of seeing David. David! His name came like a ray of light in a black sky. She must see him—Just for a second. She wouldn't want to speak to him; but just to see him and get a smile would give her a bit more courage. She went timidly to Miss Jones' desk and asked permission to go to the cloakroom for an extra handkerchief.

"You see, I've got a cold," she explained, her voice coming out much smaller than usual because of the lump in her throat.

Miss Jones was thinking of her Tom, and wondering, if somebody was to get the blame for this accident, if it wouldn't be her. It would be sickening if it was, with only a year to go before she had enough saved. But she was not hard-hearted—she knew just how Beth must be feeling.

"Yes, do, dear." She was going to add something more, but one of the sales girls came up for her signature.

Beth, swallowing hard, went down to the ground floor. She walked to the end of Groceries and up the Cooked Meats counter, and had another blow. David was not there.

She did not wonder where he was. In her present state of misery he was just the bit of heat in the icy cold, and if that heat was gone, then there was nothing. With a throat that ached from swallowing tears, and with a very white face, she went back to her own department.

Jenny was on the lookout for her.

"You're wanted, Beth, in Mrs. Nunn's room."

Beth nodded. She couldn't answer. It was plain what was going to happen to her. She was not asking for sympathy.

Mrs. Nunn was sitting behind writing. She did not look up as Beth came in, but said:

"Sit down."

Beth sat and waited, her hands tightly clasped to help her control herself. Then Mrs. Nunn laid down the pen and looked up, and Beth was startled. Mrs. Nunn had been crying. Without thinking that it was not her place to notice her buyer's eyes, even if they were red, she said:

"Oh, I'm so sorry, and it's all my fault."

Surprisingly, Mrs. Nunn laughed. She took her mirror out of her bag and examined her face.

"Dear me! Does it show that much?" She got out her powder puff and dealt with her nose. "No, you're not to blame for the state of my eyes. Today has happened to be a particularly trying one for me, and the dress business came as a climax."

"For you as well?" said Beth. "How odd! My day's been awful too."

Mrs. Nunn leant forward.

"It's not a bad thing that you should see that I'm upset. I'm at the top of this department, and you are a junior. You may think that the dress being stolen is a tragedy happening just to you.

But that isn't what happens in a big store. Some little girl—you, perhaps—is careless and makes a muddle, and the person above her is responsible for her and takes the blame, and then the managers come into it, and finally perhaps the directors, and in the end nobody remembers who made the muddle, but it's a black mark against the department, and the honour of the department is all our business—yours as well as mine."

"Is that why you were miserable?"

Mrs. Nunn sighed.

"In a way; but as well I was disappointed about that dress. It was a clever buy of mine—I had an idea of having a line like it: I'd hoped we'd do very well with them. Good dresses are rare, you know."

"You won't have to pay for it, will you?"

"Only indirectly, but if you make a clever buy you hope to do well out of it. I've a boy and girl at school wanting a lot of things, and it's not always easy to find them."

Beth was amazed. The great Mrs. Nunn with children at school, reckoning on making good sales to buy them the extra things, just as she was counting on that sale to get Eve a birthday present.

"I'm dreadfully sorry," she said. "I suppose I've got to go. I'll have no chance to work hard and make it up to you a bit."

Mrs. Nunn came back to herself with a jump.

"Dear me! I don't know why I'm telling you all my private affairs. No, of course you've not got to go. We all make mistakes—as a matter of fact I was pleased with you: you told us what happened sensibly and clearly. Now run along. You've had your lesson. See it never happens again."

Beth stood outside Mrs. Nunn's door and felt herself growing happy again.

"I'm like a plant," she thought, "that the rain's beaten down. I can feel myself rising up." For a moment she felt detached, as though she had stepped out of herself and could look at herself. "I hope I'll remember this minute: that however beaten down one may feel, one can get up. I may need to remember that later on."

CHAPTER TEN

It was Friday, and pouring with rain. Beth neither wanted to go to the dentist nor leave the dry shop for the soaking streets. The possibility of there being any pleasure in the afternoon never crossed her mind. So it was all the more lovely to open the waiting-room door and see David.

"Well, well," he said. "Who'd have thought it?"

Looking at him, Beth knew that their meeting was not an accident. She tried to appear severe, but only managed a frown which had nothing to do with the rest of her expression.

"How did you manage it?"

He pulled her down into the chair next to him, and Scissors put his paws on her knee and licked her hand.

"Now don't let's waste time over tactless questions. How's Gowns?"

Beth pulled Scissors up on her lap.

"Simply awful!" She told the story of her shoplifter. David watched her face, and loved the intense worried look of her. "And then in the end, when everything seemed terrible, Mrs. Nunn was nice." Beth's voice tailed away. She glanced at him. "Are you listening?"

He nodded.

"Listening and looking. I wish I could learn to take Cooked Meats as seriously. There's something missing in me. I don't believe I'd turn a hair if somebody went off with three galantines and a ham."

She laughed.

"All the same, though I'm laughing, it isn't a thing to laugh about. I wish I could catch that woman."

"Ah, now you're talking. If ever you do, call me—a magnificent policeman I'll make."

Beth pulled Scissors' ears through her fingers.

"How's your tooth been?"

"No better. I was here again on Wednesday. Old Piper had made a shocking blunder—muddled his cases. Your cousin was here?"

"Dulcie!" Beth got on to that at once. "That'll teach you not to go scheming. Did you talk to Dulcie?"

David gave her an are-we-all-friends-here look.

"You know, my sweet, I'm sure she's an awfully nice girl, and wonderful to her old mother and all that, but I found her not quite the girl for me."

Beth's heart bounded, and at the same time she felt a stab of shame. What a cad she was to be pleased that he shouldn't like Dulcie! She forced herself to speak firmly.

"She hasn't got a mother. She's an orphan. She's never had a chance."

"Scissors," said David, "we're crushed. We are guilty of hasty and unfair judgement." He looked up at Beth, his eyes twinkling. "According to the lady, though, she has had unusual chances. Boarding-schools and I don't know what all."

"Boarding-schools!" Beth's voice was full of scorn. "What's the good of them? What she needed was a proper home. She only had an idiotic aunt."

David moved his chair nearer to hers.

"I hate wasting time discussing that girl, who is doubtless a paragon, but unimportant to us. Will you come and have tea after your appointment?"

"But we've got to get back to the shop."

"Why? We're allowed half an hour for tea. I usually go out for mine, don't you?"

Beth considered.

"You see, I'm a junior. I go when I can be spared easiest."

"You're quibbling. They can't be counting on you if you're not there."

Beth pictured a little table in a corner, and the fun of pouring out David's tea again. It would be like Saturday.

"Very well." They heard the nurse coming. "But we mustn't be long over it."

"Half an hour, including getting back to the department," David whispered. "See how nicely I've learned my shop rules."

The nurse, having taken Beth to Mr. Piper, came back to David.

"It's no good, you know. I can't think why he doesn't give you a proper appointment. I shouldn't wait."

"I wish I could take your advice. But I can't. It's your charm—it clings, and sucks a man to you like a quicksand."

The nurse shook her head.

"You're a sad case—ought to be locked up."

"That's right. Out of my mind for love. That's what you've done, beautiful."

She giggled.

"Go on. But honestly it's no good waiting."

"Ah." David turned to Scissors. "That's all she knows. 'I shall sit here,' as the frog footman said to Alice, 'on and off, for days and days.'"

The nurse opened the door.

"Please yourself. If you like wearing out our chairs, you're welcome."

The permanent stopping did not take long. Mr. Piper handed Beth a tumbler.

"Rinse, please." He turned away and spoke over his shoulder. "Is young Mr. Babbacombe waiting?"

Beth wiped her mouth.

"Yes."

"Ah." Mr. Piper made a great show of being busy boiling his instruments. "Tell him I can't manage today. He needn't wait."

Beth eyed his back thoughtfully. How, she wondered, had David got round him?

"Shall I tell him when you want him to come again?" she suggested.

She had hoped to disconcert him, but he went quietly on with what he was doing.

"No, my dear, thank you. All appointments, you know, go through the buyers."

Somebody new was in the waiting-room when Beth came back, so David picked up Scissors without a word and joined her in the passage.

"Where shall we go? Somewhere amusing, or just a plate of cakes and a brown teapot?"

His words made Beth feel as if she were melting.

"A brown teapot."

The nurse looked out of the window at their backs.

"So that's it." She turned over the appointments book and laid her finger on Wednesday. "Old silly!" she murmured. "Why didn't he trust me? Does he think I haven't got a heart?"

"And how," asked David, "is Keith Prowse?"

Beth watched the waitress bring a brown earthenware teapot and a plate of bilious-looking cakes.

"He's grand, and he's making all the difference to Edward. Taking him for walks fills up the time now he's not allowed to go to school." She poured out his cup of tea. "I do hope it won't be long before they operate. Getting worse must be so awful."

David took his cup.

"Ghastly, poor kid!" He hesitated. "It's unfortunate how I always seem to be using Edward as an excuse to see you; but you know if you weren't such a hard-hearted Annie, and would take me into the bosom of your family, I could be quite a help. After all, I have a car. I could take Edward around sometimes."

She selected the least terrifying of the cakes.

"Even if I said yes, Dad wouldn't. He's worked in Babbacombe's since he was a boy. He doesn't approve of my knowing you. He thinks you're forgetting your place. You see, he remembers you since you were a little boy and were 'Master David', and now you're 'Mister David'. And he respects your father terrifically, and he knows your father wouldn't like it."

"I'm not so sure he wouldn't like it."

"What, with Dad one of his salesmen in Hardware and me a junior in Gowns? You know he wouldn't approve. What man in your father's position would?"

David turned the cake-stand round.

"I wonder which of those would give the easiest death. I should think that thing with arsenic icing would cut me off pretty quickly, wouldn't you?" He took the cake and bit it thoughtfully. "You realise, of course, that I'm still the worm working underground. My head will keep popping up. Today is only a beginning."

Beth looked at the clock.

"We've been here twenty minutes. It will take five minutes to get back to the shop and five to get my things off and up to my department."

David beckoned to the waitress.

"Of all vile qualities in a woman, conscientiousness is the worst. Here you are, Scissors, old man—a nice arsenic bun that master can't eat because of the lady's conscience."

Walking back to the shop, Beth felt depressed. Each meeting with David seemed to make saying goodbye to him worse. In the road leading to the staff door she slowed down.

"Of course, being in the same shop, we're almost bound to meet sometime by accident."

David restrained a longing to seize her in his arms and say, "So you do like seeing me." Instead he looked deceptively innocent and agreed with her.

"Bound to, sometime, by accident."

Babbacombe's had their fortnight of July sales. The first days of a sale are nightmares to all the staff concerned, but no one suffers more than the apprentices and juniors. Beth, as a junior, was, according to custom, called by her Christian name by all the sales girls, and in those first days of the sale it seemed to her there was not one second when she was not hearing it called by somebody.

"Beth, hang all these back on the runner."

"Beth, get this packed—Madam is taking it with her. If they're busy, pack it yourself, as Madam is in a hurry."

"Beth, find Mrs. Fosdick and ask her to come to eighteen. Tell her it's only a small alteration, and Madam wants the frock for Cowes."

Of all her jobs Beth found fetching Mrs. Fosdick the most trying. Like all fitters, Mrs. Fosdick was a law unto herself, and she was a person of very strong likes and dislikes. She had taken a fancy to Beth from the beginning, and was outspoken to her about the rest of the staff.

"Who wants me? Miss Simpson. You tell her she can go on waiting. I'm busy. What! May lose the sale? That's her funeral. I'll come along when I'm ready."

Or another time:

"Where's Miss Brown got her customer? Sixteen. Now, dear, you go in and say I'm on my way. I'm not, for I've got to do somebody in three first. But say it: it'll keep them quiet, and I'll be as quick as I can."

Whatever Mrs. Fosdick said it was Beth who had to accept the consequences: the annoyance of the saleswomen, who accused her of not giving their messages, and the fretful thanks of those who felt she could have got Mrs. Fosdick quicker if she had only tried.

Once or twice Beth found herself sent out with a parcel, when delivery was urgent and no van was available. She was glad of the air, but each time she was sent it was after tea, and as she had been running hard since nine, she could appreciate nothing but a chair. Being sent out of the shop was an aggravating business in itself, taking time, of which, during sales, there was precious little. There was a pass to be got from Mrs. Nunn, or, failing her, Miss Jones. Each time Beth wanted a pass both Mrs. Nunn and Miss Jones seemed to be involved in long conversations which she could not interrupt, and which resulted in her having to hang about looking like somebody with something important to say, but equally not interrupting, which was certain to bring down wrath on her head. Having got the pass, she had to go up to the top of the building to Mr. Smith for his counter-sign. In sales times extra staff were taken on, and they were often more trouble than they were worth, and, naturally, everything to do with them was referred to the staff manager's office, so Mr. Smith was usually engaged. Beth found herself getting quite nervous on behalf of the unknown customer whose parcel she was to take. How terrible if it was a frock for a party tonight! Just think what you would feel like, waiting and waiting and it never coming!

Once she got scolded when she delivered her parcel. It was a frock which had needed a small alteration, and had been sent up an hour late from the workroom. The saleswoman responsible for it had told Beth she would have to take it, and had better run. Beth had waited ten minutes for Mrs. Nunn's signature and another five for Mr. Smith's, and had run down to the cloakroom to save waiting for the lift, and had run all the way to the tube, and had run at the other end. It was with a little feeling of triumph that she rang the flat bell. The frock was not nearly as late as it might have been. The flat door was thrown open by the owner, who was in a dressing gown. She snatched the box from Beth.

"An hour and a half late! No, it's no good making an excuse. What's your name? I shall write to Babbacombe's and complain. Have you no imagination, my good girl? Just think of the wear and tear to my nerves sitting here and waiting for that box, with nothing else fit to put on in the house. But you don't think, you don't care; you just loiter along the streets, looking in the shop windows. You've probably been to a cinema. I don't know what's happening to your working girls today—you've not a vestige of a sense of responsibility."

"But—"

"Now don't interrupt. I can't wait now to hear your excuses. I'm late enough already." And the door was slammed.

In sales time it was often eight o'clock before Beth got away. Somehow masses of people seemed to come in just before closing time, and each of them needed dozens of frocks taken off the runners, and all those dozens seemed to be in a heap waiting to be rehung after the shop was closed. Then there was packing. In the ordinary way the packing was done by the packers, but in sales times they could not begin to cope, and the apprentices and juniors had to help. When the last parcel was done there was the usual tidying for the night, armloads of covers to be brought in and hung over the frocks.

At home Janet understood about sales time. She knew George had always wanted a chair and his house shoes just as quickly as he could get them. But George, rushed though he had been all day, was a senior salesman, and got home only the half-hour later than usual. Janet was sorry for Beth, and knew just how tired she must be, but she could not keep all the family waiting for their supper until she got in. One of the hardest parts of the sales to Beth was her lonely supper: when you are almost too tired to eat, it helps to have other people eating with you.

Dulcie watched Beth coming home exhausted with smug pleasure. Being tired suited Beth less than most people, for she was the type, if she had any charm—which Dulcie doubted—who depended on looking fresh. Not in her most optimistic moods could Dulcie feel she was making any headway with David, and for that she blamed Beth. Partly because of David, and partly because she disliked her, Dulcie chose any night when Beth was tired to insert pinpricks.

"Funny you having to stop so late and only getting a pound a week and me away sharp at six-thirty and getting twenty-five shillings."

"Beth's got sense," said George sourly. "She's thinking of the future."

Dulcie sniffed.

"I'd have to have a pretty poor opinion of myself if I thought I'd stop in that old shop long."

"Oh, well," Beth interrupted good-humouredly, "you never know. I like being safe."

Janet saw that George had something sharp to say, so she broke in:

"She's thinking of my fur coat, aren't you, darling? You wait till she's a buyer."

The more her family rallied round Beth, the more Dulcie detested her. She got to such a pitch that she, who was a log-like sleeper, lay awake at night scheming how to annoy her. It was one of these bed schemes that made Beth lose her temper.

It was the day that she had been scolded by the customer to whom she had delivered the frock. It was the second week of the sales, and in the first week she had sold a few things, with the result there was some commission in her envelope. Because of the extra money and the sales she had gone to Juvenile in her lunch hour and bought the sun-suit for Eve's birthday. It was a smart affair in orange, with gay little bunches of flowers all over it. That little suit was the one bright spot in a tiring and unpleasant day. Her supper finished, with the pleased feeling that everybody was going to admire it, she undid her parcel.

"How's that, Mum, for Eve at Bexhill?"

Edward peered at it, and lifted Keith Prowse up to have a look. "See that, old man; that's going to make the beach sit up."

Janet loved something new for the children. She felt the stuff in her fingers, her eyes shining.

"Well, isn't that sweet! And it feels as if it would wash like a rag."

George eyed the little garment with approval. "Looks like a bit of our garden. Eve will look a proper little flower."

Girda joined her mother and Beth at the table.

"Isn't it smart! Won't she look a pet!"

Quietly Dulcie slipped up to her bedroom and came back with a parcel.

"I've bought something for Eve's birthday too." She opened her parcel beside Beth's.

Inside was another sun-suit, but in a different class. This was an American model, made of the new Hawaiian material, a flaming scarlet pattern on a white ground with a little hat to match. Even in Eve's small size it had cost quite a bit—more than Dulcie would have dreamed of spending on someone else were it not that she anticipated getting her money's worth in annoyance given.

All the family stared at Dulcie's present in embarrassment. It made Beth's look just what it was—a nice little thing picked up in a sale. Beth rolled hers back in its paper.

"Yours is sweet," she said quietly to Dulcie. "But why did you buy it? I told you I was getting one. We don't get enough sun to need two."

Dulcie shrugged her shoulders.

"I didn't see why the poor little kid shouldn't have something decent for once."

The whole family were hurt. Each of them tried to think of something to say, but Beth was first.

"You can take that back, Dulcie. We all know you've more to spend than I have, and if you enjoy buying the same thing I'm going to get, only six times better, that's up to you; but you can't speak as if Eve never had any clothes. There's never been a time when we haven't all had the right things to wear—not always what you'd call smart, but always nice. You can do what you like with your money, but for goodness sake don't swank." She picked up her parcel. "I'll change this tomorrow. If you want to give a sun-suit you can have the field to yourself." She went out of the room.

Dulcie grinned at Girda.

"There's gratitude. Funny way to take a birthday present to a sister."

Girda and Edward were horribly embarrassed. They quite saw why Beth was annoyed, but, for all that, a present was a present, and it was jolly decent of Dulcie to spend all that on Eve.

"Old Beth's cock-eyed this week," said Edward. "It's the sale."

"And it's a lovely sun-suit," Girda added. "Eve'll be terribly pleased."

George cleared his throat. He was sorry Beth had spoken how she had. Dulcie was a nasty bit of work, but that was no excuse to be rude. It was good of her to buy a frock for Eve.

"We all get our tempers a bit raw sales time: I often feel like snapping somebody's head off myself," he apologised.

Janet alone did not try to cover Beth's rudeness. She picked up the sun-suit and hat and examined them; then she gave Dulcie a you-and-I-understand-each-other nod. "Must have given you a lot of pleasure buying that," she said gently, and left the room.

Janet found Beth sitting on the bottom step of the stairs. Her face was to the front door and her head bent. She thought she was crying, and sat down beside her and put an arm round her shoulders. Beth swung round, her face shining.

"Oh, Mum, how can I be such a fool as to mind what people like Dulcie do or say?"

Janet raised her eyebrows.

"What's brought about this change of heart?"

Beth handed her a letter.

"Look."

Janet read.

"DEAR BETH,

My aunt has said I can have the Castle for the first week-end in August for a party of my friends, and I would like to have you, because I always feel that some of my luck comes from you taking such trouble over my clothes. You will come, won't you? Don't worry about your clothes, because we are the same size, and you can borrow any of mine.

Yours,

Barbara."

Janet gasped.

"A castle! Wouldn't you be afraid? I would."

Beth took back her letter and folded it.

"I don't think I would with her—she's awfully simple, though she's marrying a lord, and she knows just what I am."

"But think of all the grand people who may be there. Besides, I don't know what Dad'll say. He's against people going where they don't belong."

Beth gripped her letter. Barbara was engaged to that Lord Pern, that David called "Slug". It was just possible—"You persuade him, Mum. I want to go."

Janet took Beth's chin in her hand and turned her face up to hers.

"Because it's a castle?"

Beth shook her head.

"No." A slow flush crept over her cheeks.

Janet took away her hand, her face suddenly tender.

"I'll make Dad let you go, don't worry."

CHAPTER ELEVEN

THE Carsons were dressing, for it was the Saturday evening of Girda's school concert. After a lot of fuss, Janet had bought Girda's new frock, which was of a flowered material. Girda had grudgingly agreed that since she couldn't have black satin it wasn't so bad, though she still held it wasn't a bit suitable for reciting "The Little Match Girl".

"Don't think, Mum," she had said, "that I don't like it. It'll be quite all right for parties in the winter, but it doesn't look tragic."

Janet had managed to take this gravely.

"I am sorry, darling, but 'The Little Match Girl' is only happening once, and I don't want a tragic Girda all through the winter."

"Has Girda gone?" George asked Janet, as he put on his blue suit.

Janet was buttoning the back of her brown foulard frock—the same frock that she had worn for Beth's breaking up a term ago. She did not say so, but she was sick and tired of that frock.

"Yes." She gave up thinking of herself and her clothes and turned to George. "I saw her dressed just after tea. She'll be there hours too soon, but she's in such a fuss it's better to let her go. She looked sweet, I thought, in her little flowered frock."

Beth had not wanted to make her first appearance as an old girl looking shabby, but while she had her present money she still had to depend on Janet for clothes. She gave ten shillings a week for her board, and kept what was left of the other ten shillings, when the insurance money was gone, for her omnibus fares and meals, and there was none over for frocks. Tonight she put on her shop frock. It was much the best thing she had, but she did not feel very festive in it. You can't feel a frock is smart when you wear it to work every day. Her feelings about herself were not improved by Dulcie, who was making herself resplendent in royal blue taffeta. She looked across at Beth with annoying sympathy.

"Fancy you having to wear that. Haven't you anything else?"

Beth was not going to be upset by Dulcie.

"Nothing the girls at school haven't seen. Coming back as an old girl, I'd rather wear something everybody didn't know."

Dulcie did not answer in words, but her eyes were scornful. She began to hum in a pleased way. Beth did not hear the humming— her own words had taken her back three months. Was it only three months ago that she had been to her prizegiving? Was it only three months ago that she had wanted to cry because Miss Rigg said 'Next term will be the poorer because Elizabeth Carson is not with us', and had felt that next term would be the poorer for herself because she was going to work in Babbacombe's, instead of being head girl at school? Goodness! What a fool she had been! Poorer! Of course, she had not seen much of David, but no place could be poor that had him in it.

The tickets for the concert were a shilling each, and half-price for children. Beth and Dulcie had paid for their own, but that still left three shillings and sixpence as George's share—quite a bit on their budget, and not a sum he would have felt justified in spending even for so fine a charity, were it not that the children could not well be left at home. Edward had offered to stay and look after them, but that had caused an outcry from Girda.

"It's pretty mean if you aren't all there, with me doing the most important recitation of the whole concert."

As they were shutting the house, Janet had arranged with Edward to tuck Keith Prowse up on his bed—a place he was so fond of he was unlikely to bark. Paul only realised that Keith Prowse was having the privilege just as they were leaving. His face turned crimson with anger.

"Such meanness!" he said, "and Penny, I s'pose, to be shut out in the cold?"

"But, darling," Janet protested, "Penny always has stayed outside when we go out; he prefers it. Besides, it isn't cold—after all, it's the end of July."

Paul clutched the banisters in case he should be removed before he had time to state Penny's case.

"Before he hasn't minded, but of course he'd mind now. How would you like it if Dad was inside lying on the bed, and you was told you could lie on wet earth?"

Beth had an inspiration.

"I think Paul is quite right," she said. "Fetch him, Paul. I will put him on my bed."

Paul went bounding out in the garden calling "Penny! Penny, darling! Penny, loveliest cat!"

Janet looked at Beth in consternation.

"Oh, darling! He's sure to scratch at the coverlet. He hates being shut up."

Beth laughed and put her arm round her mother.

"How badly you know the habits of your own cat! Penny is always out at this time. Paul will never find him."

Beth was right. In a few minutes all the party were walking to the omnibus, Paul still muttering now and again that "it was no wonder Penny was out with that great dog getting everything," but at least willing to start, since Penny refused to come to any call.

Girda's recitation came halfway through the programme. George, Janet, Beth and Edward waited for her appearance in that state of nervousness and self-consciousness in which relations wait for their belongings to perform: keyed up not to show shame however great a fool the relative makes of itself. They were not helped to wait calmly by Eve and Paul, who were frankly bored by most of the turns, swinging their legs, and wriggling round to look at the audience, and demanding in loud whispers, "Is it Girda yet?"

At last, after a too-long and very dull French playlet, it was Girda's turn. Beth smiled at Janet, and Janet took the smile and passed it on to George. Edward dug his elbows into Beth and whispered, "Gosh! I bet she's nervous." Eve bounced excitedly on her chair and Paul leant forward breathing heavily.

The school stage curtains were red serge. They had dropped after the playlet so that the prefects could remove the two chairs covered in gold paper which had been thrones, and the little fur rug which had laid on the bare boards to express the richness of a palace. Now the curtain rose again, and Girda walked on, but such a Girda as to be almost unrecognisable. She was wearing Dulcie's black satin frock trimmed with imitation gold leather which she had worn for her first interview with Mr. Smith. Dulcie looked common in it, but Girda looked frightful. Dulcie was a slight little thing, and did at least wear her clothes with an air. Girda was in the puppy fat stage. The frock would only just fasten, and she bulged everywhere. Bulges on a schoolgirl dressed as a schoolgirl are normal, but schoolgirl bulges under black satin are embarrassing. The fashion which had been attempted and had failed of getting women to show their petticoats had appealed immensely to Dulcie. This dress had not got lace tacked under its bottom hem, so, to add to Girda's glory, Dulcie had lent a slip which had a border of cheap lace.

Girda had not been able to get into any of Dulcie's shoes, so she was wearing her own brown flat-heeled house shoes, but she had borrowed silk stockings of a rather orange sunburn. Her hair, which was usually held in place by a slide, was fastened by an immense taffeta bow.

George, scarcely believing his eyes, leant over to look at Janet. Janet, so ashamed that she lost her sense of humour, could only throw him a glance of despair. Beth looked at Dulcie, and got what little comfort there was in seeing Dulcie blush. Eve tugged at Janet's arm.

"Mum, doesn't she look lovely?"

Paul gazed at Girda with new eyes. To him she appeared like a fairy princess.

Edward missed the excitement: his vision did not carry as far as the stage. But already his ears were training themselves to help out his eyes, and he caught a faint whisper from the row behind. "What a little figure of fun!" His ears glowed crimson.

Girda, conscious for the one time in her life of being perfectly dressed, was superbly happy. She sailed through "The Little Match Girl" full of emotion. She recited sufficiently well for her audience almost to forget her appearance, and in the end there was a lot of applause. This was the moment Girda was waiting for. Her elocution mistress had taught her a polite bow, but Dulcie had persuaded her out of it. What, she asked, was the good of her slip if it wasn't to be seen. With the door shut she had taught her to curtsy.

Poor Girda! That curtsy was her undoing. The frock could just stand the strain of her when she was upright; when she stooped and all her muscles swelled it was too much. There was a popping like champagne corks, and all over the stage there fell black satin buttons. The curtain dropped on roar after roar of laughter.

It was the interval. All Janet's shame was swallowed in pity. Poor child! Thirteen is such a sensitive age. How that laughter must have hurt! She turned to Beth.

"Go and find her. Don't say anything except we were proud of the way she said her piece."

But Girda was not to be found. Beth was surrounded by friends and mistresses, pleased to see her again and eager to know how she was doing, but Beth, with a smile and a few words, got away. Where was Girda? Surely somebody must have seen her. Coming back into the hall, she met Miss Rigg, whose face lit up with pleasure.

"Beth, my dear, how are you? And how do you like your work?"

"Very much, thank you. I'm looking for Girda. Have you seen her?"

Miss Rigg shook her head.

"No." She hesitated. "Of course your mother knows best, but—"

Beth laughed.

"I know what you're going to say, but those clothes were nothing to do with Mum. She borrowed them from a cousin. Mum would never have let her go looking like that."

Miss Rigg's face cleared.

"I thought that something like that must have happened. Silly little girl! But those buttons will have been a lesson to her."

Beth went back to Janet.

"I think she's gone. I'll go home in case."

Girda had gone home. That school concert had been the summit of her dreams. She, Beth Carson's stupid, untidy sister, to be picked out to recite. She would never be looked upon as stupid again. It was because she was self-conscious about her new grown-up curves that she had worried so about her clothes. She had been terrified of a little-girl frock accentuating that she now had a chest. In Dulcie's black satin all her fears had gone. Black satin was to her so gorgeous that any garment made of it was perfect. So secure had she been in its glory that she had not noticed the nudges of the other girls, nor the dismayed face of her elocution mistress. So comforted had she been by the richness that she had lost her stage fright and enjoyed reciting and let herself go right up to her fatal curtsy.

With those roars of laughter in her ears she had bolted off the stage into the cloakroom. There she had met her elocution mistress.

"Very good dear, but"—her eyes had twinkled—"one shouldn't recite in tight frocks."

Her best friend had found her putting on her coat. "Hullo. Going?"

Girda nodded.

"Yes. Didn't you see what happened?"

Her friend, who had been ashamed for her, spoke her mind.

"Whatever made you dress like that? Everybody was laughing even before you went on."

Girda ran all the way home. She never saw the streets, and was unconscious of the people she passed. In her ears drummed, "One shouldn't recite in tight frocks."

"Everybody was laughing!"

"Everybody was laughing!" With tea

rs streaming down her cheeks and her hands over her ears to shut out the voices of her mind, she ran to the end of the garden. She crouched against the fence, moaning:

"'Everybody was laughing!' Oh, I wish I was dead!"

Far away an engine whistled. Girda raised her head.

Down there was the line. She only had to lie on it.

Beth had come by omnibus. She was not far behind Girda. She had remembered the house would be locked, and made at once for the garden. Girda, climbing the railings, stood out clearly in the moonlight. In a moment Beth had her arms round her.

With the feel of Beth's arms, Girda's hysterics died; she leant against her, shivering and sobbing.

"All my buttons coming off—they said everybody was laughing, anyway. I thought I could never bear the shame. I was going to kill myself."

Beth drew Girda to the garden seat.

"Don't be silly, darling. Your clothes looked awful, but they didn't matter. What did matter was that you recited beautifully."

Girda raised her head.

"Really?"

"Really."

Girda sobbed on for a time, then she whispered:

"Could you keep a secret?"

"Yes."

"I want to be an actress. Only my very, very best friends know, because I'm afraid people would laugh—me being not a bit like an actress to look at. But I want to be a real one, like Gladys Cooper and all that lot."

Beth stroked her hair.

"How proud we shall be!"

"Do you think Dad will let me?"

Beth went on stroking.

"I daresay. I shouldn't ask him until you're leaving school."

Girda hugged her.

"I do love you, Beth," she shivered. "Oh, gosh, I did make a fool of myself!"

Beth leant down and saw the tears had stopped.

"Just a bit. But if you're going to be an actress it won't hurt: it'll be a good thing to learn what to wear on a stage. Besides, by next term you'll be able to laugh at tonight." Girda looked up, shocked.

"Never. I'll never laugh at it. Its horror is cut on my heart, like 'Calais' on Queen Mary's."

Later Janet came out into the garden to look for them. She stopped in front of the seat.

"Is she asleep?"

Beth nodded.

"Yes. I'll wake her. Where's Dulcie?"

"Gone to her room. She's sulking because your father and I gave her a bit of our minds."

Beth gave Girda a kiss to waken her.

"Did you? It's nothing to the bit of mind I'm going to give her."

Janet smiled.

"Oh, well, it's all over. It was just a piece of silliness." Beth turned her head towards a passing train. "Silliness!" She gave Girda a hug.

"Wake up, darling. Supper."

It was Saturday morning. All the shop was full of chatter. Monday was Bank Holiday. From one o'clock there would be two clear days of holidays ahead—two days without a sight of Babbacombe's.

Beth was so excited it was all she could manage to concentrate on what she was doing. Except for a visit to Janet's mother years before, she had never stayed in other people's houses. George had no near relations living, and all Janet's family were in the north—too expensive a journey to manage. Nothing in her world had given her even an idea what life in a castle might be like. She was prepared for anything.

At Babbacombe's there was an enquiry department where you could ask any questions you liked. On Janet's advice Beth had been down there one lunchtime.

"In a house like that," she had said, "there'll be no end of servants. I believe you have to tip some of them. Very little will be expected from you, but you ought to find out what's right, and we'll see what my box can do."

Beth had been worried at robbing Janet's box, but Janet laughed.

"Don't be silly! It's the best bit of fun I've had in years. I've always wanted to know how they carried on in those big places. I'm counting the days till you get back and tell me all about it. On the quiet, mind."

At this last Beth and Janet had giggled like a couple of school children. To be sure Beth had her weekend, Janet had practised a little deception.

"I'm not going to lie," she had told Beth, "but I'm going to reduce things a bit. By the time I've done telling Dad about that castle it won't be bigger than a cottage."

Janet had chosen one of hers and George's evening strolls to say her bit.

"Such a slice of luck!" she said casually. "That customer at Babbacombe's, Miss Allan, that Beth helped get some clothes— she's asked Beth for the August Bank Holiday weekend."

George, who had been sniffing a rose, straightened up. "Miss Allan? But we don't know anything about her." Janet put her arm through his.

"And don't need to, you old fusspot. She's just a girl like any other, I expect. The great thing is she's asked Beth. It's down in Sussex, and I'm glad she's getting the chance of some country air. I was worrying at her not being able to come to Bexhill."

"She can take a spring holiday."

Janet laughed.

"That'll be a lot of good, with all the winter to get through first." She gave his arm an affectionate shake. "What you've got to do is to tell her you're pleased, and will be glad to pay the fare. She's worrying about that, I know; but, after all, it's not so much as the one to Bexhill would have been."

George puffed at his pipe.

"Where's this Miss Allan's place?"

"Somewhere Eastbourne way."

"What's she got—a little house?"

Janet paused by a clump of carnations.

"Lovely, aren't they? Sure to have a room, anyway, or she wouldn't be asking our Beth." She rubbed her cheek on his shoulder. "Come on, don't be an old curmudgeon, spoiling her fun. She doesn't get such a lot."

George tapped his pipe out on his heel.

"I like that! Curmudgeon indeed! I'd give the lining of my coat to Beth, and well you know it. Only she's young, and I don't like her going off with strangers."

"She may be young, but she's got an old head. Come on. You know what I say:

"The worry cow
Would have lived till now
If she hadn't lost her breath.
She worried her hay wouldn't last the day
And worried herself to death."

The end of it was that George gave Beth's weekend his rather anxious blessing.

"I know you've got sense, but you want to be careful; brought up as you've been, you don't know the bad sort that are about. I'll see to your fare. I'd like to do a bit more, only we've all got to go rather careful just now, with the expense of Edward coming on."

The enquiry department at Babbacombe's had been full of what to Janet and Beth was startling information on tipping.

"If your friend's only young," the enquiry clerk told Beth, "she needn't do much. Say five shillings to the maid that looks after her, and perhaps a half-crown to the chauffeur if he's had to make a special journey for her to the station, and maybe two shillings if there's a footman carrying her cases about."

Beth had shut herself and Janet into the kitchen to impart this information.

"Isn't it awful, Mum? It would be almost cheaper to take a room somewhere."

But Janet was not at all cast down.

"I should leave out the footman," she chuckled. "Does me good to say the word even. I expect you can look the other way when he's about. But you must give the maid five shillings; and have the extra half-crown by you in case you're unlucky over the chauffeur." She opened her oven door and peered in at her pie. "Though, mind you, it's almost worth spending the half-crown to have a chauffeur and a car for once."

Beth thought of these things that Saturday as she ran about hanging dresses on the runners and fetching Mrs. Fosdick. What an angel Dad was! Her fare to Lewes, where the car was to meet her, was only eight and eleven, and he had given her ten shillings. How grand Mum was to find that seven and six! She hated taking it. Anything that put Mum's fur coat farther off was a shame. She never would have taken it if she had not made a mental reservation that secretly shilling by shilling she would put it back.

Dulcie spent Saturday morning sulking. Though her lips repeated the usual lift formula, her mind was not on her work.

"It's too sickening," she thought. "Beth gets all the fun. I'm only going out to the staff sports meeting, and here she is going away for the weekend. It's mean. Just because I'm an orphan nobody bothers with me."

Coming down at about twelve o'clock, she was startled to get a nod from David. She was so surprised that she stood and stared. He came out from behind his counter and joined her.

"Well, how's Dulcie, the pride of the lifts?"

She pouted. "Very friendly all of a sudden, aren't you?"

"I'm always friendly. You're never out of my thoughts."

"Funny way you have of showing it."

"That's the fault of Cooked Meats: we boys on this counter never have time to look up." He felt in his apron pocket and brought out an envelope. "Would you be a kind girl and drop this on the third floor? It's for your cousin, but if you give it to an apprentice they'll run through to Gowns with it."

Some people were coming towards the lift. Dulcie took the note.

"All right. Going up, please."

At the top she had a moment's rest. The letter was addressed to Beth. She turned it over—very carefully with her nail she lifted the flap.

"MY DEAR BETH [she read].

The head of the worm has appeared again. Since two people are going to the same place, must one go by car and the other by rail? Anyway, in case I can be of use I shall be outside the newsreel at two-thirty.

Yours,

DAVID.

P.S.—Scissors has been invited too."

Dulcie put the letter back in its envelope and re-licked and stuck down the flap. Her eyes, had anyone seen them at that moment, were like flints.

"Going away with him for the weekend, is she. The dirty little cat!"

CHAPTER TWELVE

BETH and George met at the check clock and travelled home together. George, in his quiet way, was pleased it was the holiday, but Beth was so excited it was an effort for her not to dance down the road. She knew she should not be pleased; she knew, if she were logical, she would travel by train and ignore David and his car, or, worse still, send a telegram to Barbara to say she was not coming at all. But what she knew about what she should do did not ruffle even the surface of Beth's happiness; for this weekend she was saying "hang" to all the oughts of this world. If nothing ever happened to her again, at least this weekend would be hers, to take out and look at, as a past generation looked over pressed flowers.

Janet had packed Beth's suitcase; it lay open on the bed waiting for last things. She came up with Beth to help her change.

"I've left out that navy linen for you to travel in, and your navy school coat."

Beth fingered the navy linen.

"I look pretty frightful in it. I mean it was all right when I was at school, but now—"

Janet undid Beth's shop frock.

"Don't you believe it. I've put you on fresh cuffs and collars, and pressed it. I've always liked you in it."

Beth looked at her mother over her shoulder.

"Honest?"

Janet finished unbuttoning, then she pulled Beth round to face her.

"You're hoping you won't be the only visitor, aren't you?"

Beth felt her cheeks flooding with colour. Suddenly, with a childish dive, she put her hand into her bag and pulled out David's letter. She gave it to Janet.

"But I didn't know he was coming—honestly I didn't."

Janet read the letter through and refolded it.

"No, you only hoped." She picked the navy frock off the bed and pulled it over Beth's head, then she sat on the bed and patted the place beside her. "Sit down a minute." She smiled. "Funny, I'm quite shy of saying this. You see, life's been easy for me—marrying Dad when I was still very young and never going anywhere without him. But you know life isn't as easy for girls in the class Miss Allan and Mr. David Babbacombe come from. They do things differently; they—"

Beth's eyes twinkled.

"You don't know any of this; you're only guessing."

Janet looked sheepish.

"Well, that's a fact; but for all that you want to be careful: be a bit more strait-laced than you would be. Don't let him or anyone else staying in the house think you aren't particular, or they may misunderstand you."

Beth giggled.

"Are you trying to warn me of dangers to young girls, darling? You know David isn't a bit like that."

Janet got up.

"Every man's like that." She changed her mind: "Well, every man except your father."

Beth buttoned her frock.

"And David."

George's voice came up the stairs.

"What's up, Janet? Aren't we having any dinner?"

Across the table Dulcie looked at Beth's pink cheeks and shining eyes.

"She would look like that," she thought; "but she'd look a lot different if I told Uncle George all I know."

But try as she would she could not see how she could tell anyone what she knew. Even if she stopped Beth's weekend there was always the future—a future in which Beth and David would meet and put two and two together as to how she had got her information. No, she would have to let Beth go, but she could make things difficult. As Janet put a suet pudding on the table she leant across to George.

"I think I'll go and see Beth off at the station. Will you come, Uncle George?"

George had been thinking of going with Beth, to carry her suitcase, but the news that Dulcie would be his companion changed his mind.

"No, I'm going to see to the garden: there's a mort of dead heads to come off. You'll go, won't you, Edward, and carry your sister's case?"

Beth threw Janet a horrified glance, and in exchange got a reassuring nod which said, "I'll handle this, don't you worry."

"That's right," she agreed calmly. "You go, Edward. But if you're going, eat up: it's time Beth was thinking of moving."

Dulcie scowled at her pudding. How tiresome of Uncle George! Edward saw so badly—it was quite likely even when she got him outside the newsreel he would not notice the car. Then she cheered up. "Oh well," she thought, "even if he can't read he can't help noticing she doesn't go in a train. You wait, Beth Carson, until we get back from the station. I'd take a bet your ears will burn." The moment she had finished eating, Dulcie, to be sure Beth did not give her the slip, raced upstairs and put on her hat.

"I can't think why you bother to come with me," Beth protested. "I mean, it isn't as if I was going for long."

"Quite long enough," said Dulcie, and went downstairs humming—at least she was being very annoying, and that was something.

Janet, George, Girda, Paul with Penny in his arms, and Eve came into the hall to see Beth off. Janet was carrying the remains of the pudding. She looked round with apparent casualness for somewhere to put it, and her eye seemed to fall on Dulcie. She shoved the plate into her unwilling hands.

"Go and put that in the larder, dear."

Dulcie wriggled her shoulders angrily.

"Why me? Can't you see I've got gloves on."

Nobody answered this, and since there was nothing else to do with it, Dulcie carried the plate into the kitchen.

"Put it straight in the larder, dear," said Janet's voice behind her.

"Really I don't know what you think I am," Dulcie growled. "Your slave or something?"

Janet did not answer, but watched Dulcie go into the larder and slam the plate on to a shelf. It was a nice little larder, with good gratings for air. Without a twinge of conscience, Janet shut the door and turned the key.

Out in the passage again Janet led all her family to the garden gate.

"Come on, dears; come and see Beth off," she hustled.

"Where's Dulcie?" Edward asked. "Thought she was coming."

Janet hoped none of them would notice the thuds on the larder door. She raised her voice.

"She's changed her mind. Now get off dears. You ought to hurry."

They watched Beth, Edward and Keith Prowse until they turned the corner, then Janet manoeuvred her family into the garden.

"Go along out, all of you. It's too good an afternoon to be in."

"I'll come and help you wash up," said Girda.

Janet gave her a little push.

"Not today. I shan't be long, and I've a feeling for having the house to myself. You go and help Dad with his dead heads."

It was not for another ten minutes that Janet walked into her kitchen.

"Hullo!" she said in a well-acted surprised voice. "Who's that in my larder?"

"You know it's me. You did it on purpose," Dulcie stormed.

Janet unlocked the door.

"You mustn't say things like that even in fun. As if I'd mean to lock you in."

Dulcie's hat was on one side, and her face scarlet.

"You did it on purpose because you didn't want me to go to the station with Beth."

Janet opened her eyes.

"What an idea! Why should I mind you going?"

"You don't want me finding out how your precious Beth behaves, or telling Uncle George."

Janet took Dulcie by the shoulders and pushed her into a chair. Her voice was icy.

"What exactly are you talking about?"

Dulcie dropped her eyes: she had said more than she meant.

"Nothing: it was only a bit of fun."

Janet let go her hold on her.

"Fun!" She went to the sink and turned on the taps. She looked at Dulcie over her shoulder. "Don't you go mixing up what's fun and what isn't. 'Tisn't often I get roused, but if you try hurting my Beth I'll rouse all right; and though I daresay there's a lot of things about living here you don't like, you'll like it a lot less, and so will your purse, if you have to live on your own. Better think it over."

"Funny," said Edward, "Dulcie not coming, and not saying goodbye or anything."

Beth thought it more than funny; she had always thought Janet wonderful, but this time she seemed to have excelled herself.

"Oh, well," she said casually, "I expect she just changed her mind, as Mum said."

Edward put Beth's suitcase beside the conductor and carried Keith Prowse, and he and Beth climbed to the top of the omnibus. After a moment Beth said awkwardly:

"There's no need for you to bother to come into the station. I mean it'll be a bit crowded for Keith Prowse."

Edward gave the puppy a pat.

"Did you hear that? You aren't afraid of crowds, are you?"

There was silence for a short way, then Beth said in rather a small voice:

"Actually, I'm not going on the train."

Edward was startled.

"Gosh! Why?"

"Well, you remember me telling you about Mr. David Babbacombe giving you Keith Prowse. Well, it's him. I mean he's driving me down."

Edward whistled. He admired Beth tremendously, but this news shook him a little. He could not help thinking that she was being rather deceitful.

"Oh, well," he said after a pause, "I suppose it's all right. I mean perhaps Mum and Dad wouldn't mind, even if they knew."

Beth felt he was struggling with his loyalties, and could not blame him. Put like that she did not feel too comfortable herself.

"As a matter of fact, Mum does know. I was going by train; only he sent me a note this morning, and—well, it seems silly to spend the money on a train when I could go free in a car."

This argument Edward approved.

"My word yes! It's eight and eleven, isn't it? You'll be that much to the good. Why, you could buy quite a lot with that."

It was Beth's turn to be shocked.

"I won't keep it—either give it back to Dad, or put it in Mum's fur coat box. It seems silly not having told Dad, but, you see, David being Mr. Babbacombe's son makes it difficult. You know what Dad is about things like that."

Edward liked being talked to in this way: it made him feel very grown-up. He took a brotherly tone.

"What's he like? I mean, well, you know—"

He did not know what he meant, but it sounded to him the sort of question a brother ought to ask.

Beth stroked Keith Prowse; it was difficult to keep the enthusiasm out of her voice.

"He's nice. I say, would you like to see him? I've told him such a lot about you."

Edward's ears turned scarlet.

"Oh—well—well, yes, I would rather. And, Babbacombe's anyhow, I expect I ought to—to thank him for Keith Prowse, I mean."

David was standing by his car looking up and down the road. Beth and Edward had walked through the station and came upon him before he was expecting them.

"Hullo," said Beth.

He swung round.

"Well, well, well, so you have turned up." He saw Edward: "Mr. Edward Carson, I presume?"

Edward liked that; he took off his cap.

"How d'you do, sir." He gave Keith Prowse's lead a tug. "Thanks frightfully for him. Do you think he looks all right?"

David gave Keith Prowse a pat.

"Grand. Come and meet Scissors."

There was a big scene on the pavement. Scissors was all one wag and twist with pleasure at getting out of the car, seeing Beth and re-meeting Keith Prowse. Edward, with his eyes screwed to get them focussed, watched the two dogs. David, looking at him, was touched.

"Your sister," he said gently, "is a hard-hearted Hannah, but I don't see why her hard heart should stand between a couple of dogs' pleasure. How'd it be if I called for you next Saturday and we took them out to Richmond or somewhere and finished up with a bit of tea?"

Edward gasped.

"Really, I say, sir. Oh, sir—"

Driving out of London Beth and David were silent for quite a while; passing the Croydon aerodrome David said:

"And, mind you, next Saturday is not one of the days when the old worm is showing his head—it's an honest-to-God invitation to Edward, with no ulterior motive."

Beth had Scissors on her knee; she tickled his nose.

"You know how I feel about us meeting. Don't let's spoil this weekend by arguing about what we'll do later on." She smiled at him. "I've not changed my mind—it's just this drive down seemed like fate."

David's hand came off the steering wheel and closed over hers.

"Anything you say, darling."

He did not take his hand away for quite a time, and both he and she were conscious of pulses beating so hard that it hurt.

As if to be certain that at least one weekend in four people's lives should be perfect, the sun shone, and it was really hot. Not that Barbara and John and Beth and David needed the weather on their side—each of them asked for nothing more than to be allowed to spend the days with the pair they had chosen. All the same, as a setting for people in love the garden in hot weather was perfect.

Ribstall Castle was a show place—so show, in fact, that it was just known as "Ribstall" to half England. The shell of the old castle was still there, together with improvements and excrescences added by various owners. Maggie Wentwood had added quite perfect plumbing, and a swimming pool at the bottom of the rose-garden.

Beth was surprised to find how un-awed she was by grandeur. Even the butler and the footman did not scare her; she was not made to feel small by Ames, the head housemaid, who was maiding herself and Barbara. It was, of course, quite well known in the servants' hall that Barbara had been a poor relation, and treated as such, until she became engaged to Lord Pern. It was therefore only to be expected that she would have poor friends.

"What will you wear tonight, Miss?" Ames had asked in the shocked tones of a housemaid who has just seen a suitcase arrive without an evening dress.

Beth, wrapped in the thought that David was waiting in the hall to show her the grounds, never even flushed.

"Miss Allan is lending me everything," she explained. "Will you ask her, please?"

She positively skipped down the staircase after that, feeling pleased with herself. "After all," she thought, "I'm going to give her five shillings on Monday, so there's no need for her to look so proud."

At dinner the four of them sat round the immense mahogany table in the huge dining-room, hung with pictures that Maggie Wentwood said were ancestors. The highly polished wood of the table glittered with the reflection of all the silver piled on it.

Round it cat-footed walked the butler and his footmen. It would have been easy to be so impressed by magnificence that conversation was difficult, but nothing could oppress David and John. They insisted on telling the girls such scurrilous stories of each other's school days, with such roars of laughter, that by the time the dessert was on the table first the footmen and at last even the butler smiled.

There was half-hearted talk of dancing to the gramophone after dinner, but before the idea was formed the two girls were upstairs getting their wraps: obviously on such a night the place to be was the garden.

They were all four sleeping in the same corridor, in what the servants, who had to clean it, called "the visitors' mile". To Beth, used to ten Penruddock Road or lodgings at Bexhill, the size of the castle was incredible. She was thankful for the custom of pinning cards with the visitors' names on them on to the doors: it was nice to feel that if she was scared she could find Barbara's room.

Walking up the corridor, Barbara suddenly put an arm round Beth's shoulders.

"Are you enjoying yourself?"

Beth nodded.

"I can't believe I'm really here."

Barbara looked at her admiringly.

"You look simply lovely in that frock."

Beth paused and smoothed her black chiffon skirts.

"It's hard to believe that it's not very long ago I took this off a runner at Babbacombe's."

Barbara laughed.

"And made me buy it when I wanted yellow taffeta, and said, 'That dress looks so good, and that will be important in that sort of house.'" She moved on. "How did you know all that?"

Beth shook her head.

"I didn't. I guessed."

"So lucky you've got that sort of natural taste; it will probably come in very handy."

Beth was not sure what she meant, so she changed the subject.

"What shall I wear in the garden?"

Barbara gave her arm a tug.

"Come on. I've got a cape with a hood my aunt gave me; it will suit you marvellously."

David and Beth walked to the rose-garden. There was a moon, and its reflection lay like a silver ball at the bottom of the swimming pool. David put his arm through Beth's.

"It's a bit much, isn't it? Like the transformation scene in a pantomime."

Beth turned and looked across the roses to where above them the castle stood. In the moonlight it took on a fairy quality, as if it housed the Sleeping Beauty.

"It's lovely! Like something out of a fairy story."

He looked down at her. Her face gleamed white against the black of her hood.

"It is a fairy story, complete even with a princess."

She turned to him, her eyes laughing.

"And are you the prince?"

"Of course. And Barbara is the good fairy. I don't quite know what 'Slug' is. Perhaps a prince in disguise."

"There's no bad fairy," said Beth.

David put his arm round her.

"Oh, there must be. After all, the princess must be put under an evil spell, or where does the prince come in?" He raised her chin in his hand. "Or perhaps she is under a spell—a spell which makes her run away from the people who are fond of her."

Her face was shocked.

"Didn't we agree that you wouldn't argue this weekend?"

"This isn't an argument. I'm telling you a story, and we haven't got to the end yet. The spell that the princess was under could only be broken if she was kissed by a prince." He took her in his arms. For a moment they did nothing but stare into each other's eyes. Beth felt as if she were floating. Then he kissed her lips.

They were brought back to themselves by enthusiastic barking from Scissors, followed by Barbara's voice.

"They must be down by the swimming-pool. Listen! There's Scissors."

David leant down to Scissors and spoke severely:

"You're a damn tactless dog. Don't let me catch you butting in like that again."

CHAPTER THIRTEEN

BETH found the weeks following the August Bank Holiday almost unbearable. Since that first night at Ribstall, when in the magic of the garden she had let David kiss her, she had never been herself. She was not sorry they had kissed—it had been lovely and something to remember—but she had not let it happen again. David had been hurt when she refused, and she had not been able to explain that just one long kiss like that was beautiful, but that lots of kissing was what her mother meant when she said "Don't let him or anyone else think you aren't particular." Kissing could be cheap if you did much of it with a man you could never marry.

That was the trouble. She knew—unbelievable though she found it—that David was fond of her—really fond of her. But of course, however fond he was, they could never be more than friends. Naturally he wouldn't think of marrying her—a girl so different from his set. She knew, too, he would never ask her for more than a few kisses. The other juniors at Babbacombe's whispered and giggled and suggested that all men had only one idea; but she knew that was not true—certainly not true of David. Because she knew these things she had been strong-minded. The Sunday and the Monday at Ribstall had been glorious, but she had managed to arrange them so that there was no kissing, and had managed to refuse to see him ever since. But, oh, how it hurt! How barren the days seemed! How her heart pumped when Edward was going out with him. At least there would be news—she would know he was well.

Janet, seeing Beth's pale cheeks and feeble appetite, probed her gently.

"You don't look too good, darling. Is it young Mr. Babbacombe?"

They were in the kitchen. Beth turned to the window, tears pricking her eyeballs.

"Yes. Silly, aren't I?"

"What's the trouble? Why aren't you seeing him?"

"It's so futile, and, besides, it will spoil his chances with his father. Of course, he wouldn't like him going about with somebody like me."

Janet stirred a sauce.

"He's dependent on his father, I suppose?" Up went Beth's chin.

"Not really, he isn't. He's invented a frightfully good seaplane, and when the Admiralty start making it he'll give up the shop and be an inventor."

Janet smiled.

"Has the Admiralty bought it?"

"Not yet, but I'm sure they will. You ought to hear him talk about it."

Janet stirred for a time in silence, then she said:

"So you're refusing to see him?"

Beth rubbed her finger up and down the window.

"Yes. It's such a muddle. I mean it's no good seeing a lot of people—"

Janet went on stirring.

"I daresay you're right. I wonder how he feels."

The first weeks in September were repulsive; all the family went to Bexhill, leaving Beth and Dulcie, except for a woman who came in to do the work, and Penny, alone in the house. It seemed to Beth, already low-spirited, that they were the longest two weeks she had ever known. She particularly dreaded the evenings. She found it hard to get through an evening alone with Dulcie without quarrelling with her. She was not helped by a letter from David.

"DEAREST BETH,

Can't you relax just a little while your family are away? Wouldn't it make a nice break from Dulcie the pride of the lifts? We could eat some place and do a cinema. Be reasonable.

Yours,

DAVID."

Having made up her mind to be strong-minded, Beth stuck to her resolutions, but it hurt her to do it. She wrote to David.

"DEAR DAVID,

I wish I could come, but honestly I think it would be silly. After all, it's not so long now before your six months are up, and it would be idiotic to spoil your chances of a proper job, wouldn't it? Of course I don't think you'll need a job because of your seaplane, but just in case."

She was worried about the ending. She wanted to put "love", but of course she couldn't, and "yours sincerely" sounded so formal. She ended by copying David and putting "yours", but she thought it looked wrong for her—it was not the way she would sign anything.

At the end of the second week, when her spirits were very low—for she missed the family, and Dulcie was growing more difficult every day—Miss Jones sent her to Ribbons. As there was no hurry, Beth went down the three flights of stairs which finished in the marble entrance. As she turned the corner to the bottom flight, she suddenly stood still, her breath coming in short stabs. The commissionaire was swinging round the revolving glass doors, and inside them, coming in, was her shoplifter.

Beth drew back into the shadow, and wondered what to do. She did not know by sight any of the detectives on the ground floor, and the chance of any of the staff believing a junior from Gowns if she said she recognised a shoplifter was nil. The woman was walking up the shop. Beth ran down the remaining stairs and looked after her, and then, not knowing what else to do, she followed her.

The woman walked along purposefully, looking neither to right nor to left, through Ribbons, Flowers, Haberdashery, and then she turned off towards the food section. Beth, behind her, found herself hurrying. What a piece of luck! This really was fate. They bustled through Confectionery and into Cooked Meats.

David was slicing beef for a customer when Beth came by. She paused at the end of his counter, and he looked up. At once, disregarding his customer, he came over to her.

"Well! You can't have come to call."

"No." Beth, conscious of the customer, dropped her voice. "Do you see that woman?" David looked down the shop.

"I see about fifty women."

"The one in the black coat and skirt, with the white and black flowers in her hat."

"Yes. What about her?"

"That's my shoplifter."

The customer, her eyes flashing with temper, called to David:

"My good man, will you please finish with my order? I haven't all day to waste."

"Get after her, duckie," David whispered to Beth. "I'll join you when I'm through with this old mare."

Beth's woman went into the food market and ordered meat. Beth stood a discreet way off and tried not to look like a sleuth. David came and stood beside her.

"What's she up to, Mrs. Sherlock? Am I right in supposing she has just slipped three legs of mutton and a piece of beef into her handbag?"

Beth giggled.

"Shut up! Don't make me laugh. Already all the assistants are wondering what I'm doing."

"Oh, that's easy." David looked professional. "You've come to buy a joint for the annual outing of indigent salesgirls. It's to be cooked and we're going to handle it in Cooked Meats and—" He flicked her sleeve. "Heave up the anchor: we're off."

The woman, having ordered what she wanted, turned and hurried back through Cooked Meats.

"Glory!" said David. "She's going up in the lift."

"Oh, goodness, what shall we do?"

David walked on.

"Go up, too, of course."

"But what about Dulcie?"

David twinkled at her.

"She can't say anything. Come on."

Dulcie brought down her lift, and stepped out to let her passengers pass.

"Ground floor, confectionery, cooked meats, food market, ribbons, flowers, haberdashery—" She broke off, her eyes goggling, as she saw Beth and David. "Lampshades, linens, lace, handbags. Going up, please."

"Keep in front of me, David," Beth whispered. "She may remember my face."

Dulcie was nearly blowing up with rage. Of all the sauce, for David and Beth to get into her lift. She was certain Beth had planned it just to annoy her. It was all she could do to start the lift.

"First floor: boyswear, menswear, inexpensive millinery, perfumery, gloves, post office, library, rest room."

The woman got out. David and Beth followed. As he passed Dulcie David gave a slight bow and raised his chef's cap. Dulcie wished she had her hands on Beth; she would love to have hurt her.

The woman seemed in less of a hurry. She wandered casually along, through Boyswear and Menswear, and "inexpensive millinery". In the Millinery she paused now and again to look at the hats. She examined them with an amused smile. It was clear they weren't in her class. In Perfumery she stopped, and pulled up a chair and sat down. David drew Beth round a counter out of sight.

"You hang about and snoop. She looks as if she's parked for a bit. I'll find the floor 'tec."

Beth dared not go round to the front of the counter. It was unlikely the woman would remember her face, but some people remembered all faces, and she dare not risk it. At the corner of the counter was a tiered stand holding bottles of scent. Each shelf had mirrored sides. Beth found that at a certain angle she could see the woman and the counter in one of the mirrors. She watched an assistant come forward.

"Good morning, Madam."

"Good morning. I want something new in the way of a scent. Have you got something amusing?"

Beth watched the assistant falling, just as she had, for the poise and obvious richness of the customer. The counter became littered with expensive bottles, and quantities of different perfumes were sprayed on to the woman's hands. She sniffed at them with obvious interest. She was clearly particular about the scent she used. At last she seemed pleased.

"This is delicious. What is it, did you say?"

"It's Moudrée's new flower scent, 'Lime Avenue'."

"How much?"

"Five guineas these big ones, then three guineas, thirty shillings, and fifteen shillings for the little sample size."

The woman gave another sniff at her hand.

"Heavenly. I'm sure I adore it, but I suppose I'd better start off with a sample."

The assistant nodded.

"Account, madam?"

"No, cash."

The assistant turned away to get the small-sized bottle, and at that moment, with a quick look left and right to see no one was watching, the woman opened the large patent-leather bag she was carrying and swept into it the five-guinea bottle.

Although Beth knew she was a thief, she felt quite winded to watch her actually at work.

"Goodness," she thought; "and she'd get away with it if I wasn't there." She looked round for David. He was just coming into the department. With him was another man. Beth went to meet them.

"She's taken a five-guinea bottle of scent."

The detective stopped.

"Can you swear to that?"

"Yes. It's in her bag."

"Good! We'll let her move on. Don't want to put the wind up her. She took a dress from your department, I hear. You'd better come with me." He turned to David. "You can go back to your work."

David opened his eyes.

"What a dirty trick! You'll need me, you know. I'm David the detective's aid."

The man laughed and nodded to Beth.

"Come on, Miss."

David caught her arm.

"You couldn't be such a cad as not to tell me the end of the story. Will you have a bit of food with me tonight?" Beth wavered. "Be fair. Would you like to be sent back to Cooked Meats when there was a real live thief to catch?"

Beth was torn. Apart from longing to say "yes" on her own account, she did see his point: it was mean he was to miss the end of the story. Suddenly she gave in.

"All right. Where shall I meet you?"

The detective was looking annoyed. David spoke quickly.

"My club, where you had that drink with me, as near half-past six as you can make it."

The woman seemed to have bought and taken all she wanted. With the stolen scent in her bag, and the bought scent swinging from her finger, she went to the lifts and down to the ground floor. Beth, squeezed into the corner behind the detective, wished it was Dulcie's lift. She would have enjoyed seeing her bewilderment. Dulcie did so hate not knowing what was going on.

In the marble entrance the detective laid his hand on the woman's arm.

"Excuse me, Madam, would you come to the office for a moment?"

David and Beth sat on two of the chromium-and-jade stools and sipped their drinks.

"And what did she say to that?" David asked.

"Nothing." Beth took a nut. "I felt sorry for her. She just went sort of greenish, and just nodded, and followed him."

"What happened then?"

"Well, I waited outside for ages, and then I was called in. Two of the managers were there, and the bottle of scent was on the table. She looked awful—her skin kind of stretched with trying not to cry. The manager asked me to tell him what had happened."

"And he said, 'Well done. The firm will double your wages.'"

Beth shook her head.

"No, he didn't: he asked how I happened to be there at all, and I explained that Miss Jones had sent me to Ribbons, and about how I recognized her as the person who had stolen our model."

"What did the woman say to that?"

"She gave me a look, that's all, and then I explained how I had followed her—"

"And what did you say about me?"

She flushed.

"I just said going through Cooked Meats you were the first person I saw—and that was true—and I asked you to help me."

He lit a cigarette.

"And what happened then?"

"They said I could go, and I got into an awful row from Miss Jones, because after all the fuss I forgot the ribbons I went for."

David signalled to the barman to give her another cocktail.

"I wonder what'll happen to the thief?"

Beth shrugged her shoulders.

"Nothing, I should think. The dress came back in the afternoon; it was hardly worn at all. Mrs. Nunn said she didn't suppose they'd prosecute. I'm glad. I was sorry for her, and now we've got the dress I don't mind any more." David raised his glass.

"I'm drinking her health. Here's to you, shoplifter. Thanks for this evening."

CHAPTER FOURTEEN

THERE was to be a fancy dress ball arranged by the sports club. A terrible mine disaster had horrified the world, and the Lord Mayor of London was sponsoring a fund for the relatives of the dead men. Usually shop balls were expensive—for Babbacombe's Christmas ball the tickets were a guinea, and only the heads of departments and the more dashing of the staff went. For this ball it was decided to make the tickets only half a crown, so that everybody could be there.

"Only half a crown," said George. "I reckon we all ought to go."

Janet was charmed at the thought of George at a fancy dress party. The news of it first came up one Saturday over lunch.

"Certainly you ought to go." She looked round the table, her eyes wrinkled with amusement. "What d'you reckon Dad ought to go as?"

Paul bounced up and down on his chair.

"Oh, Dad, go as the devil. There was a picture in Mum's paper of a fancy dress of a devil. It had horns and a tail."

George grinned.

"No, son—doesn't sound my cup of tea."

"If I was asked to a fancy dress party," said Eve, "I'd be dressed as a fairy. Couldn't Dad go as a fairy man?"

She was sitting next to Janet, who stooped and kissed her.

"No, pet."

Girda leant her chin on her hands.

"I know—Hamlet. You'd look lovely in black velvet, Dad."

Edward giggled. He did not look up—his eyesight was so dim now he could not see George if he tried.

"How about a huntsman? And I'll lend you Keith Prowse."

Dulcie laughed loudly.

"How about something comic? You're more the cut for that, Uncle, than anything else."

There was a cruel edge to her voice. The family looked at George in a shamefaced way. With his thinning, greying hair and narrow, anxious face and pince-nez, he was perhaps funny to look at, if you had not the eyes to see the man inside. Beth was the first to recover.

"What are you going as, Dulcie? An angel?"

The family shrieked—not because they thought Beth very funny, but because they were thankful the embarrassing moment had passed, and they could take their eyes off George.

Dulcie had given a lot of thought to what she should wear. She had convinced herself that the fancy dress ball would be her chance with David. She had called out to him from the lift, "Coming to the fancy dress ball?" and he had replied, "You bet," and from then on the fancy dress ball became in her mind her great opportunity. When she was alone in the bedroom, she gazed at herself in the glass, planning what would suit her best. She had no delusions as to her charms. She was small and fragile and full of exciting curves, and whatever she wore must be designed to show off these beauties. On an occasion like a fancy dress ball she felt sure that Beth would be a negligible quality—first of all, she would not spend any money on her dress, partly because, thank goodness, she hadn't any money to spend; but still more because she would think it a waste.

Two dresses had seemed to Dulcie perfect for her type. The first was to go as a child, with a little frilled frock halfway up her thighs, and socks. Little-girlishness she knew to be endearing, and she saw herself much sought after, and making a big success of an evening spent talking baby talk. On the other hand, there were men who might forget that she was a woman, and a very desirable woman, if she was dressed as a child. She was not quite certain that David was not the sort that treated someone dressed as a little girl as a little girl. As the one thing she was determined to establish was that she was easy to know, and not stand-offish in her ways, on the whole she decided on her second choice—a bacchante. There had been a picture in one of the illustrated papers of some chorus girl dressed as a bacchante, and it had stuck in her mind. In the photograph the girl had worn some strips of chiffon which seemed to be attached nowhere and showed masses of leg. Dulcie schemed a dress on the same lines, a dress made of bits of coloured chiffon which would fall into a little short ragged skirt when she stood still, but which any man who was a man (and she was sure David was that) would discover could be lifted by the flick of a finger, to show almost invisible shell-pink trunks.

Though she would not admit it, Dulcie was slightly nervous of George and Janet. It was not that they could do anything to her, but they had, as she frequently told herself, a way of looking which was downright rude. She had an idea that they would wear the downright rude look if they saw the sort of dress she intended to wear, so for that reason she decided on secrecy until the night itself, when she appeared in all her glory. Now she faced Beth's question with that blank secret expression which was certain to infuriate anyone who saw it.

"It's a secret." Then she added, still being slightly in love with the small-girl idea: "Ickle Dulcie is going to give everybody a great big surprise."

Edward might not have his eyesight, but he certainly had his ears. He made repulsive retching sounds and buried his face in his handkerchief, heaving his shoulders.

Paul was deeply interested in this new outbreak of Dulcie's. He leant across the table politely.

"Why did you talk like that? Eve doesn't, and she's only eight; and Penny doesn't, and he's only three; and Keith Prowse doesn't, and he isn't six months yet."

Dulcie had never been fond of Paul. She looked at him witheringly.

"Little boys can't understand grown-up people—it takes a man to understand."

Paul turned to his father.

"Did you understand, Daddy, why Dulcie talked like that?"

George was on his best behaviour, trying his hardest not to let his very real hurt at Dulcie saying he looked comic force him into an unkind thought.

"You shouldn't make personal remarks, Paul," he said severely. "Maybe Dulcie can't help herself."

Janet was shocked to find how much she enjoyed seeing Dulcie snubbed. Nevertheless she was determined to keep mealtimes peaceful. She gave an easy laugh.

"I don't see why it matters so much how Dulcie talks, and there is no reason for her to tell us what she is going to wear if she doesn't want to. The question is, what's Dad to wear?"

As it happened, George was not to wear fancy dress, after all. The sports committee, in order to make the fancy dress ball a really shop affair, decided to invite an old and established man from all those departments where men were employed to be MCs, and George was invited to represent Hardware. From his early days in Babbacombe's he had possessed a dinner jacket which came out for a function about once in two years. For the fancy dress ball it came out again. George was so thin the clothes still fitted, though the cut was old-fashioned and the cloth turning a little green; but he and Janet had never seen smart evening clothes, and a dinner jacket was a dinner jacket. Pressed and steamed by Janet, it seemed to them both that he would look as smart as any man in London.

Dulcie had been quite right when she had decided that Beth would not get herself a good fancy dress. Beth would not have wanted to go to the dance at all were it not for the chance of David being there, and David, as she knew, liked her in anything that she wore. She considered a fancy dress a shocking waste of money, with Edward's operation hanging over the family, and she planned to wear her old navy blue linen frock with an apron and a white cap and go as a waitress; but Janet was having none of that.

"Oh, we can do better than that," she had said when Beth had told her what she had meant to do. "The old fur coat box can manage something. You leave it to me."

Leaving it to Janet meant that on the first day when she was free she had gone up to the West End, to one of the large drapery stores, and there discovered some very inexpensive blue-grey casement cloth. Out of this, and with some white muslin, she had made a perfectly charming Quaker dress, which suited Beth's wide-eyed, innocent face to perfection.

On the night of the fancy dress dance Janet made a bit of a festivity for all the family: there was a special supper with a trifle, and Paul and Eve sat up for it, and each of the three who were going was expected to make an entrance. Janet arranged the chairs across the living-room.

"Come on, all of you, sit down; and, Edward, you go and announce each of them—Dad first, then Beth, and then Dulcie—and we'll give them a good clap."

George was used to playing his part in these little family affairs. As Edward flung open the door and announced "Lord George Peasoup" he came in with his red M.C. rosette well in prominence and swaggered round the room while Janet and the girls curtsied. Edward went outside to ask Beth what she was calling herself, and came back grinning.

"Mistress Honesty."

Beth, with her hands folded and her eyes cast down, came demurely in at the door. Janet gave George a dig in the ribs.

"Doesn't she look a duck?"

George glowed.

"Bit of all right, old Beth."

"Go on, Beth," said Edward. "You ought to talk to them all in 'thees' and 'thous'."

Dulcie had come down the stairs with her dressing-gown over her shoulders. She had dressed in the bathroom, so that not even Beth had seen what she was wearing. In the bedroom in front of a looking-glass she had felt something almost new to her, embarrassment. Was it possible that she had gone a little too far? Of course the bit of artificial leopard skin going over one shoulder and under the other as it did really covered all that mattered, but still it would be awkward if it slipped. Then of course there was plenty of skirt really—nowadays, seeing what bathing dresses were like, there was no excuse for anyone to be fussy—but it did seem as if she had been rather mean with the chiffon; it was transparent, and somehow the trunks didn't quite look as if they were there. Of course it would be all right when she got to the ball: there'd be a lot there with far less on than she had. It was only showing herself to her Uncle and Aunt she did not like. They were such a silly, strait-laced lot. It was just like them to make all this fuss before starting, showing the dresses to the kids. Why bother about the kids, anyway?

"Come on, Dulcie," called Edward. She hung her dressing-gown over the stairs. "What shall I announce you as?"

"Just 'bacchante'." Dulcie rearranged the leaves and cherries in her hair. "And get on, because I don't want to hang about here all night. I'm cold."

"'Bacchante'," yelled Edward, opening the door.

The bacchante dress suited Dulcie to perfection. Her yellow hair had been piled up in a mass of curls and wound in and out of green leaves and cherries, and her pert, made-up face took on a strangeness, rising above the scanty bit of leopard skin. But that audience was not the one to appreciate her. Bexhill was the only place at which the family saw the latest bathing styles. It was not the sort of place where anything very *outré* was worn. Besides, the Carsons always chose a quiet bit of beach. There had never been any money for theatres. A pantomime at Christmas was the only entertainment in the year, except for an occasional film, and the people on the films or in pantomimes were actors and actresses, and therefore had a quality of unreality which covered anything they said or wore. Dulcie, standing in the living-room doorway, with her fragmentary coloured strips hung round her waist and her slim white legs finishing in silver sandals, through which showed her painted toes, struck a note in ten Penruddock Road that had never been seen there before, and which George, at least, hoped never to see again. He stood up, quite pale with shame.

"Dulcie! You can't go like that. It isn't decent."

Edward felt his loss of sight more acutely than usual. His ears red with excitement, he peered eagerly in Dulcie's direction.

"Not decent! What's she got on? You said you were a bacchante. Are you dressed as Lady Godiva?"

Girda's eyes swam with admiration.

"Oh, Dulcie, you look lovely! Oh, I do wish it was me! Might I try it on tomorrow?"

George raised his voice.

"You will do nothing of the sort. If Dulcie has no idea what's proper, that's not to say I'll have her putting ideas into your head."

Paul got off his chair.

"I'm going to fetch Penny. I do think it's a shame he shouldn't see. He'll like to tell all the other cats for miles and miles."

"But what's she got on?" said Edward.

Janet might not ever have seen anyone dressed like Dulcie, but she did read her picture papers, and realised that probably at the ball itself Dulcie's appearance would be less startling and less what she considered unpleasant. She got up and patted Dulcie on the shoulder.

"You'd better put on a coat: you'll catch cold while we're having supper. Come on, everybody; supper. You people want to be off."

David, in Elizabethan dress, got to the ball very early, and planted himself in the entrance of the hall. The sports ground was on the outskirts of Battersea, and the dance-hall attached to it. He had found out that George was an M.C., and therefore would have to be early, and seeing where the hall lay, he knew the Carsons would walk.

They came round the corner: George walking deliberately in the gutter, to keep as far away from Dulcie as possible; Beth with her coat partly covering her long grey skirts, and Dulcie well coated, with bare feet in her walking shoes, and her silver sandals dangling in her hand. David drew back behind the door, and let the three of them file past him; then he moved over to a vantage point behind some pot plants where he could watch the door of the ladies' cloakroom. Beth was out again in a minute. He had always thought she was perfectly enchanting to look at, but tonight in her Quaker dress she made his heart stand still. He put his hand on her arm.

"Oh, darling. Don't you look lovely!"

She glanced down at her grey casement-cloth frock and was surprised.

"It's very ordinary." His hand on her arm made her heart hammer so it felt as if he could hear it. She looked at his striped trunks and velvet doublet. "You're awfully grand. Are you Sir Walter Raleigh?"

"Round about the old boy's date." He held out his hand. "Can I have your card? This evening's mine, you know." Beth felt a thrill at his possessive way of speaking, but she shook her head.

"Goodness, no, of course it isn't. Why, your father's going to be here, and if you were seen dancing with me all night the shop would never stop talking."

She looked so charming, and he felt he had been so patient in these last weeks, that he lost his temper.

"If you think I'm going to let these yobs dance with you the whole evening you've made a big mistake. You'll dance with me, or I'll dance with nobody."

Beth kept her head; she moved him back behind the pot-plants.

"Don't be difficult. You must see that I can't dance only with you. Just imagine what everyone would say."

"Who the hell cares what they say! Look here, Beth, I'm just about fed up. I know all you've said about waiting for the six months to be up and all the rest of it, but it's not reasonable. I came here for nothing but to dance with you. Be nice."

She took his card.

"Suppose I give you two in each half?"

He had been afraid he was only going to get one dance, and was slightly mollified.

"And a bite at the buffet in the interval?"

"No, I can't possibly give you the interval. You'll have to have that with one of the women buyers." She looked up at him. "Don't you see you aren't just David of Cooked Meats tonight—you're Mr. Babbacombe's son. It's a kind of test night for you. Your father is sure to be watching, seeing that you do the right thing. And dancing with a junior isn't the right thing."

"And if I do the right thing, what then? It'll only mean dreary jobs in Babbacombe's, and I'm already fed up with it."

She wrote her name on his card.

"You may still hear about your seaplane. It's silly to lose heart. Look, I've given you the first and the last in this half, and the third and the seventh in the second half. How's that?" She wrote down his name on the same numbers on her own card. "Don't look so cross."

The band struck up, and he peered in at the door, and saw the word "Extra". He grinned at her.

"Sorry. This is an extra. Can I have it as well as number one?"

She wanted to dance with him so badly she did not even answer that, but without a word followed him to the floor.

Old Babbacombe was dining with Mr. Piper before coming to the dance. They were very old friends, and enjoyed an evening together. They sat facing each other across the port and puffed at their cigars. Old Babbacombe looked at the clock.

"Have to be movin' soon for this damned dance. Very good cause and all that—splendid of the sports committee to get it up—but nuisance havin' to go."

Mr. Piper tapped his cigar ash neatly on to the tray.

"Young David will be enjoying himself, I suppose."

Old Babbacombe gave an appreciative sniff at his glass of port.

"I'm pleased with him. Doin' very well, so they tell me. I was going to have him up in February when I see all my people, but I'm plannin' now to see him a bit before then."

Mr. Piper laughed.

"I had him in for his teeth in the usual way. I hear you've put him into Cooked Meats. What was the idea, Ginger?"

Old Babbacombe smiled.

"Testin' the boy. Don't want any more foolin' round. Time he was settlin' down in a good job and gettin' married. I could do with a grandchild or two."

Mr. Piper could remember old Babbacombe's wife. He had come round to see him the day she had died. It was wintertime. He could still see Ginger looking smaller even than he was, crouched in a big armchair before a few dead coals, too sunk in misery to notice that his fire had gone out. It must have been lonely for him all these years with no one but the boy. He pitied David, and knew how hard it must be to be forced into a career in which he had not got his heart, but he saw his friend's point. He had nothing but the boy. Naturally he wished him to carry on in the business. If there were grandchildren, what a difference it would make to the old man's life! A clutter of kids coming to call and climbing over his chair. He thought of Beth; and David's efforts to see her.

"Be a fine thing if the boy got married," he agreed. "Any signs yet?"

Old Babbacombe shook his head.

"No, nor likely to be until he's got more money. But since he's been in the shop he's stopped foolin' around with all those painted little idiots with more money than sense that he got to know up at Oxford."

Mr. Piper passed the port.

"You wouldn't mind, then, if he married a girl without any money? Working girl, perhaps?"

Old Babbacombe poured out another glass of port.

"I don't care what a woman does: it's what she is that matters. My wife was a different class from me, as you know, but I didn't love her because she was a Barton and the daughter of a baronet—I loved her because she was my Rose, and she would still have been my Rose if I'd found her selling apples in the Old Kent Road."

Mr. Piper nodded.

"That's sense. Well, you may get David settled down quicker than you think."

Up shot old Babbacombe's eyebrows.

"What are you drivin' at?"

"Probably nothing in it, but there was a girl—a nice girl, too—that he was interested in when he came to my surgery. Made me alter my books to fit him and her in at the same time, the young devil."

"Eh!" Old Babbacombe leant forward. "Does she work in my store?"

Mr. Piper nodded.

"Nice girl. Now what was her name? Carr? No, that wasn't it. I have it—Carson." Old Babbacombe looked thoughtful.

"Carson. I wonder if that's the same girl. There was a girl that got shut in the lift with David. It was her, as a matter of fact, that told him that he shouldn't be taking money off me which he didn't earn."

Mr. Piper gave a snort.

"Sounds a girl of sense. She looked that sort."

"If it's the same, she was a girl of sense. A relation of Carson in Hardware. I wrote it down on a pad at the time: 'Keep an eye on Miss Carson.'"

Mr. Piper sighed contentedly as his port trickled down his throat.

"Funny the way things work out, Ginger. You may be keeping an eye on Miss Carson for the rest of your life. You never know."

It was the seventh dance in the second half—a waltz. David looked down at Beth's upturned face.

"You've given me an awful evening. I had supper with Mrs. Kitson. She's the oldest buyer in the place, and she's put on an extra stone for every year she's been in Babbacombe's. My word, the sandwiches that woman put away. Have you had anything to eat?"

Beth nodded.

"I had a cup of coffee and a sandwich with Dad."

David looked out of his eye at Dulcie floating by.

"Your cousin's cutting a bit of a dash. She ought to go in for a beauty competition or something." Suddenly he tightened his arm round her waist. "I've been a good boy all the evening. Could I have a prize? How about cutting the last dance and sitting it out with me."

To Beth the evening had been rather a dreary waste, with four oases. Somehow, though she was ashamed of herself for feeling it, she hated to see him dancing and apparently amused with other girls; especially she had hated it when she saw him dancing with Dulcie. She hated it now when he said that Dulcie ought to go in for a beauty competition. She knew he was not really interested in Dulcie or anyone else, but she wanted him to herself. It would be heavenly to find one of these sitting-out places, and stop there until the dance was over; but she had him to think of first. Old Babbacombe had arrived about halfway through the dance, and had been escorted to a seat on the platform by the organisers, and had sat there benignly beaming at his staff while he chatted to the heads of his departments. All his people were pleased to see him there, and nudged each other, "Look! The O.M.'s arrived. See old Ginger Babbacombe getting off with Mrs. Nunn." But for all the gossiping he did, Beth noticed his eyes—the way he, without seeming to, kept his thoughts on David. He would be the first to notice if his boy left the room and sat out for the rest of the ball, and would be the first to find out who he was sitting out with. There would be plenty only too willing to tell him. The whisper would go round in a minute: "It's a girl in Gowns—just a junior." She looked up at David, regretfully shaking her head.

"I'd love to, but I'm sure it would be a mistake. Your father would hate it. I know he's watching you all the time. Besides, there is my father to think of. He'd be terribly shocked."

David wriggled his shoulders angrily.

"Are we to spend all our days fussing what our fathers think?"

"Not all our days," Beth explained. "But, after all, there is your job. I hate you in Cooked Meats. I hate you wearing that beastly chefs cap. I want you to do something more fitting."

David had spent a dutiful but trying evening. He had not enjoyed seeing Beth dancing with other men, any more than Beth had enjoyed seeing him dance with other women. He thought that he had done a good deal to please her tonight, and that it was only just that he should have his reward. His tone was bitter.

"I like that—to care what I wear and not to care what happens to me. Shoving me off to dance with every Mary and Molly the whole evening. You used not to be like this. You weren't a bit like this when we bought Keith Prowse, or at our weekend at Ribstall."

She had to laugh.

"You sound like a cross little boy when you talk like that. Rather like my brother Paul. You know perfectly well that your father would not approve of you knowing me, and my father does not approve of me knowing you. Dad believes in people stopping where they belong. In a way he's right, you know. I mean, in the end you have to stop in your own world, and though it's heavenly going out of it sometimes, it's sort of upsetting."

He stopped dancing and drew her to the side of the room.

"What are you talking about—the world where you belong and stopping there?"

Beth wished she had never tried to explain herself or her father's point of view. It seemed a very difficult subject to have started on.

"Well, you see—I mean—perhaps I shall marry—"

He gripped her arm so tightly that it hurt.

"Marry! Who are you marrying?"

She was frightened of his face. He looked in the mood to make a scene. Inquisitive eyes were already staring.

"Nobody—I mean when I do—oh, please don't look like that—everybody's looking at us."

"Well, come and sit out and talk things over."

She glanced at the platform, and saw that old Babbacombe was looking at them.

"I can't. Honestly, your father's looking at us."

He let her go.

"Very well. You are the most impossible person: I never see you, I never get a chance to talk to you, and when I do see you at a dance you never dance with me. Go and speak to your father. He seems the only person you're interested in."

Beth was so stunned to find they were quarrelling that for a moment she stood still, just staring after David. Then, feeling a smarting behind her eyeballs, she made for the cloakroom.

David went to the bar. He ordered himself a whisky and soda and sat down hating himself. Lord, what an idiot he was! Whatever had induced him to speak like that to Beth? What must the poor kid be feeling? She couldn't know—how could any nice girl know?—just what torture it was to have to dance with her, and then, with all his pulses throbbing, spend the rest of the evening dancing with other people, trying to make small talk, while he watched her trotting round in other men's arms. What the hell had she meant about the man she was going to marry? Was there some man? Was there some secret? Something she hadn't said? At the mere thought, he got up. He'd go and find her and talk things out. He couldn't, he wouldn't leave things like this: it was driving him mad.

Dulcie was having a riotous evening with the young, gay and not too particular. She was conscious that all the older women and some of the men were eyeing her with disapproval; but what did she care? She was a riot with the boys, so what did the old fogeys matter? As a climax to her evening she had danced with David. Only once, but she congratulated herself that it had been a pretty successful dance. David had said that she ought to go on the films, and if that didn't mean he was falling for her, what would? For all that, she was not going to be satisfied with just one dance, so she spent the rest of the evening with her eyes glued on David. So it was that she did not miss that Beth and David had quarrelled, nor that he had gone into the bar alone. Seeing his departing back, she gave her partner's shoulder blade an affectionate pinch. "Ickle Dulcie 'ants a d'ink."

Her partner had had a good many drinks already, and was cherishing the hope that Dulcie would allow him to see her home. He gave her a squeeze round the waist.

"Righty ho, girlie. Just give the name to your gargle, and it's yours." He put his arm through hers and led her towards the bar. Halfway there he gave a twitch to one of her chiffon strips.

"Are all the goods in the window?"

"'ou's a naughty boy: 'ou shan't look." Then, to take the harshness out of her words, she leant her shoulder against his. It was the bare shoulder without the leopard's skin. Shivers of excitement ran down his spine.

"Come on, girlie, let's see what a gargle will do for us!"

They ran into David just as he was deciding to leave the bar. Dulcie stood in front of him, her hands behind her back, her chin childishly raised towards him.

"Will you have a d'ink, Mr. Cooked-Meat Man?"

He moved her gently to one side.

"No, thank you. I'm dancing this with your cousin."

Dulcie lied quickly.

"Then she's dancing with two other people. I saw her with Mr. Grey—he's the buyer in Hardware, and a much more 'portant person than you, Mr. Cooked-Meat Man."

David turned back to the bar, his heart sinking. Beth couldn't be caring that they had quarrelled if she could at once go and dance with another man.

"This," said Dulcie, pointing to her partner, "is Joe. He's awfully nice. Aren't you, Joe?"

Joe put his arms round her.

"I know somebody else who's awfully nice."

"Let me go," said Dulcie. "You're pulling up my skirt."

The thought of pulling up Dulcie's skirt elevated the already over-excited Joe. With a whoop he lifted Dulcie on to the bar.

"Now I've got you. You can't get down."

Two other men came in to have a drink. Seeing Dulcie and her legs, they came over to join the fun. David suddenly decided to drown his troubles, and ordered drinks for everyone, and Joe, not to be outdone, ordered a second round. In a few minutes the party was going. Dulcie squealed delightedly and kicked up her legs, while the four men pulled at her chiffon skirts, pretending to lift the pieces.

"Let go, you naughty boys. Oh, you naughty, naughty Mr. Cooked-Meat Man!"

It was at this moment that old Babbacombe, escorted by Mr. Smith and two or three of the committee, passed along the passage at the end of the bar on his way home. He paused in the doorway just as David gave a tweak at a piece of orange chiffon, and Dulcie squealed and kicked her legs. He turned to Mr. Smith, jerking his head towards the bar.

"My boy seems to have had a drink or two. Don't like to see that sort of thing at our staff parties. Better break them up." He moved on, then a thought struck him. "Who's the girl?"

Mr. Smith was sorry that old Babbacombe had happened to come on that scene. His voice was stiff with disapproval.

"Her name's Carson. She never was our sort. I said so from the beginning, but I had to take her on. You see, she's a relative of Carson in Hardware."

Old Babbacombe got into his car. As it moved off he shook his head.

"So that's the girl, is it? Grandchildren indeed! I'll see young David in the morning."

CHAPTER FIFTEEN

DAVID woke up feeling like death. For a moment he did not remember why he was so wretched, then, like the surge of the incoming sea, remembrance flooded over him. He had quarrelled with Beth. He sat up and ran his fingers through his hair.

"Lord, I am a blasted fool! She was quite right when she said I was behaving like a child. Strewth! Will she ever forgive me?"

He got out of bed and fetched some notepaper and an envelope. He tapped his pen on his teeth. He was sure he hadn't the gift to say what he meant—never had been much of a hand at writing things down. All he felt like saying was "Oh, darling, darling, I'm sorry," but that seemed a bit wet, and not likely to pull much weight with a sensible girl like Beth.

After much thought he wrote:

"DARLING BETH,

I am an ass and an idiot. I made such a crashing mess of last night that I feel in a sweat this morning. If you can forgive me, will you meet me at my club after work? I shan't ask you to stay long, but I feel so frightful that I must see you, if it's only for a minute.

Yours all over dust and ashes,

DAVID."

Having written this, he felt a whole lot better, and as he bathed he whistled. After all, even making an ass of yourself had its brighter side if it meant seeing the girl the next day.

He got to the stores early and gave the note to the timekeeper.

"Be a sport, old man, and keep a lookout for the lady, and here's a little something to buy a drink."

The doorkeeper grinned.

"Yours is the first," he said, propping the envelope up on his shelf. "Funny we can go on for weeks with nobody making a date with anybody, but after a dance I'm fair snowed under with letters. Seems to stir people up—dancing together does."

The doorkeeper had a great reputation in Babbacombe's for reliability. Although there were close on two thousand employees he had some strange system of keeping a track on them all.

A note given to him never misfired. With a feeling of something accomplished, David went whistling to the dressing-room.

In the middle of the morning old Babbacombe sent for David. David laid down his carving knife and called to the man next to him on the counter.

"I'm sorry, I'm seeing the O.M. You can look after this lovely bit of raw beef."

The other man had overdone his drinking the night before; beads of sweat broke out on his forehead.

"Don't, old man—not even as a joke. I've already had my breakfast back, and I'm trying to steady up to hold a little lunch."

David looked at him with an experienced eye.

"You come out with me presently. I'll get a chemist to knock you up a prescription that would settle an inside that rocked like the sea. Meanwhile"—he lowered his voice—"if a note should come for me, park it till I come back. Mind you, I don't want a note: no news is good news in this case."

Old Babbacombe was sitting at his desk. He glanced up as David entered.

"Sit down, son, and take off that damn silly hat."

David sat.

"That's no way to speak of my badge of servitude."

His father laid down his pen.

"I'm not in a jokin' mood this morning."

David looked sympathetic.

"Sorry to hear that. It's these staff parties: you can't help doing yourself too well."

Old John glowered.

"Now you be quiet and listen to me. I've had very good reports of you. Accordin' to your buyer you have done uncommon well."

"Thank you."

Old John had lain awake half the night planning this conversation, but now that he had come to it he found himself failing for the best words, and, although it was urgent he should speak calmly, suffering from nervousness.

"This good report of you comes at a very fortunate time, very fortunate—comes at a time, in fact, when I'm in a position to put you in the right place."

David's face lit up. This was good—this was something to tell Beth tonight. She certainly wouldn't be cross when she heard this news.

Old John saw the light on his son's face and lowered his head. Damn difficult this was being. Why on earth did the boy want to go making a fool of himself?

"Yes, very fortunate." He hesitated. "As it happens, you can start right away."

David lit a cigarette.

"That's fine. As a matter of fact, I shall quite miss my cooked meat. I've got a soft feeling even for a galantine."

Old John went on as if David had not spoken: "So you see you can start when you like. Well, I mean you'll have your packin' to do."

"Packing!" David sat up. "What on earth do I want to pack for?"

Old John tried to look surprised at himself.

"Oh, didn't I explain? This vacancy we have is in our Scotch branch. You go to Glasgow."

"Glasgow!" David repeated feebly. "Glasgow. Oh, but I say, Dad, I can't go there."

Old John knew very well David did not want to go there, nor anywhere out of London. His fear of a row made him bluster.

"You'll go where you're sent. You're not a director yet, you know, and you'll do what you're told."

David looked wildly round the room. This was a knockout. What on earth was he to say? He couldn't go to Glasgow—why, it was miles away. He would never see Beth at all. On the other hand he would get no sympathy from Beth if he turned the chance down. He decided, in spite of all Beth felt on the subject, to make more or less a clean breast of the situation. His father wasn't a bad old stick and would probably understand. He drew his chair forward.

"As a matter of fact, Dad, it's not awfully convenient. You see, there's a girl. Her name's Beth Carson, and—"

The last thing old John wanted was to hear about that girl. He had remained in many ways young in heart, and he remembered just how bitterly he had resented any interference in his life when he was David's age. Much better make this Glasgow job sound real and never mention the Carson girl at all. He nodded.

"I daresay, but one bit of skirt is much like another; you'll find somebody in Glasgow."

To hear Beth described as a "bit of skirt" made David see red.

"I'll thank you not to speak like that about the girl I happen to love. I should like to know what you'd have done if grandfather had called mother 'a bit of skirt'."

Old John turned white. To hear his Rose put in the same class as that creature he had seen sitting on the bar seemed to him sacrilege. His voice trembled.

"You be quiet. You've no right to speak that way. How dare you class your blessed mother with that slut!"

David got up. For one second he was near murder. Then he got a grip on himself. "I'm going."

Old John came round his desk.

"Don't be hasty, lad. Maybe I spoke as I shouldn't. But I saw your girl last night—she was pointed out to me by the staff manager. You're young, and don't see so clearly, but there's only one word for her sort. Smith said the same."

David clenched his hands to control them.

"So this Glasgow job is put up to get me out of the way."

Old John was cornered. His voice was gentle.

"Just for a time—give you time to think."

David came slowly across the room and stood facing his father.

"I don't want time. I'm in love with the most perfect girl in the world, and if she'll have me I'm going to marry her."

Old John's hand shot out and caught David's arm.

"You can't do that, lad. Think of your mother. What would she say? Why, she didn't even know there were girls of that sort in the world."

David snatched his arm away.

"Shut up."

Old John decided it was time for clear speaking.

"Now, look here. I've been patient because I know what it's like to be young, but I'm not standin' for any more of this talk. You're going to Glasgow, and you're goin' damn quick."

David shook his head.

"Oh no, I'm not."

Old John was not used to being crossed; his temper rose.

"Oh yes, you are, or else you're out. Out of my shops, and out of my house, and without a penny. You'll see how your girl likes you then."

David opened the door.

"Right. When you come back tonight I'll be gone. Goodbye."

Left to himself, Old John sank down at his desk and mopped his forehead. "Silly young fool!" he thought—"gettin' in such a state about a girl like that. But it wouldn't last—not two minutes it wouldn't, not when the girl knows the boy hasn't a shilling." He knew her sort. To make assurance doubly sure she could go too. Without a penny between them they'd soon get tired. Smith had said the girl never had been their type. It wouldn't be difficult to find a just excuse for giving her the sack. That sort of minx was always a nuisance: sure to be the wrong side of her buyer. He pressed the bell. "Mr. Wills," he said as his secretary came in, "I want you to do a bit of confidential work. I want you to see Mrs. Nunn in Gowns and get a report on a girl in her department called Carson."

Beth had spent just as wretched a night as had David. It was a miserable thing to have left him feeling like that. She blamed herself for what had followed; not, of course, for Dulcie making such a show of herself and Dad being asked by Mr. Smith to take her home, but for David being one of those who was fooling with her. It was quite unlike him, and he would never have done it if he had not been miserable. It was not until it was nearly light that she dropped asleep. She was woken by cries from Dulcie.

"Oh gosh, Beth, I feel terrible! I'm going to be sick."

Beth ministered with as good a grace as she could, but she felt it was an act of justice that Dulcie should be ill—that would teach her not to go drinking too much and making nice people like David drink too much.

Beth got David's letter from the doorkeeper as soon as she reached the shop. He pulled her arm to draw her out of hearing of George.

"This is for you. No need to tell your Dad all your business."

Beth would like to have retorted that Dad did know all her business, but it certainly wouldn't be true, and today would be a rotten one to start confiding. She and George had come to work alone, as Dulcie was feeling too ill to get up. George was so bitterly ashamed about last night that he had only spoken once, and that was to say, "I thank God, Beth, you aren't the sort to go fooling about with men." No, it certainly wasn't the moment to let him see her get a letter from David.

From the first reading she knew she would meet him. She was doing what she thought right in refusing to see him, but her right did not include an occasion like this. He had made an awful ass of himself. Her heart melted as she remembered his cross-little-boy face. Naturally he wanted to put things right.

David was at his club half an hour before Beth could possibly get there. He had seen his neighbour of the Cooked Meats counter at lunchtime, and over a pick-me-up had learnt that there had been no note for him. But that did not make it certain she would come. Perhaps they were busy in Gowns; perhaps she was not in at all today; perhaps—

It seemed to David that as Beth walked into his tawdry, glittering bar that it was just cardboard scenery, and that really he and she were alone in an open space.

"Darling." He seized her arm. "Will you marry me?"

Her eyes stared up to his so fixedly that he felt as if he could dive into them.

"Marry?" she whispered, and then again, "Marry?"

"Of course. You know I've been wanting to ask you for ages, but I couldn't because you were so silly about my father; but now I'm free. You see, he's given me the sack."

Beth was concerned.

"Why? What did you do?"

He had his answer ready.

"I cheeked him. Oh, don't be cross, darling. I can't tell you why I did, because it's a private quarrel between him and me, but honestly he deserved telling off."

"But what'll you do now?"

He drew her to the bar counter and they clambered up on two stools.

"I've got myself a job. It's in a garage at Hounslow." He beckoned to the barman. "Two champagne cocktails, please."

"Champagne!"

"Of course. To celebrate our engagement." Beth, too happy to think coherently, blinked at him.

"Hounslow! That's a long way."

"Not from where I'm living. I've got myself a room nearby. Twelve and six a week. My landlady looks like a black beetle."

"But why aren't you going to keep on living with your father?"

He laid his hand on her knee.

"Because we've quarrelled, darling. He's turned me out without a farthing. I've no future unless my seaplane turns up trumps. I'm just a garage hand. Do you think your father would let you marry me, and, more important, would you marry me?"

Beth suddenly grasped that all this was true. He was free, and he wanted to marry her.

"I want to marry you more than anything in the world."

CHAPTER SIXTEEN

GEORGE was not easy to satisfy. It might be Mr. David had quarrelled with his father—young men often did—but it didn't last. It would make things worse if he got engaged to Beth. Gentlemen should marry in their own station; there was no getting away from that.

"But what is my station?" David asked. "I'm just a garage hand."

"That may be, Mr. David," George retorted, "but I know my Beth's place, and that's what I'm thinking about."

In the end George, urged by Janet, agreed to a half-and-half arrangement. Beth might meet David at the weekends. There was to be no official engagement, and no ring until after February. In February Mr. Babbacombe started interviewing every member of his staff, seniors first. It was then he went over their sales sheets and rises in pay occurred, or sometimes the sack. George was past pay rises, and, he hoped, secure against the sack, but Mr. Babbacombe saw him in the usual routine way. That would be his chance. At that interview he would bring up the question of David and Beth. Until then nothing could be settled.

David and Beth did not mind. Every Saturday afternoon they met and had tea together, and every Sunday when it was fine they went into the country. Sometimes when it was wet Beth brought him to Penruddock Road. Janet loved him and so did the children. It was nice for Scissors and Keith Prowse. Even George got used to him at last and brought himself to drop the "mister" and to call him David. On weekdays Beth on her way home from the shop called at the post office.

David, cutting himself right off from his father, had given orders for his letters to be sent to a post office. Every night receiving the letters across the counter was an adventure. Eagerly Beth turned them over. The letter from the Admiralty would have something on the back. Had it come tonight? Every night as she posted the letters on, one of her own went with it. Two people were never more in love.

Because Beth was so much in love, the ordinary things of life passed her by. She was not conscious of interests which had no bearing on herself and David. She worked as well as ever, but was not as observant as normally, and so she missed the fact that Mrs. Nunn was keeping an unusually interested eye on her.

Mrs. Nunn had been drawn to Beth since the day when the frock was stolen and she had reminded her of her daughter. She considered her one of her most promising juniors, so it had been a big surprise to her to find that Mr. Wills was cross-examining her as to how the girl was getting on, and still more of a surprise when she realised the enquiries came from old John himself. She would have been more surprised still if she could have seen old Babbacombe in his office hearing Wills' report.

"Mrs. Nunn says the girl is one of the best juniors she has?" Old Babbacombe enquired. "Well, that's funny."

"As far as I can make out, sir," Mr. Wills assured him, "she is obliging, and shaping well, and has put through one good sale. There was some trouble about a shoplifter, but the girl was not to blame, and afterwards was herself responsible for getting the woman caught and the dress returned."

Old Babbacombe nodded his dismissal.

"All right, Mr. Wills, you can go. Mind you, I don't want anyone to know I've been asking questions. I never dismissed a good employee yet, and I'm not starting now."

Alone he shook his head.

"Funny, very funny. I could have sworn a girl like that would have put Mrs. Nunn's back up at the start. She didn't look a good worker to me. I must keep my eyes open."

Because the enquiry had been made, Mrs. Nunn felt it her duty to watch Beth closely. An enquiry like that must mean that something was wrong, but she couldn't imagine what. The more she saw of Beth the more she approved of her. She was quick, willing, and eager, and had about her, as well, a quality of radiant happiness which she found particularly endearing.

Beth, living through her weeks for her Saturdays and Sundays, was less observant now, too, about things at home. She took her share in the little family arguments—Paul's defence of Penny, and Girda's emotional crises over her clothes—and she tried to think of things that would amuse Edward. But, wrapped away in her own happiness, other people's emotions passed her by. So it was that she missed the fact that Janet was pretending to be bright and was not feeling it, and that George was becoming more silent every day.

It was a few weeks before Christmas. They had been busy in Gowns, so Beth had missed both George and Dulcie, and came home on the omnibus alone. On the way her mind churned a number of thoughts: David spending Christmas Day with them; the new frock she was buying at the store; of how she was meeting David tomorrow night. As she came in at the front door Janet called her:

"Is that you, Beth?"

Beth went into the kitchen.

"Hullo, Mum." Then she stopped, seeing Janet's face. "Whatever's up?"

Janet clasped her hands and swallowed before she spoke.

"They're going to operate on Edward tomorrow."

Beth gasped.

"So soon? But I thought it would be months."

Janet shook her head.

"No. Dad and I knew, but we didn't trouble you—you had other things to think of. The doctor wants to make it as sudden as possible so as not to upset Edward."

Beth put her arms round her mother.

"Oh, Mum, you should have told me! Poor Edward! Does he know?"

Her mother shook her head.

"No, we'll tell him tonight. It's a nasty business for him; he'll need to keep his pecker up. They give you something, but you're conscious all the time—you can't have chloroform, it seems." Her voice tailed away wretchedly. The thought of her child, what Edward was to endure, had haunted her since she first knew what was wrong with his eyes. Now, with the operation so near, her courage flagged. She twisted her apron into a pipe. "Oh, Beth, why must he have to bear this? If only I could go through it for him."

Beth looked at her mother with a warm feeling in her heart. Their positions were reversed. Janet, who all her life had been there to prop and comfort her children, was now asking one of those children to prop and comfort her. She gave her mother a hug.

"Don't fuss, Mum. I don't suppose Edward will. If you come to think of it, it's a good thing he's ready for the operation, for the sooner he's ready the sooner he'll see."

Janet gripped her convulsively.

"Or doesn't, as the case may be."

Beth gave her a little shake.

"Don't be silly, Mum—that's no way to talk. Now I tell you what, I'll stop out tomorrow and go with you and Edward to the hospital."

Janet's face lit up.

"Oh, could you? Dad wanted to, but it seems they're short-handed. But you're very busy, aren't you?"

Beth laughed.

"Not so busy they can't carry on without a junior. Do them good to hang their own dresses and run their own messages for a change."

Janet looked cheered.

"Well, that will make a difference. Then there's another thing. I can't help feeling that you'll tell Edward better than Dad will. Dad's so worried that he'll make it sound serious, and so will I. Perhaps you could tell him in a light way, so it doesn't sound so bad."

Beth went up to her room and took out her writing paper.

"DAVID DARLING,

Edward is having his eye operation tomorrow. He's going in the morning, and they're doing it in the afternoon, and I'm stopping out to go to the hospital with Mum. I hope I'll be able to get away for the evening as we planned, so

be at Lyons Corner House at 6.30 in case. If I don't turn
up come on to the house.

Much love,

BETH."

She folded the letter and put it in an envelope and addressed
it, then she went to her bag for a stamp.

Since the fancy dress ball, Dulcie had been going out with a
lot of boys from the store. They filled in her time and amused her,
but they were not what she wanted. She had watched Beth and
David with ever-growing fury. But she had not lost hope. She was
always waiting for her chance to break things up. She was dressing now to go out to a film, and she glanced, in passing, at Beth's
letter. She did not suppose she could do anything with it, and had
no particular idea in her mind, except that the mere thought of
getting hold of a letter from Beth to David held vague promise.

"Shall I post that for you?" she asked casually. "I'm going out
with Joe."

Beth looked round gratefully.

"Oh, would you? I've got to go to the hospital with Mum and
Edward tomorrow, and I may not be able to meet him in the evening. I want him to get it first thing. You won't forget it, will you?"

Dulcie shook her head.

"Not me. I won't put it in my bag—I'll carry it, then I can't
forget."

Dulcie was meeting Joe in the Piccadilly Tube Station. On
her way to the omnibus she stopped and opened Beth's letter,
and an amused smile came over her mouth. At the post-box she
stopped and tore the letter to fragments and pushed the pieces
down a drain.

With the family's connivance, Edward and Beth had the sitting-
room to themselves. Edward felt his way to the fireplace and sat
down on the mat, and turned Keith Prowse upside down and
rubbed his tummy.

"Aren't you getting a great big boy?"

Beth sat on the rug beside him and played with Keith Prowse's ears.

"Feeling like having a shock?"

Edward's hand stopped rubbing.

"What? Am I going to have my operation?"

"Guessed it in one."

"When?"

"Tomorrow."

Edward said nothing for a moment, then he began rubbing again.

"That's good! I'm fed up with hanging about waiting." Beth felt a lump growing in her throat. How difficult it was not to be upset when people were brave, especially a person like Edward, whose ears gave him away by turning scarlet! She forced herself to answer.

"That's what I said you'd be. How did you guess?"

Edward picked Keith Prowse up and hugged him.

"People fussing. You know. Dad brought me home a box of sweets, and Mum asking what I'd like for supper. I suppose to them I seem like a man going to be hanged."

Beth's eyes smarted with tears.

"Old idiot, aren't you?"

Edward hugged Keith Prowse tighter.

"I talked to that doctor for a bit when Mum wasn't there. He says it isn't too bad. He said while they are doing it I ought to think only about being able to see again."

Beth ran Keith Prowse's tail through her fingers.

"I'm going with you and Mum to the hospital."

His face lit up.

"Oh, good! Then you'd take Keith Prowse back. I'd like him to come with me." He flushed. "I feel better when he's about." His voice, to his great shame, broke. He jumped up. "Come on, Keith Prowse. Come on, old boy. How about you going out? Cats. Cats. Cats."

*

Taking a person to a hospital or nursing home is bound to be a depressing business. It was all right during breakfast, with the children about, although there was an awkward moment when George went off to work. He wanted to say something and didn't know what; he managed a "Good luck, son", and then hung about feeling for the right words. Janet gave him a friendly push.

"You get along, or you'll be late, and that'll be a nice thing, with Beth staying out. Don't want all the family getting a bad mark."

Dulcie for once said the right thing. She was hard and self-centred, but she was touched by Edward that morning.

"Don't stop too long in the hospital, or Keith Prowse'll be growing up, and you know what that means. Don't want to come home and find him with a wife and six puppies."

The idea of Keith Prowse as a married dog proved a most lucky topic—it engrossed the whole family until it was time for them to start off for school.

"If Keith Prowse marries," said Eve, "I'll lend his wife a wedding veil. It's on my baby doll."

"I don't see why he should marry," Paul protested. "Penny's much older than him, and he's never thought of it."

Even Janet smiled. She wondered what Paul thought Penny did with his evenings.

When the children had gone off chatting up the road, time hung heavily. There was the housework to do and Edward's case to pack, but these things did not employ Edward, and he fumbled his way in and out of the bedrooms and kitchen, with Keith Prowse at his heels, trying to seem natural and at ease, but touching Janet and Beth unbearably by his scared white face. They were thankful when it was time to start.

At the hospital Edward suddenly became very aloof, as if he were afraid that his family might disgrace him and cry.

"Don't you bother to hang about, Mum," he said, seizing his suitcase.

The sister gave Janet a you-and-I-understand-them smile.

"Come back about five," she said. "We'll have everything over by then and some good news for you."

Looking back, neither Janet nor Beth could remember much of what they did with themselves for the rest of that day. They went home, of course, and the children came in to lunch; then part of the afternoon, because it was wet and cold, and neither of them cared to sit about, they went to a cinema, but they had no idea what the picture was about. Very early Janet began to get restive and sat looking at her watch. They were back at the hospital far too soon, and were shown into a waiting-room.

All waiting-rooms are depressing. It seemed to Janet and Beth that aeons of time passed before the door opened and a sister came in.

"Mrs. Carson?"

Janet had got up and stood gazing anxiously with the expression of a dog begging for a bone.

"Is he all right?"

"It's difficult to say yet about his eyes." The sister's voice was gentle. "He was a bad case, as you know. He stood the operation very well considering."

Janet made a little movement.

"Could I see him? Just for a minute?" The sister shook her head.

"I'm afraid not. It isn't a visiting day, you know, and in any case he's better quiet. You see, he will be in a good deal of pain."

Janet's hand quite unconsciously went to her throat.

"If he's in pain, sister, he'd like me by him. You know how children are about their mothers. They seem to get little again when they're ill or anything like that."

"I'm sorry, Mrs. Carson."

Beth laid her hand on her mother's arm.

"Come on, Mum. It's visiting day on Saturday. It's only three days."

Beth, with her arm through her mother's, led her out of the hospital, down the steps into the street. Janet said nothing, but walked along with her head bent. At the street corner she swayed.

"It's silly of me, Beth, but I feel queer."

Beth gave her a quick look and saw she was nearly fainting. With her arm round her she helped her up the street and into a chemist shop. The chemist was a kind-hearted man; he gave Janet a stiff dose of sal volatile.

"That's a nasty turn you've had," he said sympathetically. "Do you often have them?" Beth explained about Edward, and he was even more sympathetic. "Enough to turn anyone up. I remember how my wife was when our little girl was taken bad and went to hospital."

"Is she better now?" Beth enquired.

He shook his head gloomily.

"No, we lost her."

Fortified by the sal volatile, but not by the chemist's sad story, Beth and Janet walked slowly to the omnibus. Beth out of the corner of her eye saw a clock. It was after six; no chance of meeting David.

"Come on, Mum," she said cheerfully. "What we want is a good fire and a pot of tea. David's coming along to see us presently; that'll cheer us up."

Dulcie left her lift promptly at six and dashed out of her working clothes and into her outdoor things and scurried off. The Corner House was big, and Beth and David might have a special place of meeting. She didn't want to run any risk of missing him.

Far from missing him, Dulcie very nearly ran straight into him, which was the last thing she intended. She did not want to see him before she was perfectly certain that Beth would not turn up. He was standing by the chocolate counter examining the boxes. She took herself as far away as possible and waited. Half-past six came. David looked at his watch and turned his head to the doors and raked with his eyes everybody that came in. At a quarter to seven, Dulcie decided it was safe to come out. She wandered across the shop and managed a meeting that looked like an accident.

"Hullo, David." She sounded startled and nervous. "Well, who'd have thought of seeing you? Well, I mean . . ."

He noticed her hesitancy and was surprised. Hesitancy was the last thing you expected from Dulcie.

"I'm waiting for Beth. I expect she's been kept late at the store."

"Waiting for Beth!" Her eyes were round.

"But—But she wrote, didn't she?"

"Wrote! What about? Isn't she coming?"

Dulcie made a little movement as if to get away.

"I don't know anything about it."

He caught her arm.

"Wait a minute. What's the mystery?"

She looked scared.

"Oh, there isn't a mystery. She said she was going to write to you. You see, she had to meet somebody else."

David was puzzled. He hooked his arm into Dulcie's. "Come and have an ice or a cup of coffee or something and tell me what you're driving at."

Walking into the restaurant, Dulcie was thinking rapidly. This was working very well. He was at least going to sit and talk to her—which was something. But whatever story was she going to put up? He would meet Beth again, if not today, then certainly tomorrow, and the truth would come out. Then she flung up her chin. Oh, well, who cared? She could always say she did it for a joke.

Over coffee and cream buns she told her fairy story.

"You know that Mr. Grey that's buyer in Uncle George's department. He's always been interested in Beth. And yesterday he asked Uncle George if he could take Beth to the theatre tonight. I think Uncle George hopes that he'll marry her." She stretched out her hand and laid it on his. "I don't mean that Beth isn't awfully fond of you. Everybody knows that she is, but you see he's got plenty of money, and it would be a frightfully good marriage."

He dragged his hand from hers. He was not going to discuss Beth with Dulcie.

"Drink up your coffee. I ought to be going. I came straight here from work, and I suppose her letter missed me."

Dulcie lingered as long as she could over her cream bun.

"Of course it's easy for Beth to do things. You see, when you've got a father and mother you don't have to decide things for yourself. But I'm an orphan. When I meet a man that I'm fond of I shall be so glad I've got somebody to look after me that I shall never look at anyone else, certainly not go out with them."

David looked at her with an amused smile. He had no illusions about Dulcie.

"That'll be wonderful for the man. You ought to make a splendid wife."

She looked at him reproachfully.

"You're teasing me. I shall make a wonderful one. You don't know how wonderful I'd be for the right man."

David was impatient to get at Beth's letter. He took up the bill chit.

"Well, if you've finished I ought to be going."

She got up slowly and brushed a crumb off her coat. She turned up her blue eyes, and blinked through her lashes.

"Thank you so much for being so kind. I shall never, never forget this day."

Outside the Corner House she looked after him doubtfully. Had she done any good? "He's such a funny sort," she thought resentfully. "He never takes you seriously. Still of course if anything did happen, and he and Beth really quarrelled, he might remember about me. I'm just the sort that men would turn to if they quarrelled with people like Beth."

Back in Hounslow, David threw open the door of his room and looked round. There was no sign of a letter. He went to the stair rail and called over the banisters:

"Mrs. Pirn. Mrs. Pirn. Have you got a letter for me?"

She came out of the kitchen wiping her hands.

"No, sir, there hasn't been a letter all day. You know I always put them in your room."

"All right. I expect it got sent to the garage. I'll go and fetch it."

At the garage they were surprised to see David back.

"I thought you had gone to the West End with your best girl," said Nobby, a fellow mechanic.

David went towards the office.

"Has a letter come for me, do you know?" Nobby shook his head.

"No, I took them in myself. There's bad news for somebody. That Morris we had brought in by the breakdown gang is to be taken up to Edinburgh. The boss wants somebody to go. You aren't looking for a long, cold drive, I suppose?"

David did not answer, but strode into the office and went to the rack where the letters were kept. It was perfectly true there was nothing for him. He came out to Nobby.

"Where is the boss?"

Nobby jerked his thumb towards one of the garages.

"In there. Why? You don't want the job, do you?"

David stood still, turning over the question in his mind.

Did he? He was in such a bad temper that he had lost his reasoning powers. He knew Beth loved him and he loved her, but she couldn't go treating him like this—going out with another man and not even troubling to let him know. It was a low-down way to behave, and he'd damn well write and tell her what he thought about it. It might be a good idea to go up to Edinburgh with that car and give her time to come to her senses and apologise. He turned to Nobby.

"Yes. I'll take it; and I don't care how soon I start."

CHAPTER SEVENTEEN

IT WAS a miserable evening. In the upset over Edward, Janet forgot that Beth had said that David was coming. The children caught the feeling of nervousness and depression in the house.

Girda burst out crying quite suddenly, and Eve was tearful when it was time to go to bed. All of them in their different ways looked to Beth for support. Each one seemed to feel that if Beth was being her normal self things were not so bad with Edward; he would be all right in a day or two; and somehow Beth managed to be her normal self. It was uphill work, because inside she was feeling wretched. Apart from Edward, what could have happened to David? Why didn't he come? Had he got mixed up in some car accident? But all this worry she kept inside, none of it showed in her face, as she tucked Eve up in bed, and read her "Peter Rabbit", and agreed with Paul that (if he would stay) for this one night Penny should sleep on his bed, as it would be rather lonely for him upstairs by himself. She even succeeded in making Girda laugh, telling her that she was fussing too much and giving an imitation of her behaving like an agitated hen.

The worst part of the evening was sitting over the fire with Janet and George. They tried to be cheerful, but George's pipe hung unlit in his fingers, and Janet made a poor show at dealing with a basket of mending. However hard Beth tried to keep some sort of conversation going, there were long pauses, and her heart sank lower and lower. She dare not think of Edward, lonely and in pain in the hospital, as she was sure she would break down and cry; and she dare not think of David. Why hadn't he come? Oh, why hadn't he?

For once it was a relief when Dulcie came in. She had been out dancing with a boyfriend, she told them truculently. Beth wondered at the truculence. No one had the spirit to scold her, and in any case she personally did not care where Dulcie had been as long as she was out.

When she had got her mother to bed and given her some hot milk to make her sleep, and had given George a goodnight hug and told him not to fuss, Beth still hung about, unwilling to go to bed. She was too worried to feel like sleep, and in no mood for Dulcie's chatter. She crept downstairs again and sat by what remained of the fire, and there in the dark she let herself go.

She buried her face in her hands and sobbed, while she prayed incoherently "Oh, please God, let Edward get all right, and oh, please, don't let anything have happened to David."

After a wretched night, in which she had slept in fits and starts, Beth got up early and helped her mother get the breakfast. In spite of her night she succeeded in sounding cheerful.

"Buck up, Mum. You wait till you get to the hospital; you'll laugh then at the state we've been in."

It was she who heard the letters fall into the box. Without a word she put down what she was doing and ran. With a bounding heart she saw David's handwriting. So he had written. What a fool she had been to fuss! The letter was quite short; she read it in the hall.

"DEAR BETH,

I don't mind you going out with other men, but you might let me know. If I hadn't run into Dulcie I should never have heard. I shan't be seeing you for a day or two, as I am starting to Edinburgh early in the morning returning a car.

Yours,

DAVID."

For a moment, reading that letter, everything for Beth went black. What could David mean? What in the world had Dulcie said?

"Beth! Beth!" called Janet. "The porridge is ready. Will you take it in?"

Beth stuffed the letter into her pocket and went into the kitchen. Janet had enough to worry her this morning; she must not know about this.

But Janet, full though she was of her own anxiety, still had eyes for her other children. She noticed Beth's white face and the pitiable attempt she made to eat her breakfast. This was not the Beth that had come down that morning. Something must have upset her. Thinking this, she suddenly remembered David. Beth had expected him last night, and he had never turned up.

As soon as it was decent, Beth got up from the table. A moment later Janet followed her. She came up to her bedroom, and put her arm round her.

"Something's upset you. What is it?"

The direct question was too much for Beth. In a moment she was sobbing, and had given Janet the letter.

That letter did Janet more good than a bottle of champagne. One form of emotion is an antidote to another, and the blind rage that shook her drove for a time anxiety out of her heart. She had always disliked Dulcie, but this time the girl had gone too far. She gave Beth a hug.

"My word! You wait till I've told Dulcie what I think of her."

"It won't help," sobbed Beth. "He's gone up to Edinburgh thinking that about me, and perhaps he'll run into something and get killed, and I'll never have a chance to tell him it wasn't true."

"What! A good driver like him? Don't be such a goose! Of course he'll be all right. We'll get on to his garage and find out where he's gone and send him a telegram. Now you go to work, and don't worry. It'll all come out in the wash. You leave this to me. I shan't talk to Dulcie now—there isn't time to say one half of the things I want to say."

Because David was coming last night, Beth had not been to the post office for his letters. She went for them that morning. The post office girl handed her three. As was her custom, Beth turned each of them over, then she drew a sharp breath. The third was an ordinary inexpensive buff envelope, but stamped on the back was a crest surmounted by a crown and round it was written "Admiralty S.W."

Never in her life had Beth considered opening somebody's else's letters. It took her quite a time to bring herself to open this one; but what was she to do? Suppose it was an appointment. She was the only person who knew about the seaplane. He might be angry with her at the moment, but she was sure he would like her to open this letter.

The letter was quite formal, couched in the usual Government manner, but the news in it took away Beth's breath. It was guarded in what it said, but it did hint that they were interested, and they would like Mr. David Babbacombe to call on them on Friday morning next at eleven o'clock. Friday morning! And this was Thursday, and David was somewhere on the road to Edinburgh.

To Beth the Admiralty were customers, and people with inventions like David's were the store. It seemed to her clear that if the Admiralty were suddenly in the mood to buy something, and the person who had the goods was not there to sell them, that quite obviously they would buy elsewhere. Horrified, she faced the picture of David missing his one great chance. How awful if he need not have gone up north with that car, but just said he would go because he was cross with her and glad of something to do! If that was the case, it was her fault. Somehow he had got to be brought back.

All the way to the store she turned the problem over in her mind. How could anybody catch a car on the road? Of course it could be broadcast for; but she had no idea how to persuade the BBC that this was the sort of case to be broadcast. There seemed to be only one way to catch a car, and that was send a faster car after it. Desperately she thought over the people she knew who had cars. It did not take her long. There was only John Pern, and she had not the faintest idea where he lived. Anyway, he seemed to spend most of his time in the country. Then quite suddenly she thought of David's father.

Nobody in Babbacombe's ever went to see old John without an appointment: all the business of his staff was conducted through Mr. Smith. Beth knew that it would be perfectly hopeless to attempt to ask to see him, but because it was for David and the matter was so very urgent, she was prepared to do a thing she would never have done for herself, or even for her father—she was prepared to walk in without asking.

It was well known in Babbacombe's that old John went to his office promptly at ten o'clock every morning and that alone in his office he opened and read his letters before ringing for Mr. Wills. At ten o'clock sharp, and with knees knocking together with fright, and the precious letter clutched in one hand, Beth climbed to the top of the building. Old John's office was at the end of a long passage. With her back against the wall, making herself as invisible as possible, Beth sidled to the door, opened it and walked in.

Old John heard the click and looked up scowling from the letter in his hand. What was this interruption? Nobody was allowed to interrupt him until he rang, nor ever had been. At sight of Beth he stuck out his chin and frowned so fiercely that his red-and-grey-striped eyebrows met over his nose. What was this chit of a girl doing here? He stretched out his hand to ring his bell. Beth hurried forward.

"Please don't ring. I've come about David."

Old John did not admit even to himself how badly he was wanting news of his son. He had been too proud to make enquiries, but he had often been near it. It would be easy to put a private agency on to tracing the boy, and there would be no need to say anything, but good to know how he was, and not ill or needing help. It wasn't that he was worrying, he told himself fiercely, but just his sense of responsibility. After all, the boy was his son. He drew his hand back from the bell.

"What have you got to do with him?"

Beth took the letter out of its envelope and laid it on the desk.

"He's invented a seaplane. He never told you because you weren't interested. Now he's got an appointment, and he'll miss it, because he's on the way to Edinburgh, and you must go in your car and get him back."

Old John read the letter. He was amazed. Seaplane! Idiot of a boy! Why hadn't he told him? Might have known he would be interested. Of course these service fellows always wrote guardedly, but the letter did seem like business. He looked up.

"What's this about Edinburgh?"

"He's working in a garage, and they sent him up there this morning to return a car."

"How d'you know?"

"He wrote."

"Why?"

She turned crimson.

"It's no good being angry with me just now, and of course you will be—it's only to be expected. But, you see, David and I love each other."

Old John blinked.

"Love each other, but—"

"Yes, I know," Beth broke in, "and honestly while he was working in the shop I said it couldn't be, and so did Dad. But now he's only a garage hand it's different."

Old John leant forward.

"And what might your name be?"

"Carson. Beth Carson. I'm a junior in Gowns. My father works in Hardware."

Old John shook his head.

"That's wrong; you aren't the Carson girl."

"I'm sorry," said Beth, "but I am. And please don't let's talk any more about me. Please send for your car. You can see it's important. David should know about that letter." Old John picked up the telephone receiver.

"Send my chauffeur up." He beckoned to Beth. "Come a bit closer. Turn your face to the light." Beth obeyed. He shook his head again. "Must be gettin' blind in my old age. Could have sworn your hair was yellow."

"Perhaps you've seen my cousin Dulcie. Her hair is yellow."

"Dulcie." Old John's jaw shot out. "Who's she?"

"Well, just Dulcie—Dulcie Carson. She works on the Lifts."

"Lifts!" The old man saw daylight. "And she made a fool of herself in the bar at that fancy dress affair?"

Beth sighed. How unlucky that story should have reached him!

"Well, yes, I'm afraid she did. Dad was terribly upset." The old man's voice became suddenly gentle. "How long have you and my boy cared for each other?"

Beth considered.

"We met first on Paddington Station. I was meeting Dulcie, who was coming to stay with us, and I fell over Scissors. I think I've loved him ever since."

"And it was you he was shut with in the lift?"

"Yes."

The old man banged his fist on his desk.

"Gosh! I've been all kinds of a fool. Callin' a decent girl the things I did. No wonder he walked out on me. Can't blame him." The chauffeur came in. "Ah, there you are, Parkinson. We're goin' Edinburgh way, starting at once."

Parkinson looked surprised.

"Any luggage, sir?"

"No; haven't time. If we need any we'll buy it on the way." He turned to Beth. "Where's the garage, my dear?"

"Hounslow."

"And we're going first to Hounslow to pick up a mechanic and get an address." He turned back to Beth. "Could you start in ten minutes?"

It was just before Barnby Moor that David got his puncture. He had taken on the job of driving the Morris up north in so foul a temper that he had not bothered to look the car over, and the garage, leaving the job to him, had not looked either, so it took a puncture to tell him there was no spare tyre. David swore. It was bitterly cold; all round heavy grey clouds shot with a pinkish shade were piling up; the least weather-minded eye could tell it was going to snow.

"Blast!" said David. "Blast! blast! blast! Look at that, Scissors."

Scissors did not mind about snow, but he did mind motoring. He thought it an inferior way to get about while people had their legs. Now, with pleased barks, he leapt out on the road, and trotted cheerfully up the grass verge, sniffing as he went. David blew on his hands and opened the toolbox, and took out the jack.

"It's all very well for you, Scissors," he said morosely. "The good God provided you with gent's natty suiting in black sealskin, and nobody is expecting you to work. Oh, strewth!"

His exclamation was because of the jack. There are jacks and jacks, and this one might well have been used by Noah after the Flood when the Ark needed cranking up out of the mud. There was no possibility that it would work. David lit a cigarette and waited for help.

He was not the only person to notice the threatening clouds. In fact, after a few minutes the weather ceased to look threatening and became a definite snowstorm. It was nearing two o'clock, and every passing motorist seemed to be hurrying to a late luncheon and managed to avoid seeing David's raised arm. Then round the corner came a Rolls Royce. With very small hope of attracting the chauffeur's attention, David raised his arm again. Just as he supposed, the car went by, then, when it was a few hundred yards past him, it stopped. The door was flung open and out scrambled Beth.

Scissors had found the grass unpromising, and was trotting up the side of the road when Beth came out of the car. Pleased to see a friend so far from home, he bounced up, wagging his tail. Beth, with eyes for nobody but David, fell over him. Completely bemused at seeing her at all, David could only laugh.

"Ducky," he said, picking her up, "do you always have to fall over my dog?"

It was good news of Edward. Janet, with a song in her heart, waited for George to come in. She heard his step in the hall and ran to meet him.

"Edward's splendid. They say he ought to do well, and we'll get him home by Christmas. Just look at this." She held out a telegram. "It's from Beth. She says she won't be back until late. She doesn't say what she's up to. The telegram's been sent off from Barnby Moor." She heard Dulcie's high heels clicking up the road. "Make yourself scarce, there's a dear. I've got to have a few words with that young woman."

Dulcie faced her aunt sulkily.

"Well, I only said it for a bit of fun."

"Fun!" Icy scorn rang in Janet's voice. "Fun! You did nothing of the sort, Dulcie. I've watched you. Ever since David's been coming to this house you've been after him. What you want to waste your time for I can't think. Anyone with half an eye can see they're so much in love that nothing could separate them."

Dulcie bridled.

"I don't know so much about that. You should have heard the things he said to me at Lyons yesterday. He didn't sound so much in love as all that to me."

Janet looked at her niece with loathing.

"Ever since you've come to this house, Dulcie, you've upset us. You haven't tried to fit in, and you haven't tried to learn. Now, I don't want to be hard on you, but after Christmas I'm going to find somewhere else for you to live. You're not a good influence about the place, and I don't want you upsetting the children."

Dulcie threw up her chin.

"If that's all, you needn't wait till after Christmas. As a matter of fact I was going to tell you; I'm going back to stay with my aunt for a bit."

Janet, delighted though she was at the news, was shocked.

"What about your job?"

Dulcie fidgeted with her bag.

"I'm leaving. In fact, I've left."

Janet took hold of her arm.

"Have you been given the sack?"

Dulcie lost her temper.

"Yes, I have, if you want to know. And I'm glad of it. It was never the right sort of job for a girl of my education. And I wasn't doing anything, either. I suppose there's no harm in a girl being kissed once in a way. I never knew there were people waiting for the lift. A lot of tell-tales going to Mr. Smith."

Janet drew back.

"Well, I don't often admit myself beaten, but I'm beaten by you. I just don't know what's going to happen to you. I'm sorry for your poor aunt; but I've got my children to think of."

Dulcie flushed.

"I'm glad I'm going. I'm sick of you—sick of the house, sick of everybody in it. All you wanted was my money. You never tried to make me happy. I've sent my aunt a wire, and I'm going up now to pack."

Janet looked at the slammed kitchen door, then she shrugged her shoulders.

"Well, my conscience is clear. We've done what we could. It's a funny world. I'd take a bet some fool of a man will marry that girl. My word, I pity him."

Janet, in anxiety, breathed heavily through her nose. No one made a better plum-pudding than she did, but every year she felt in the same state—unable to relax until she saw it standing black and shining on its plate.

"There, Beth," she said in the awed voice proper in one beholding a masterpiece. "It's ready for the holly."

Beth stuck the holly in the top and handed the dish to her mother, then she threw open the dining-room door.

"Ready."

The family jumped to their feet and sang heartily, if without much voice, the first verse of "God Rest You Merry, Gentlemen."

Janet carried the pudding in and turned laughing to old Babbacombe, who was sitting on her right.

"You mustn't mind us, Mr. Babbacombe. We've sung that carol every Christmas since Beth was a baby. The first year we had her in her high chair. Just as I was cutting the pudding she began to cry. 'Sing something, George,' I said, 'to amuse her,' and, seeing it was Christmas, he sang that carol, and we've sung it ever since."

Old John looked at the pudding, then he turned to Eve, who was sitting next to him, and spoke in a hoarse whisper:

"I suppose it would be expecting too much if I hoped there were things in that pudding."

Eve bounced up and down on her chair.

"There are, there are! A sixpence, a threepenny bit, a heart, a bag of money, two little dolls, a thimble and a ring. If you get a ring you'll be married, and if you get the thimble you'll be a spinster, and if you get the dolls you'll have babies."

With the eyes of them all on her, Janet inserted the knife and cut a slice.

"It was a very fair division of mascots. Eve got the ring, Paul the sixpence, Girda the bag of money, George a silver cat, David the heart, Edward the threepenny bit and Beth the pair of china babies."

"Well, I do call that mean," said Paul to Mr. Babbacombe. "You and Mum haven't got anything."

Old John turned to Janet and gave her a nudge. His voice was drowned by the chatter.

"If there's any truth in what comes out of a pudding, and some day Beth and David have those babies, I reckon they're a present for you and me, eh, Mrs. Carson?"

Janet had a sudden vision of the nursery of her dream—a nursery she had always wanted for her own children and never been able to afford. Grandchildren! Babies of Beth's! It made her quite dizzy to think of them. She could only answer old John with a smile.

After the plum pudding, dessert was put on the table and crackers.

"We'll be a bit noisy now, Mr. Babbacombe," said George anxiously. "Maybe you'd rather come in the other room for a smoke."

Old John shook his head.

"No fear, not me! I haven't had a Christmas like this since I was a boy. Besides, I've a little something of my own to hand out. You know where you put those parcels, David lad; bring them in."

Christmas presents in the Carson family had always been on a modest scale. The look of the parcels which David brought in drew an awed gasp from all the family. There was a square box for Janet and a heavy parcel for Edward, an enormous parcel for Paul and something exciting for Eve. There was a little parcel for Beth and envelopes for George and Girda.

"And first," said David, "to show there's no ill feeling, there is a present from Scissors to Keith Prowse. Come on, Scissors, old man, hand it over."

"Well, I call that mean," said Paul. "Hasn't anyone brought anything for Penny?"

David grinned at him.

"Wait a minute. I was coming to that." He put a paper bag on the table.

Paul opened it. It was a carton of cream with "To Penny, with deep devotion from Scissors and Keith Prowse" written on it. Paul took the gift seriously.

"Penny's out, but he'll be very gratified when he comes in."

Old John's parcels caused screams of excitement. Eve had a doll's perambulator, and Paul a bicycle; Edward a wireless set, and Girda an order on the store for a frock. For Beth there was a string of pearls. Old Babbacombe clasped them round her neck himself.

"They were my wife's, my dear. She'd like you to have them. I've a feeling that you're just the kind of girl she would have wanted our boy to marry." He winked at George. "Your Dad doesn't think we're good enough for you. Puttin' up all kinds of arguments, but you can't name the day too quickly to please me."

George looked anxiously over his pince-nez.

"Oh, no, Mr. Babbacombe, sir. I didn't say that. But I still feel it isn't fitting that the daughter of one of your salesmen—"

Old Babbacombe held up a hand to stop him.

"Have you had a look in that envelope I gave you?" George opened it, while all the family watched. Inside was a letter. He read it through. When he looked up his face was quite pale.

"It can't be true. It's a thing I should never expect."

Old Babbacombe turned to Janet.

"I've appointed your husband one of our managers. Feel myself lucky to get him."

Janet gaped at George, speechlessly. She was brought back to herself by a clamour from the children.

"Open your box, Mum."

"See what's in your parcel, Mum."

Old Babbacombe put a hand on it.

"Before you open that I must tell you it's not a present from me. It's a present from David. There was a bit of a cheque to buy himself something, but he said he would rather have that for you."

Janet lifted the lid and pushed back the layers of tissue paper, and in an awed hush brought out a Persian lamb coat. The hush was succeeded by shouts.

"Mum's fur coat!"

"She's got it at last."

"There's no need for her fur coat box."

"Put it on, Mum."

Janet put on the coat and stood smiling shyly at them all, unaccustomed to her finery.

"Thank you, David."

Beth held her mother's hand.

"Don't you think it's time we had our toast?"

Janet picked up her glass.

"Here's to us all, especially Edward. May he soon get rid of his dark glasses. And here's to Beth and David." Then she turned smiling to George and Old John. "I'll link you two together. Here's to Babbacombe's."

THE END

FURROWED MIDDLEBROW

*titles available in paperback only
**pseudonym of Noel Streatfeild

Printed in Great Britain
by Amazon

24049360R00121